the piper's son

the piper's son

MELINA MARCHETTA

CANDLEWICK PRESS

Copyright © 2010 by Melina Marchetta

Lyrics to "Here If You Want" by the Waifs (p. 50), "Smokers Outside the Hospital Doors" by Editors (p. 102), "Your Ex-Lover Is Dead" by Stars (p. 279), and "32 Flavors" by Ani DiFranco (p. 280) all reprinted by permission. Lyrics to "How to Make Gravy" by Paul Kelly (p. 101) reprinted by kind permission of Paul Kelly and Sony/ATV Music Publishing Australia. Excerpt from "Japan" from *Picnic, Lightning* by Billy Collins (p. 210) copyright © 1998 by Billy Collins. Reprinted by permission of the University of Pittsburgh Press.

First Candlewick Press edition 2011

First published by Viking/Penguin Books (Australia) 2010

Library of Congress Cataloging-in-Publication Data is available.

Library of Congress Catalog Card Number 2010039168

ISBN 978-0-7636-4758-2

10 11 12 13 14 15 BVG 10 9 8 7 6 5 4 3 2 1

Printed in Berryville, VA, U.S.A.

This book was typeset in Sabon.

Candlewick Press
99 Dover Street
Somerville, Massachusetts 02144

visit us at www.candlewick.com

*For my dad, Antonino, whose dream it is to have his children
and grandchildren living under his roof, and for my mum, Adelina,
who'd love us to live next door. This novel could be as close as it gets.*

And in memory of Morgan J. Hill, who loved Joe Satriani.

prologue

The string slices into the skin of his fingers and no matter how tough the calluses, it tears.

But this beat is fast and even though his joints are aching, his arm's out of control like it has a mind of its own and the sweat that drenches his hair and face seems to smother him, but nothing's going to stop Tom. He's aiming for oblivion.

And he hears them holler his name because the song's ended and he's still going, strumming strings to their foundations. And suddenly the room is spinning and when he hits the ground, headfirst off that table, his life doesn't flash before his eyes because Tom can't remember his life. Can't remember the last year, anyway.

But then memory taunts him and he's back at that cemetery where they're burying his uncle in an empty grave. And Nanni Grace is there alongside his step-grandpop, Bill, and Auntie Georgie and Tom's dad, and they're all just dead inside. Georgie says it's what happens to you when you bury your little brother. Nanni Grace says it's what happens when you bury your youngest son. Tom's dad says nothing.

Beyond where they stand, there's another empty grave that belongs to them. Of someone even younger than his uncle Joe.

"It's what I've been doing for most of my life, Tommy," Nanni Grace tells him. "Burying the men in my family in empty coffins."

She's always said it's why they have the right to own the world. Because their family's blood is splattered all over it. Long Khanh, Vietnam. That Tube station in London. Different types of wars, someone else's fight, but it's the Finches and the Mackees who have paid.

When he opens his eyes, he's four years old again and his dad clicks the seat belt into place. "We're on our way, mate," Dominic Mackee says, like he does every single time they go through the ritual. For a moment their hands touch and it turns into "This Little Piggy."

And Tom feels like he's flying.

Because he and the piper are on their way.

chapter one

He's just Tom.

"Thomas Finch Mackee?"

The everyman with the most overused name.

"Come on, mate. Try to keep awake," the voice says.

Even the Bible was hard on them. The doubter who didn't trust his band of brothers and had to see the proof for himself to believe. He never liked that story. It made the Toms in history look piss-weak.

"Thomas? Is it Thomas or Tom? Come on, mate. Keep your eyes open."

In Year Eleven, the girls knew him as Thomas because it was the name they heard at roll call. Took years to get them to call him Tom. At home, it became a game within the family. Another day, another Tom.

"Tom Thumb, what's the story, little man?" his uncle Joe would ask him.

And when he was seven and they lived down the road from Georgie's place on Northumberland Street, she'd come over for dinner and make him do Tom Jones impersonations in front of the family, twisting with him as she held both his hands while he sang "What's New Pussycat?" in a Welsh accent that always had his mum, Jacinta, and Georgie killing themselves laughing until they almost wet their pants.

Then came Peeping Tom and *Tom Sawyer* and *Uncle Tom's Cabin* and *Tom Brown's Schooldays* and Little Tommy Tucker and "Tommy Trot, a Man of Law." The Toms in literary history had let him down and he hated them all. They were all a bunch of Prufrocks. He wanted his name to be Huck. Or Ishmael. Yossarian would do just fine.

"Tom?"

Different voice. A nurse. He can tell because she sounds like Sister Terri from *All Saints*.

"Tom, can you hear me? You're at the hospital, *Tom*. Your friend is here to collect you."

Let it be her.

Has he said those words out loud? Tom thinks he's said her name, anyway. Hasn't seen her for two years, but he prays that she's come to collect him because Tom needs collecting. Because he can't get her out of his mind. Sees her every time he closes his eyes. Sees the thousand things about her that turned him on. There was that lopsided way she walked because the satchel of her uni books weighed her down, and there was the fringe that covered her eyes, and no matter how many times he looked into them, he couldn't tell if they were green or brown, just somewhere in between. She told him once that the girls convinced her to do stuff with her hair. Foils, she called them, and he didn't understand foils, so she showed him using tin foil and he thought, *How bloody stupid*, until he saw what the foils did to her hair, all gold mixed with brown, and the way it was cut jagged around her chin, making her look scruffy one minute and cool the next.

It amazed him how they went from being best mates and just hanging out to having a bit of eye contact that lasted just a tad too long, turning their relationship into all things confusing. It had happened that time they were watching a band at the Sando with some of his mates from uni. He had stood with his arms around her and his chin resting on the top of her head. Nothing new about that. They were a tactile bunch, all of them. But she leaned back to say something and that was it. Again. And he couldn't let go. Not when they were sitting at the Buzz Bar in Newtown having a hot chocolate and his hands were playing with hers and she was letting them play, and not when they were crossing King Street to go back to one of the guys' houses in Erskineville and he was holding her hand and she was letting him, and he knew that if he tried to kiss her, she'd let him. But he didn't.

He was never afraid when it came to girls.

Unless it was Tara Finke.

When the nurse calls out his name again and he opens his eyes, Francesca Spinelli is sitting there, wearing fifty emotions on her face like she always did when they were at school together. He doesn't tell the nurse that she's lying. They're not friends. He has no idea how the hospital even tracked her down. These days his contact with her is limited to the unavoidable once or twice a week they cross each other's path at the Union, one of those incestuous inner-west pubs where everyone ends up drinking or working. And you know how it happens. One day you pass strangers by and think, *I used to hang out with them.* But that was a world before dropping out of uni and parents splitting and two nights of everything with a girl whose face you can't get out of your head and

5

relationships falling apart and favorite uncles who used to call you Tom Thumb being blown to smithereens on their way to work on the other side of the world.

Talk of Francesca these days is frequent among his flatmates. Two of them work with her, and most nights Tom is subjected to rants and tirades about the "wack job" in charge of the rosters at the pub. Tom walks away each time because the moment the insults enter his ears, he'll be an accessory, and he's never in the mood to come to her defense just because he spent three years almost surgically attached to her and the others. And Tara Finke.

Tom's always enjoyed being a coward like that.

But here Francesca sits calmly by his bed, clutching his backpack, and he hates her for that look in her eye. Compassion. Empathy. It's a killer. It disarms you when you least want to be disarmed. After his uncle Joe's death, two years ago, he hated looking at any of their faces. Tears constantly welling up in their eyes. "How are you, Tom?" they'd ask, and he'd want to tell them to shut the hell up and stop asking questions. It's what he's enjoyed most about living with his flatmates this past year. They drink, they smoke their weed, they play their music, they have no ties with whomever they have sex with, and the days pass in a pleasant haze where nobody analyzes how he feels, how he's supposed to feel, how he'll feel the next day, how he feels about the present, which is shaped by the past, which will impact on the future. With his flatmates, Tom just exists.

"I'll drive you back to my place, Tom," Francesca says. "My parents are overseas, so you don't have to talk to anyone and you can just rest."

He doesn't respond.

"The nurse says you should try to stay awake because they're worried about the concussion. You've got ten stitches because you fell into a glass."

"I'm going home," he mutters, holding a hand to the bandage on his head. He stares down at his fingers, which are taped. "But if you can drop me off at the Union, I need to get the key to the flat from Zac and Sarah," he says, referring to his flatmates.

"They're not there," she says quietly.

"Then they'll be home. Drop me there."

He still hasn't looked at her properly. Sometimes back in high school they'd compete over who could stare each other out. Francesca was hopeless. She would fail in the first five seconds, every single time. Tara Finke held out the longest, for three minutes most times, and something always happened between him and Tara in the thirty-third second that felt like a punch to his gut. He didn't get what it meant back then.

"Stani had to let them go, Tom," Francesca says. "Both of them." Her voice is firm as though she's prepared for his reaction. "They never turn up on time and I always have to cover for them and do double shifts. They didn't even tell us you had an accident, Tom."

"Why would they?" he snaps, sitting up. "Are you my next of kin?"

He grabs his backpack from her, fumbles through it for his phone, and rings Sarah's number. It goes straight to voice mail, so then he tries Zac, but no one picks up.

"And anyway . . ." Francesca continues, but he blocks her out. For someone who was a basket case the first six months they knew her, she turned out to be the most resilient and coordinates the rest of the girls with an efficiency born of a hidden Fascist gene. "She's Mussolini's bastard child," he once confided to Jimmy Hailler, the only other male in their group at the time.

". . . the being stoned thing got a bit boring," she finishes.

He wants to hit someone. "So you sacked them because they smoke dope?"

He's out of bed and standing over her. Although there's alarm on her face and a little bit of fear, she doesn't move away.

"I don't give a shit what they do, Tom, except when they don't turn up to a shift and Justine has to come in when she needs to be at a gig," she says fiercely. "Each to their own. They can stick whatever they want up their nose, down their throat, and up their arse."

"I live with them," he spits.

"I don't care. They're—"

But he holds up a hand to cut her off and grabs his clothes, which are hanging off the bed. "You're everything they've ever called you behind your back, you stupid bitch," he mutters.

"If you swear at me again, Thomas . . ."

"What?" he sneers. "You'll tell Trombal? Where is he now? Last I heard, he was pissing off overseas to get away from you."

Francesca takes a visible breath in front of him and picks up her bag and pushes past him. But she hesitates for a moment and turns back.

"For your information, your friends call me those names to my face. And they're thieves as well. So while you guys were hanging out spending the money they were bringing in, take note that most of it came from Stani's till at the Union."

She shakes her head and there are tears in her eyes.

"I know you're sad, Tom. But sometimes you're so mean that I wonder why any of us bother."

8

. . .

It's dark outside, but Tom can't see the time on the clock of his phone because the glass face cracked, presumably at the same time as his head. He rings the landline at the flat but is warned by a recorded message that he's almost out of credit, so he hangs up before the answering machine sucks up what's left. He has a hazy recollection of having topped up his phone card and can't for the life of him remember where it's all gone, but nothing seems to be making sense to him at the moment. He stops twice from the dizziness and sits on the brick fence that lines the hospital on Missenden Road, watching an ambulance drive in and offload some drunk that they've probably picked up off the streets. He clutches the phone, willing it to ring. For Zac and the guys to be pissed or high and start belting out, "Ground Control to Major Tom," which got old a long time ago, but tonight he needs to hear it to make sure everything's okay.

The moment he's off the main road, a part of him panics. Although he's close to home, where he stands there are no hospital lights to keep him alive to the world. He doesn't want to collapse in the back streets of Newtown in front of one of these ugly flats, which according to his aunt should have been demolished the moment they were finished. His aunt Georgie has a strange idea of justice. Rapists, pedophiles, and architects of redbrick flats built in the 1970s all belong in the same jail cell. Out here tonight, under the dullest of moons, Tom feels as if he's the last man on earth. Six blocks east from the home he grew up in. Three blocks south from the university he dropped out of a year ago. Four blocks north of the bed he shared with Tara Finke that last night together when life made sense for one proverbial minute, before everything blew up.

9

Outside his flat, the moon sheds light on the garbage strewn all over the front lawn, and it's not until he's up close that he realizes it's not garbage at all. It's his stuff. There's not much of it, but he can't believe they've left his guitar out here for anyone to pinch. Zac and the gang haven't gone to the trouble of packing or asking questions about allegiance. They've just chucked everything over the balcony. It's what happens when their only two sources of a steady income, notwithstanding a dole check or two, have just been sacked courtesy of someone who belongs to Tom's past. He hammers on the security door, but no one answers and then he steps back to look up to the balcony.

"Sarah!"

Some nights she crawls into bed with him when she's between boyfriends. She isn't one to deal too well with her own company and who's he to refuse if it's on offer with no strings attached. He likes the fact that she can keep sentimentality and emotion out of it. Until now. He makes the mistake of believing that sex between them will make a difference.

"*Sarah?*" he yells, and it almost breaks open his stitches to put that much effort into speaking. When no one answers except the guy on the top floor to tell him to shut the hell up, he goes back to his stuff on the lawn and crams some of his clothes in his backpack and begins to feel around in the dark. All he wants is his guitar and his *Norton Anthology*. But the photos usually tucked inside the poetry anthology are missing, probably scattered all over the grass, so he crawls around until he finds all three. He doesn't know which one's which, but knows he's not leaving until he has them all. He grabs his guitar and tucks the photographs back into the book and then he heads back toward the hospital, weighing up his options. Georgie is the obvious one, but he knows he can't turn up to his aunt's place in the middle of the night with ten stitches in his head. She'll ring Brisbane in an instant, and then he'll have to deal with his mother's anxiety. And so he realizes, with a lack of shame or guilt born of desperation, that he'll call Francesca Spinelli because after tonight he'll never have to see her again. There'll be no hanging out at the Union now that his flatmates have been sacked. It's a bed she can offer with no questions from her mother and father. He's got enough credit for one more phone call and he rings her because he's a prick. He knows Francesca will come and get him no matter what he said to her tonight. He knows she'll expect nothing in return.

He's outside the front of the Mobil petrol station ten minutes later, and once his body has been stationary for a while, the painkillers begin to wear off and the cold snaps at his bones. At this time of night, Parramatta Road looks like some sci-fi movie. Massive lights from the servos and traffic lights, and not one car to be seen except a ute coming toward him from Annandale. Which means Will Trombal is driving. Mostly Tom's pissed off, except for a sliver of enjoyment in knowing that he's probably disrupted Trombal's night. There's never been love lost between Tom and Francesca's boyfriend. The filthy look that Trombal sends him and the five-minute drive of silence to Francesca's house, while the three are squashed in the front seat, prove it.

When they get to her place, Francesca touches Will's hand, and Tom watches as Will clenches hers. "I'll just go unlock the door for him," she says quietly, waiting for Tom to get out first. Will gets out as well and leans against the ute. Tom can't see his expression in the dark, but he feels the bastard's eyes drilling a hole into him. Will Trombal was in the next year up from them at school, and Tom can't believe Francesca's still with him after five years.

"Thanks." Tom mutters the word. He doesn't mean it but says it all the same.

"Don't," Trombal says quietly. "You'd still be out there, and I wouldn't give a shit if you were bleeding all over Parramatta Road, if it was my choice. You know that."

They have a quick verbal exchange but only get to cover the alphabet from A to F, outdoing each other with the most choice of words. Trombal kind of wins this round, courtesy of having hung out with engineers in Asia for most of the year. Then they're shoving each other and Tom sees more emotion on the other guy's face than he has in the years he's known him. Francesca's back between them, trying to push them apart, but it's Trombal she's facing and they start kissing in the middle of his fight—*they start kissing*—and it's no longer about Tom, and he makes his way to the open front door, looking back once.

Trombal has her pressed against the door of the ute and they're going at it like they've got no time left in this world together and Tom can hear that she's crying and any time she comes up for air, Francesca's saying, "Be careful, Will, *please*," and Tom's not an idiot to realize what he's interrupted. Will Trombal's some wunderkind in engineering, sponsored throughout his uni years by one of the top companies. Now Trombal's taking a break from studying and it's payback time, so he's had to spend most of the year working offshore in Sumatra.

12

Francesca's still crying when she comes inside and makes herself busy doing up the sofa bed for him in the lounge room.

"When's he leaving?" Tom asks quietly, more out of the need for something to say than real interest.

"In the morning."

"Go be with him, then. I'll be fine."

She fluffs up the pillow and throws it on the bed before looking up at him coldly.

"As if I'd leave you here with my little brother."

chapter two

Georgie makes a list. Her hand is steady as she writes and she nods and records. It's part of the job description to stay neutral.

flannel shirt
metallic-blue nylon tracksuit pants
wool sweater
Adidas running shoes
gray parka
thin gold-plated chain with the name Sofya *engraved on it*

A Bosnian woman sits facing her. Georgie can see by the information on the form that they're almost the same age, the woman maybe a year or two younger. The woman looks older, but so would Georgie if she had waved good-bye to her husband with the nylon tracksuit pants and her son with the Adidas shoes and her father with the wool sweater and her uncle with the gray parka and her cousin who loved a girl named *Sofya* and never saw them again. Sometimes the woman takes her hand and begins to weep, and Georgie lets her hold it while she continues to write. And when the woman lets go, Georgie wants to beg her to keep holding on. She wants to weep with her.

She's not doing too well these days, although she's only thrown up twice today. Earlier, while she was puking up morning sickness that doesn't seem to discriminate between morning or afternoon, she made another list. She wants to stop making the lists, but she can't. It's become her little addiction, list making.

So she tries to call them rules. Ignore the first rule of not getting pregnant at forty-two because of the risks, because it's not as though she planned this and it's too late anyway. First real rule: no smoking. And no alcohol. Not even a glass of wine. Deformities, they say. No stone fruit. Not good for the baby's intestines. And of course she'll breast-feed. According to midwives, nothing beats the nutrients in breast milk because they keep the baby strong. Except if you live in Ireland, where ninety percent of them don't breast-feed, so they must have strong immune systems to start with for some reason. She'll sleep it on its tummy so it won't die during the night from crib death. Or is the rule sleeping it on its back these days? And no pool. According to the stats, backyard drowning is the leading cause of injury for children under five, ahead of violence, poisonings, falls, burns, and motor-vehicle crashes. Of course her baby's not sitting in the front seat because air bags can decapitate young children. She'll vaccinate. She won't give it peanuts. She'll never leave it overnight at a friend's because according to statistics ninety-five percent of all molestations happen at the hands of a family friend. There'll be no Internet. Pedophiles are lurking everywhere. And she'll holiday at home, thank you very much. No tsunamis here, or earthquakes.

And won't he grow up to be the healthiest of young men, all because she kept him safe? Ready for the world. Ready to one day conquer it. To travel. Get on a train. Go to work. Get blown out of her life.

Maybe she should be having that glass of wine and cigarette after all.

15

chapter three

The stone top step of his aunt's front porch is cold under him, but Tom's not budging. He's got all the time in the world and nowhere else left to go. Across the road at the park, he can see people letting their dogs off the leash for that final run before they go home for dinner and lock out the world behind them.

He sees Georgie before she sees him. Coming up Percival Street from the station, and he can see it's her ex, Sam, by her side. Georgie and Sam haven't been together for seven years and they don't look together now. Their bodies are stiff, their heads down. When they stop at the park across from him, Tom watches as Sam's hand reaches out to Georgie for a moment, but he seems to stop himself and then she's walking across the road toward the house and there's that look Tom's become used to in his life with his aunt. It's the unconditional love that flashes across someone's face before they remember the shit. Before they remember that their only nephew hasn't made contact for months and that he's a big prick. She can't hide her joy for a moment, not Georgie, and Tom knows the instant she sees his stitches because she has a hand against her chest and the eyes give it all away. But that's Georgie. Her pain was awful to watch the day they buried his uncle Joe, or whatever the hell you call it when you have a service with no body. Georgie's grief was worse even than Nanni Grace's, who refused to allow anyone to comfort her. "Take care of Bill," Nanni Grace said over and over again because Tom's step-pop was crying like nobody's business. No one had ever seen Pop Bill cry. "Take care of Bill," Nanni Grace said, "because he's falling apart without his boy."

When Georgie reaches him, he stands up and she gives him a hug with such force that he can't let go. Nothing's felt this good since that night two years ago when he was holding Tara Finke in his arms. And there it is again. A memory he's kept at bay for so long and all he needs to do is fall into a table to bring it back.

"What happened?" Georgie asks, touching his face.

He doesn't speak. Can't.

"Tom, what happened?" she asks again.

"Can I stay here?"

"Are you in trouble with the police?"

He shakes his head. "It's just stuff."

The moment of unconditional love is over. All Tom's life, Georgie has tried to be the cool aunt. The good cop to his father's bad cop. The one who'd let him get away with anything. But she failed most times.

He stares at the front yard, the roses all pruned and the grass cut. He thinks of Sam walking her home and what that means. Back in the nineties, Georgie and Sam had bought this three-story Victorian because Sam was making a shitload of money and the property market hadn't gone haywire yet. It was cheaper to buy on the Stanmore side rather than in Leichhardt because of the planes and flight path. When they broke up seven years ago, Georgie refused to move out and insisted on paying Sam rent. Sam moved onto the next street just to make things more complicated for all involved.

"Is he living here again?" Tom asks.

"Who?" she says firmly. "*No.* Who told you that?"

"Settle, petal," he says, pissed off that he's about to enter crazy family territory. "Give me the keys. You look like shit." Suddenly he's angry and he doesn't know who he's angry at.

"Bad day," she says.

He nods. He knows bad days. Bad days take him completely by surprise. They make him not trust the good days because it's likely something's lurking twenty-four hours away.

Georgie sits on the step and he knows they're not going through that door just yet.

"You sure you're okay?" he asks.

Georgie works for some branch of the Red Cross where they track down people's relatives who have disappeared in conflicts. Tom read somewhere that this year they were trying to identify bodies from mass graves that had been dug during the Bosnian War, more than ten years ago. That would mean Georgie spends most of her days interviewing survivors who immigrated here, recording what their dead or missing family members were wearing on the day they were last seen. Tom can't think of a worse job for a Mackee.

"If you let me move in, I can pay my way," he says. He can't believe he's twenty-one years old and begging his aunt to let him move in with her.

"Where are you working?" she asks, finally standing up, digging around for her house keys in a ridiculously oversize bag until she ends up chucking the contents of it onto the patio floor.

He hesitates for a moment. "I get money . . . from Centrelink."

She stops searching and stares. She has what Tom's mother calls classic looks, same as his little sister and Nanni Grace. Like those gorgeous actresses out of a 1940s war film with wavy dark hair, red lipstick, and what Tom's mum called alabaster skin. If his little sister wants to know what she'll look like at forty-two and sixty-three, she just has to look at Georgie and Nanni Grace. It's all in their eyes. A dark-gray mass of bullshit detectors, with a bit of meanness thrown in. *"Don't you look at me with those eyes, Anabel Georgia Finch Mackee,"* his mother would warn his sister.

"You're on the dole?" Georgie has her arms folded and she's angry.

"Yeah, like I said. Centrelink," he says, instantly on the defensive.

"Just call it *the dole,* Tom."

"What's wrong with that?"

"Your father would have a fit and so would your pop Bill."

"Well, seeing as the great Dominic Mackee is probably facedown in some gutter at the moment, I just might not take his opinion into consideration."

He knows he's gone too far. His father and Georgie are twins, and it's against Georgie's commandments for anyone to criticize her brother. Or brothers.

"What a thing to say," she says, shaking her head with fury. "What a little shit you are, Tom. Don't you dare talk about your father like that."

He simmers for a moment, crouching down to throw her stuff back into her ridiculous handbag.

"You're a hypocrite," he accuses back. "You've said worse about *your* father. I've heard you go on about Bill."

19

"And since when have you been allowed to call your pop *Bill*?"

Since everyone who used to make the rules nicked off on me, he wants to say.

"You don't even go by Bill's name anymore, Georgie *Finch*," he exploded. "You haven't for twenty years, and you and my father have never called him *Dad*. It was always *Bill*. The double-standard crap in this family shits me to tears."

She finally gets the door open and he follows her down the corridor. He knows he's going to be blasted with memories any minute now. Georgie'll have a thousand photos all over the place. Mostly of Tom and Anabel and his uncle Joe. The first he'll see in the lounge room is of Georgie and his dad at seventeen. Georgie's wearing a boob tube, minus the boobs, and is standing between his father and Joe, both of them wearing those tight boardies from the eighties. Uncle Joe was ten in the photo, all skinny arms and legs like Pop Bill. But not Dominic. Pop Bill may have given them his name, but Dominic Mackee was all Tom Finch. He was Georgie and Dominic's father, who had married Nanni Grace before he went to Vietnam to fight the war and never came back. In the corner, with the best view of the TV, is the ugly green vinyl armchair that his uncle Joe once found by the side of the street on his way home from the station. Joe had lived here with Georgie before he went to London to teach, and she put up with anything, although she hated the chair with a vengeance because it clashed with her period furniture.

"It's an eyesore, G," Tom's father, Dominic, would say. "Get rid of it when Joe's at work one day." Before his job at the trade unions, Tom's father had made furniture, so the armchair was a monstrosity to anyone with good taste. Tom hadn't minded the chair. He'd fight his uncle Joe for it, and whoever got there first wouldn't budge for the rest of the night. One time he even dislocated his shoulder, diving from one end of the room to beat Joe to the chair. That was the year Tom turned seventeen and things had been crap at home between him and his father. They had always been tight, but that year everything ended up in a fight. With Georgie living just around the corner, Tom ended up there most of the time.

Georgie disappears into the kitchen, and Tom joins her just as she finishes listening to her messages. He hears his mum saying, *"Hey, G. Give us a ring."* He wants to ask Georgie to play it again, just to hear the voice.

"When did you last speak to her?" he asks quietly.

"A couple of days ago. Anabel played a piece on the trumpet over the phone."

"What did my mum say?" he asks.

"Same thing as always," Georgie says, turning on the coffee machine. " 'I'm worried about Tommy. I send him a text message every second day and he doesn't respond.' "

He's quiet for a moment.

"Yeah, I do. Sometimes."

"Liar."

"Night before last, I returned one. Know what she sent back?"

Georgie doesn't answer.

"Same thing as always. *I'm worried about your auntie G.*"

He doesn't add the part, *Find out if it's true that she's pregnant.* Although he can tell that she is. Either that or Georgie's had a boob job.

Georgie holds up a mug and he nods. The beans begin to grind, and he smells memories with that sound. Of them snuggled in this kitchen. He couldn't remember one Sunday morning without Georgie and his mum and dad and Anabel and Uncle Joe eating croissants from Le Chocoreve and drinking espresso and hot chocolate.

"I think she's having a hard time," Georgie says.

He doesn't say anything, because no one gave his mother, Jacinta, a harder time than Tom. He had refused to go to Brisbane with her, even though he was flunking uni, because there was no way he was leaving his father behind. She said it would only be for a few weeks while his father sorted himself out, so Anabel wouldn't be affected by what was going on with Dominic's drinking. That was a year ago.

"She did the right thing going up there," Georgie says. "Jacinta needed to be with her mother, no matter how much your grandma Agnes goes on."

He goes to light up a cigarette and offers her one, but he knows she'll say no.

"Outside," she orders, and he's close enough for her to reach out and touch his face.

"You look awful, Tommy."

"Can I stay?" he asks again, and there's pleading in his voice. He knows she can't resist him. Not Georgie. Her obsession with her brothers, Dominic and Joe, continued on with Tom and his sister, Anabel.

"No drugs and only if you get a job."

"You'd think I was a junkie the way you go on. It's weed, Georgie. Less harmful than booze."

"Don't give me a lecture about drugs and alcohol. I told your father the same thing. He can come back here, but not if he's drinking."

"Well, he better not fucking come while I'm staying."

"And stop swearing."

"Yeah, 'cause you've never sworn in your life."

He takes the coffee from her, needing fresh air because if he doesn't get out of this room, he'll suffocate from memories. He's felt like that for more than a month now. There's no particular reason for it, but sometimes he feels like he can't breathe, like his body is shutting down. Two weeks back, he rang Nanni Grace because the hyperventilating was scaring him shitless and she was the only person he could speak to without the guilt and without the questions.

"It's called grief, my beautiful boy," she had murmured over the phone. When Tom was born, Grace and Bill were still in their early forties. There was no *Grandma* and *Grandpa* for them. Nanni and Pop was as close as they allowed.

But he didn't get the grief thing. It had been two years since Joe's death and all of a sudden it was there again.

"Ring your mother, Tommy," his nan had sighed. There were no in-law issues in his family. His mum and Nanni Grace had a great relationship. "She's up there with Anabel, missing you so much."

"How's Auntie G?" he'd asked, as if he hadn't heard what she'd said.

"Everyone's saying she's pregnant."

That had surprised him. "Why don't you just ask her?"

"Because Georgie will tell everyone when she's ready, and we have to honor that."

"So when her water breaks and she's in labor, you'll pretend to sound shocked when she announces that she's been pregnant for the past nine months?"

23

Nanni Grace chuckled at that. It had made Tom smile. His pop Bill would laugh at the sound of it whenever they were up to visit from Albury. "There's a bit of evil in that chuckle, Gracie," Bill Mackee would drawl.

"Whose is it?" Tom had asked, referring to the baby.

"Sam's."

"Shit. Does it get any more complicated than that?"

Later, he goes inside and Georgie's already upstairs. He doesn't want to ask whether he gets the attic. He figures he'll just take it and sort things out himself, but when he reaches the third floor, Georgie's already left sheets and blankets on the bed. The room is a memory fucker. The first thing he sees is the Slade LP stuck on the mirror where he left it that night two years ago. Then he sees the Joe Satriani *Surfing with the Alien* poster. The hyperventilating starts again and he can't get the window to work. He bolts down the stairs but doesn't get past Georgie's room. She's on the floor, rummaging through the chest at the foot of the bed. She's anxious in her searching, and although she's his aunt and twenty years older than him, her expression is like a kid's. Like his sister's when she was scared and nobody but Tom's dad could calm her down.

"What are you looking for, Georgie?"

She doesn't answer, as though she can't hear him, and he walks in and sits on the floor in front of her. She's holding a small green square of cloth attached to a necklace of the same material. "Is it religious?" he asks, feeling its texture.

She nods. "It's a scapular. Kind of a Catholic token of devotion." There are two of them. "This belonged to Dominic," she explains. She laughs. "They're a bit outdated now."

24

Tom spent a lot of time trying not to think of his father, and most times he failed because Dominic's name kept coming up in conversation. There's always someone Tom comes across in the area who wants to know where Dom Mackee is. Everyone loves Dominic. They should do a sitcom about him. Stanmore's favorite son and husband and brother and friend and father.

"He'd force me to tie it around my undershirt strap when we were kids," she says. "Your pop Bill would always say that they'd be able to identify our father's body in Vietnam one day because Tom Finch wore his scapular tied around his undershirt strap. So Dominic and I had to be the same."

Tom swallows hard. His pop Bill had mentioned something about Tom Finch a month ago, when they last spoke.

"Is it true what they're saying? About finding Tom Finch's body soon?" he asked.

Her eyes bore into his.

"Where did you hear that?"

"Saw it on the news. How those old-timer vets found two of the others guys back in June. They reckon it'll be Tom Finch soon."

She's still looking at him, scapular gripped in her hand. He can tell. This is the beginning of the ritual. Georgie's preparing to bury her father after forty years. Tom can't imagine what that's going to do to his family.

Not after Joe.

"Pop Bill sounds choked up every time he brings it up."

"They were best friends, Bill and Tom Finch," she says. "Knew each other all their lives."

And they both fell in love with Nanni Grace.

"Do you think it's true," he asks, "about the scapular?"

25

She shrugs. "Don't know. But when we were kids, Dominic wouldn't go anywhere without it. It's like he thought if he was wearing it, maybe Tom Finch would find us somehow."

He sighs, standing up. There are too many subjects he wants to avoid. "Thanks for the sheets and stuff."

There's a soft smile on her face. "When I walked into the attic, it was the first time I didn't think of it being Joe's room," she says. "I thought of those gorgeous girls you used to hang out with in high school and at uni. What was the name of the one whose mother worked at the Red Cross before me? She stayed here one night and you both looked . . . I don't know . . . frisky."

"Tara," he says, his voice husky. "She's in Timor."

Tara Finke, whose voice was suddenly stuck in his head, *"Talk to me, Thomas. Just talk to me."* If he was going to dream up any words from her, they'd be angry ones, not ones said with such empathy.

"Do you want me to make you something to eat?" she asks.

He nods. He doesn't know whether it's the food or the normalcy of it all, but he follows her down and watches as she tosses some veggies and chicken around in a wok. They eat in silence, but it's a better silence than he's used to, and then he goes to bed and he lies there studying the photos he carries around. One belongs to him and the other two belong to his father, but Dominic Mackee left them behind like he left everything behind when he nicked off. Tom's favorite is of Nanni Grace's four men, as she'd like to call them. Tom with Joe, Pop Bill, and Dominic. He remembered that day when his nan took the photo just as Joe's tongue snaked into Dominic's ear. "Oh, you're a silly boy, Joseph Mackee," she had said with a laugh. And then there's the one of Tara and the girls with Jimmy

26

Hailler and Tom, back when they were in Year Twelve. Tara had her hand up over her eyes, trying to block the sun, while Tom's arm was around her shoulder. It was one of those photos taken under the instruction that they had to huddle up to fit in the frame. He remembers keeping his arm there for ages after. The last is of Joe and his girlfriend standing on Solsbury Hill in Somerset back in 2005. Peter Gabriel's "Solsbury Hill" was Tom's father's favorite song, so Joe sent him the next best thing.

And in his dreams that night, it's not just Tara Finke's voice he hears but Joe's. So clear. As if they had both just spoken to him the day before. And he wants to stay asleep so he can hear their voices for as long as he can.

chapter four

"Georgie?" She hears Lucia's voice as she balances the phone and tries to find the keys to the front door. "We're in Norton Street. Are you coming down?"

It's not really a request; it's a Lucia order. It's what she specializes in. She has bullying down to perfection. Lucia's the one that Georgie gets to ring up and complain to if she's having a problem with a telco or insurance company. Lucia handles the Charbel household of three kids under eight while still doing conveyancing for family and friends. She volunteers for the Saint Michael's Parents and Friends group, the tuckshop, writes articles for the Law Society, and still seems to have more energy than all of them. On the day of the bombing, when they received word that Joe was on the Piccadilly line between Kings Cross Station and Russell Square at 8:50 a.m., it was Lucia who spoke on behalf of the family outside Georgie's house. The rest of them could hardly speak. When the press refused to go away, she was the one who shouted, "Can you please respect this family's privacy, you fuckers!" while shoving between the vultures with her pram. They all used to snicker at the people who made scenes on the six p.m. news. Until someone decided to stick a camera and microphone in front of their dead brother's father and ask Bill how he was feeling.

"Abe and I have a babysitter," Georgie hears her say, and she can hear Abe in the background organizing everyone. "You know how rare that is."

Georgie doesn't budge from where she's standing at her front door. "I'm not up to company," she says. All she has to do is put the key in the lock and she's home free.

"Come on, Georgie. Jonesy reckons he can hardly remember what you look like."

"Probably because he's looking down and text messaging every time I see him," she says tiredly.

"A little antipasto dish and bread sticks and you'll be home by seven thirty — I promise. Everyone's here but you."

Not everyone. Jacinta's up north and Dominic's down south.

"Is Sam going to be there?" Georgie asks.

"Yes."

Silence.

"Georgie," Lucia says patiently after a couple of moments. "Despite the fact that we're not talking about your obvious weight gain, can I be blunt in saying that if you and Sam can exchange bodily fluids, then the rest of us can enjoy both of your company together?"

There's a standoff. The win/loss ratio has always ended with Lucia slightly ahead. One moment's hesitation costs Georgie.

"We're at Scalia's."

Sam is smoking his lungs out beyond the glass door of the café, which looks out onto the street, while Lucia and Abe are talking kids'

29

birthday parties and a dwindling social life. Abe belonged to Georgie and her brother Dominic first. They met at sixteen at an Antioch religious retreat. Abe loves telling the story. How he was the good boy who had never broken a rule in his life until Dominic Mackee offered him a cigarette and said, "How about we nick off tonight? My sister's coming, too." Abe said it was as though Dominic was promising him a better life if he followed, and about ten years later Dominic made good on that promise and introduced Abe to Lucia. Then Lucia brought Sam along because they worked together at a law firm and were united by what they called death by conveying. Dominic and Sam hit it off in an instant and Georgie ran after Sam for a year before he finally figured out how he felt. They spent the next seven years together until Georgie called a break and then things fell well and truly apart and everyone got caught up in the ricochet.

"Four parties in one weekend"—Lucia's counting with her fingers—"McDonald's, bowling, Jamberoo, and a disco party." Lucia's sister Bernadette joins them, squeezing between Georgie and Jonesy. Jonesy's the baby of the group, who's taught with Abe for a couple of years.

"So we said to Daniel, 'Honey, no clowns, no jumping castles, nothing. Just good-old-fashioned pin-the-tail-on-the-donkey and a piñata, and for the sake of equality, we'll invite the whole class.' Very simple," Abe explains. Abe and Lucia are always a tag team in the way they tell a story.

"But then all these parents, who haven't been to a backyard party since they were six years old themselves, decided to turn up with the whole family. So we had ninety people at my son's birthday and no one wanted to go home. We ended up having to feed them."

"It was like the loaves and fishes," Abe said.

"No, the wedding feast at Cana, because we had to give them booze."

Abe and Lucia's daughter is going to communion classes and they can quote every parable in the Bible these days.

"And Lucia forced me to be in charge of the piñata line," Jonesy complains.

"He handed out detentions," Lucia says.

Georgie laughs. "Jonesy, you're a dick."

"Next time, *you* do it, Georgie. *Nothing* scares me more than a bunch of kids beating up a goat full of lollies."

"It's about downgrading," Abe explains to whoever is listening. "I've told the kids there'll be no Christmas presents this year. We're donating to an orphanage in Sierra Leone and buying a goat from Oxfam."

"Lovely," Georgie says as Abe leaves and joins Sam outside.

When he's out of listening distance, Georgie and Bernadette send Lucia a look of disbelief.

"Let him think he's saving the world with that goat," Lucia says.

Jonesy looks at everyone's empty glasses and starts working out the round. "You want a beer, Georgie?" he asks.

"No," Lucia answers for her. "She'll have mineral water."

A look passes among them all.

Jonesy taps at the window to find out if Sam and Abe want another beer, and Georgie continues to stare at Lucia. With none of the men around, everything is just about to get more complicated.

"You can't have pâté either," Lucia tells her as Georgie digs her water cracker into the mini feast before them.

"And why is that?"

Lucia doesn't respond.

Just ask me. Just say the words.

"Because it doesn't taste nice," Lucia says, taking the biscuit out of her hand as if Georgie is her six-year-old son whose mouth she's about to clear of whatever object he's just put in there.

Georgie looks through the glass doors and her eyes meet Sam's as she tries to ignore the scrutiny she's receiving from Lucia. It's why she loves hiding in her house. Because she doesn't get to see that look in people's eyes.

She stands just as Jonesy returns with the drinks.

"I'm going," she manages to say.

Jonesy looks from one to the other. "Ah, come on, G. Sit down. You just got here."

She shakes her head and she wants to cry because these days it's too hard not to.

Her eyes meet Sam's through the glass door again and she sees him sigh, the way his body slumps as he stubs out a cigarette, and next minute he's poking his head through the doorway. All these years and he hasn't forgotten the SOS plea in her eye.

"I've got to pick up the boy," he says.

And there they are. Her options. Sitting among friends who don't know what to say to her anymore. Or picking up a six-year-old who represents the greatest betrayal of her life.

She walks alongside Sam as they make their way up Norton Street. Years ago it's what they used to do during the week at this time of the night. Come down for a coffee or a quick pasta and glass of wine. They loved it here on weekdays because it belonged to the locals. All the people they wanted in their lives lived within a ten-minute radius. Her brother Dominic had started the vow of not moving away from each other just because they'd be able to afford bigger houses in the outer suburbs. "Let's stick together, no matter how poky our houses are," he had made them all promise. "Better to be able to pick up each other's kids and hang out together than have bigger backyards and rumpus rooms."

Outside Sam's mother's house on Crystal Street, the kid waves up at her like he does every time they do this.

"Hi, Georgie."

"Hi."

Sam's mother watches from the patio of her tiny semi, and Georgie has no choice but to walk toward her. The older woman kisses her, clutching her tightly, as confused as everyone is, and Georgie hears her whisper, "It's a miracle, Georgie. It's a miracle." Which is strange because Sam grew up with people who didn't believe in anything. And she thinks of those times she'd joke with Lucia and Jacinta and Bernadette that she was the only one of the four who wasn't named after someone who saw an apparition of the Virgin Mary. Georgie didn't believe in miracles. It was as though God had said she didn't deserve them.

They walk toward Stanmore with Sam between her and Callum. As always. As he would when he waited for her at the station in those numb days. The boy was four when Joe died and didn't question who Georgie was or why she was so silent. She remembered once, when they stood at the lights and Sam's phone rang and it was time to cross, how the kid took hold of her hand as if she was the only person who could get him to the other side alive. And Georgie felt eleven years old again, holding her little brother's hand.

When they reach Sam's house, on Myrtle Street, he unlocks the door and sends Callum in.

"Why don't you stay?" he asks quietly.

She shakes her head. They have a strange silent agreement. Georgie being under the same roof with Callum isn't part of it.

"Don't let Lucia stay upset at you for too long."

"How do you know it's not me upset with her?" she asks sharply.

"Either way, it will cut you up. You know that."

He knows her well. He had slept beside her often enough to know that Georgie needed to be connected to her world. Years ago he'd reach over and grab the phone and hold it out to her. "Ring them and sort this out, or I don't get to sleep," he'd snap.

But this is now. He doesn't say anything. They neither greet nor bid farewell with a kiss or a touch. Their physical relationship only happens in bed. So the unspoken lingers between them. He's a stranger, this man, with his vulnerability and his empathy. She liked him better with the arrogance. She could fight that with sharp tools of her own.

"They're hurt," he says.

"Sorry?"

He sighs. Everyone sighs in front of Georgie these days.

"They're hurt that you haven't told them about the baby."

"Why can't they just ask?" she asks bluntly.

"It's not their business to. It's yours to tell and they can't understand why you won't."

She sees it on his face, the recognition of her shame.

Because you don't get pregnant by a man who's betrayed you and boast about it to the world. Because you don't forgive his relationship with another woman, no matter how nonexistent or brief it was. *This is shame,* she wants to shout at him. *Not getting pregnant, but getting pregnant by* you. You don't forgive a child coming out of that relationship. Not unless you're desperate or part of some *Cosmopolitan* magazine article. And he knows.

"I don't know what to say to you, Georgie."

Behind him, Callum's standing by the door, clutching a book in his hand.

"Your son wants you to read to him," she says, turning around and walking away.

To: mackee_joe@yahoo.co.uk
From: georgiefinch@hotmail.com
Date: 10 July 2007

I end my day, Joe, the way it begins. Listing items of clothing. Because that time when I traveled to London to try to bring you back home to Mummy and Bill and Dominic, your Ana Vanquez told us every detail of your last couple of hours.

That you wore brown corduroy pants.

A blue cotton shirt.

Your fake Rolex from some marketplace in Morocco.

A black band around your wrist.

Black leather boots that you bought when you guys traveled to Spain to meet her family.

And I can't stop thinking of that woman I interviewed. How she told me that she cries when she thinks that her husband and son and father and uncle and cousin knew where they were heading that day in Srebrenica. Because they had those hours on that bus, Joe, understanding the inevitable and it makes her sick to the stomach to think of their fear. Of her boy's fear.

But did you, Joe? Did you have a moment to fear? Or were you thinking of your beautiful Ana Vanquez? Or me, your sister? Were you thinking of the table your brother, Dominic, was making for Mum and Bill so we could all fit round it when you came visiting with your girl? Were you thinking of your nephew, Tommy, hogging your space up in my attic and your niece, Anabel, being the only person apart from Mum who has your father eating out of her hands? Was there a tune in your head? Were you listening to a song? Thinking of those kids you were off to teach? Were you smiling, Joe? Looking the world in the eye?

chapter five

He gets a part-time job at some data-entry place near Central Station, working from ten to three every day. To his left sits a guy called Mohsin. Mohsin the Ignorer, Tom calls him. Tom speaks; Mohsin taps away at his computer as if he hasn't heard a thing. Language isn't an issue because he's heard Mohsin speak to the guy on his other side who persists in talking cricket all day and it's clear to anyone with intelligence that Mohsin is a rugby league man and cricket talk annoys him. Tom can tell by the amount of sighs he hears during those five hours at work whenever the cricket freak opens his mouth and talks LBWs and all-rounders. Once or twice he's seen Mohsin read the league pages, but each time Tom offers his opinion, total silence ensues. So now when Mohsin the Ignorer turns his way, Tom gives him a "talk to the hand" look and pretends he can type a hundred words a minute.

Today he's restless and checks his e-mail. Before he can stop himself, he types Uncle Joe's name in the search space and retrieves one of his e-mails. And for the first time in a long while, Tom laughs.

To: tomfmackee@hotmail.com
From: mackee_joe@yahoo.co.uk
Date: 28 June 2005
Subject: Nothing Comes of Nothing

My delusional, numbskulled nephew,
How long is this going to go on, mate? This obsession with the psycho Tara Finke—your words, not mine—whose name you haven't stopped saying since you were sixteen. Conquer this passion. Do something about it! Yeats it, Tom. STD.

My advice? Get out the *Norton* I left you, and you better bloody still have it because if you lost it like you did my *Slade Alive!* LP, I will hunt you down, son. Page 1902. "Japan." Not about the Japanese, but about moments of perfection. Commit it to memory and make good use of it. Because if I come home and you're still pining over this little girl without having given her a chance, I will call you a chicken shit for the rest of your life. C. S. Tom, for short.

And can you please clear your crap out of Georgie's attic? She reckons you use her place like it's a hotel. Don't expect me to bring my girl to a hovel.
With much love and affection,
Joe
P.S. Tell your father to get stuffed about the Roosters getting beaten by the Tigers. One text message a day is enough gloating.

In Tom's family, there's "before London" and "after London." The 28th of June 2005 was "before." It was easier to remember the "befores." That morning, he had googled Yeats and worked out that STD was all about seizing the day and not some sexually

38

transmitted disease. He knew that all along, he'd tell his uncle, Mr. Expert on dishing out advice about footy and women. He was always curious to know if Joe worked out the subject line before he began the e-mails or after. Joe was an English and history teacher, so everything had a theme. Most times it was the Shakespeare he was teaching. Tom could tell it was *King Lear* those days because the subject line the week before was "Poor Tom's a-Cold," just because he wrote to complain about the windchill factor at Brookvale Oval.

In the kitchen that morning, his mum had been putting some fruit and a muesli bar into her lunch bag and peering out the back window.

"Check your father out," she said.

Tom stood beside her that day "before London," dwarfing her, because she was so tiny. All ginger hair and freckles, Jacinta Louise Mackee was. Half the time she looked like a kid and not someone who advised the government on how to treat their immigrants. The morning light had blinded him for a moment as he'd watched his dad hunch over the timber.

"He pencils a line," she explained, still intrigued after all these years, "and then he stands back for hours, thinking about whether it's right or not. Next, he's going to run his fingers along the timber and if there's one little splinter out of place, he'll file it back. With my nail file, mind you. *Prick*."

But it had been an insult laced with affection. She picked up her satchel and kissed Tom's cheek.

"Tell him it's time to go to work and that we've got Anabel's confirmation talks tonight, and don't forget to move your crap out of Georgie's attic, Tom. You know she wants to get things ready for Joe." She knocked at the window and held up a hand in a wave and then she was off.

He poured his cereal into a bowl with milk and walked out back to watch the master at work. It had been bloody freezing and he'd regretted not putting on any clothes except for the boxers.

"You're going to be late," he said with a yawn. On the bench was a good slab of timber, a river red gum. His father was making Nanni Grace a table for when Joe and his girl came to visit from London.

"Straddle it, will you?" his dad said, grabbing hold of the electric saw. "Hold it still."

Tom hadn't been happy with the suggestion. "You better not get that too close to you-know-where," he muttered, swallowing a mouthful of cornflakes and putting down the bowl.

His father stared at a spot he missed and began filing again before he put on his goggles and switched on the saw. When it was over, Tom was shaking his head with disbelief, pointing to his private parts. His father was grinning.

His dad was looking good, he had thought. Not like the year when Tom turned seventeen and Dominic was heading toward some meltdown, courtesy of too many liquid lunches and union negotiations between a hostile government and disgruntled workers. But forty was looking good on him. His father took off the goggles. "Listen," he said. "Georgie wants you to—"

"I know," Tom interrupted. "She wants me to get my shit out of her attic. You'd think a king was returning, the way she's going on."

His dad had shrugged. "He's her little brother. You know how she is about Joe."

"Like you're not," Tom scoffed. "His woman's going to be with him, you know, and he's not going to be able to do all the stuff

40

you've got planned. Can't imagine Penelope Cruz going to a footy match or at the pub every night." They called her that because she was Spanish. Georgie called her Pen for short.

His dad lifted his arm to stretch out a muscle and Tom had reached over and poked him in the gut.

"What's this? Looks like flab, Dominic."

Tom loved calling him that too, just to piss him off.

"Little shit," his father said, holding his gut in and slapping his abs. "Watch this body. It's what yours'll look like one day."

"Mum noticed it from the kitchen," Tom had lied, grinning. "She was like, 'Check out that carcass, will ya!'"

Before he could duck, his father had hooked him around the neck with his elbow and they struggled for a while. They were both killing themselves laughing and neither gave in. It was allowed to get as vicious as they wanted, without any repercussions, and those days it was the only physical contact they had with each other. Tom got the upper hand, but he knew he could lose it any moment.

"She didn't seem to have a problem with it last night," his father managed between grunts when they hit the ground.

Tom shoved him back and had tried not to choke at the idea of whatever his parents had got up to the night before. He'd just been given a reason to be in counseling for the rest of his life.

Later, they carried the slab of timber onto the grass. He could tell the table was going to be beautiful and he could understand his father's obsession with getting it right. They both stared at it for a moment. The smell of it, mingled with the silky oak and lavender in the backyard, made him smile.

"Nice," Tom said.

"Getting there."

"Can I borrow fifty bucks?"

He got the look.

Tom laughed. "I can't fit a job in between band and uni, and they pay peanuts for gigs these days."

"What about the contacts your mum had?" his dad asked.

"I rang and spoke to four very polite computers who gave me all these options and then cut out on me. Then I tried the post office, because they were advertising, and I spoke to another computer. Very rude, that one. Don't think it recognized 'Are you shitting me?' as an option."

"You know why that is?"

"Why is that, Dominic?" Tom had asked drolly, because he knew he was going to be told why.

"Because we don't live in a society anymore, Tom. We live in an economy. We're not citizens. We're customers. That's what this government's done to us."

"Can't I just ask you for fifty bucks and you be Marcel Marceau?"

His father, the smart-arse, mimed out the handing of the money and they were both grinning again.

"As long as I don't have to chase you to pay it back." He looked at Tom suspiciously. "What's it for?"

"Membership for the Young Libs."

"Yeah, very fucking funny."

Tom had laughed at the expression on his father's face. "I'm wooing a girl."

He remembers seeing Tara that night and how he kissed her and how they ended up in Georgie's attic. And how one week later they ended up going all the way in her parents' house. Then his life became all about "after London" and now Tom's taking those deep breaths, like the ones a counselor told him to take, because he thinks he can't breathe. Until he sees it there in the in-box and his heart lifts: tomsister@hotmail.com. At thirteen and three quarters, as she persists in reminding everyone, Anabel's news is limited to what their mum won't let her do and the ongoing bitter battle with Trixie Pantalano, her nemesis, in a bid for top of the class for Year Eight, and someone called Ginger who fights her on everything to do with the social justice committee. But the soap opera she's filming to document her life makes him laugh every time she sends him the next segment. The kid can do deadpan better than anyone he knows, better even than their father. In today's episode, she's sitting at Grandma Agnes's table lamenting her life in a sonnet. She's got the iambic pentameter down to perfection. He can hear the click of a computer in the background and imagines that his mother is holding the camera while she's working on some legislation. He gets a quick image of his mum when Anabel's back in possession of the camera and he can't help but notice those laugh lines around her eyes that seem to be all about age these days and little to do with laughter. In the old days, his mum and Georgie spent most of their time killing themselves laughing at absolutely everything. "You girls are going to wet your pants," his father would say in his typically dry tone, but most of the time it was Dominic who made them laugh. Tom could do it too. And Joe. They were perfect mimics.

The film ends with Anabel dancing around the kitchen, playing the trumpet. Tom's impressed with the speed of her playing and her ability to keep the notes in check. His parents wanted her to play the violin, but the moment Pop Bill showed her Tom Finch's trumpet, Anabel wasn't interested in any other instrument. The screen freezes on a kiss that she throws out to the world, but it's the wedding photo of his parents on Granny's mantel behind Anabel that he stares at. He magnifies the screen until he sees both their faces. *Shit*, they were young. So young that his mother's parents flew down from Brisbane to talk Dominic and Jacinta Louise out of "ruining their lives." But Tom's mum and dad had already gone and done it at Saint Michael's with only Georgie and a couple of their best friends in attendance. Six months after the wedding, Tom was born. Nanni Grace and Bill insisted that they move to Albury, but Tom had heard his father say more than once that he would never have been able to look his in-laws in the eyes if Jacinta didn't finish her degree in politics. So his father dropped out of law to look after Tom, and instead of taking his wife home to his parents, he took her home to his twin sister and they all moved into a cramped two-bedroom fibro in Camperdown and lived off Georgie's wage as a paralegal while Dominic started fixing people's furniture.

His father's face in the wedding photo freaks Tom out. It's like looking at himself in the mirror. Worse still, it's like looking at a photograph of his grandfather, Tom Finch, and he can't help thinking that when Tom Finch and Dominic were his age, they were fathers. By the time Tom Finch was a year older, he was dead.

He looks back at the keyboard and begins typing.

To: tomsister@hotmail.com
From: anabelsbrother@hotmail.com
Date: 16 July 2007

Dear H-anibal,
How goes it, fugly girl?

44

Make sure Agnes of God doesn't get Mum down, and tell her I'm staying with Georgie and, yes, she has put on weight and will be losing it in about four months.
Love, the better-looking sibling,
Tom
P.S. The Mackee pride goes down the toilet if you let chicks with names like Trixie and Ginger get the better of you.

He takes the bus home, already bored, which is a worry when it's only three thirty and the highlight of your day is an e-mail from your little sister. The thought that this will be his timetable for the next couple of months makes him feel as if he's gagging from lack of air. At least if he was with his flatmates, he could waste the day away and not realize it was even over until it was two in the morning and one of them would point out that the home-shopping show was on.

The worst part of the day is always walking past the Union hotel. Today Stani, the owner, is out front smoking. Tom could keep walking and forgo the long history his family has with the place, but he can't. Because Dominic and Joe Mackee drank here. Georgie still does with his parents' friends. And then there's the story of his grandparents and this pub. Two best friends traveled from the Burdekin in North Queensland sometime in the 1960s and walked into the Union and fell in love with Grace. Tom Finch was the smarter talker of the two and won first round, marrying her before his name came up in the lottery sending him to Vietnam on a tour of duty. He never returned. The heartbroken, patient one, Bill Mackee, grieved a best friend and married the love of his life, adopting the twins when they were four years old.

"Tom," Stani acknowledges.

45

He still speaks with a heavy Eastern European accent, although he's been in the country long enough to have lost it. Tom had met him briefly in the days when he hung out with Justine Kalinsky, Stani's niece, but the old guy's never used his name before. Tom knows he can't spend the next couple of months walking past and being on the receiving end of Stani's accusing stare each time. He can handle people thinking that the Mackees were a bunch of ratbags. He imagined that his uncle would have been kicked out once or twice, too. Joe could be a bit of a yob when he was drunk. And God knows how bad his father was in the end. But what Tom's ex-flatmates had made him, by association, pissed him off. Mackees weren't thieves, nor were Finches. He thinks he'll make it easy and just give Stani the money from his final dole check.

When he turns back, Stani's already disappeared inside, so Tom follows him in.

It's a small pub. No slot machines. No big-screen TV. No jukebox. The room at the back has good acoustics for rehearsals and is hired out for small parties. On Sunday afternoons there's a regular bunch of locals who sit around the table near the door and play. Sometimes Tom turned up, not because his flatmates worked there but because of the sounds. A fiddle, two guitars, and vocals, with a fierce passion to the music. He liked what he played over at the Barro hotel, from time to time, but it was beginning to bore him. It was like the stuff he used to play when he was fifteen. Before the girls came into his life.

"It's shit punk," Tara Finke once pointed out bluntly on the way home from one of those combined schools extravaganzas during their last year at school. The music teacher had asked him to accompany the orchestra for a number that needed guitar, and Tara had been sent along as a prefect representative. "That doesn't mean I think punk is shit," she continued. "It means that when someone plays punk in a shit-like manner, it's excruciating. So either find yourself a good punk band or move on, Tom. Because it kills me to say this, but you're actually a tiny bit gifted."

"How would you like it if I said to you, 'It kills me to say this, but you're actually a tiny bit beautiful'?" he had asked, pissed off.

She hadn't said anything then, which was rare for her.

"Would you have been lying?" she said after a long silence.

"Lying about what?"

More quiet.

"About me being a tiny bit beautiful."

"Shit, yeah."

But later that night, he had sent her a message on MSN.

Of course I was lying. The "tiny bit" part, anyway.

Stani looks up at Tom from behind the bar, surprised to still see him there.

"Francesca reckons Zac and Sarah took some money," Tom says.

He doesn't want to make it sound like a whine or an accusation, but it comes out abruptly. Stani doesn't speak.

"So around how much are we talking about?" Tom asks briskly.

Stani waves him off. "They're gone. You go too. Let's call it even."

Tom shakes his head. He focuses on the bottles lined up behind Stani's head.

"Just tell me how much it is and I'll pay you, and *then* we'll call it even."

Tom's getting frustrated. He wants to get on with his life. He

47

wants to get off the bus every afternoon and walk past the pub without feeling guilty.

He hears the music from the back room: someone stumbling over guitar chords and then the sound of the accordion. He knows Justine uses the back for rehearsal, and he wants to get out of here before he has to face her. Seeing Francesca the other night was bad enough. "Just tell me how much it is," Tom says again, forcefully.

Stani already dismisses him with a look, but Tom won't budge.

Just tell me how much it is, you old bastard, he wants to shout.

"It's over two thousand dollars, Tom. Got that kind of money?"

Tom can't hide his reaction. Tries to, but can tell from Stani's expression that he fails. The money in his pocket seems pathetic, and he wants to punch something or someone. The guitarist in the back room who doesn't know the chords makes him want to barge in there and smash the instrument into pieces.

"Why didn't you sack them?" he blurts out. "You would have known what they were doing."

Stani leans forward over the counter. He's led a hard life, and it's stamped all over his face.

"Because I promised Dominic Mackee that I wouldn't let any of my employees sign a workplace agreement. It would have been easier if I did."

"My father didn't represent your union."

Stani shrugs. "A union man's a union man."

Tom gives up. He doesn't have two thousand dollars.

The guitar playing continues, and he notices Stani taking a deep breath of total sufferance.

"Wrong chord," Tom mutters to him, and then walks away but stops before he makes it outside.

"I'll work for you," he says from the door. "Until I pay it off."

Stani shakes his head. "Like I said, don't return here with your friends, and you and me, we're square."

Tom shakes his head. "*No.* I work here until the debt is paid off."

"No."

"You think I'm going to steal from you, don't you?"

His voice is aggressive, but he can't help it. He's back at the counter, fists clenched at his side. He tries to remember what his counselor in high school would tell him during their "how to combat the bully in you" sessions that Tom was forced to attend in Year Eight.

"I do," Stani says flatly.

Wrong chord again.

"Bloody bastard," Stani mutters. *"Wrong chord, Frankie!"*

Great. Francesca. That's all Tom needs. Both girls.

"Change the chord!" Stani calls out again.

"To a G," Tom tells him.

"To a G!"

The guitar playing stops.

"What if I promise?" Tom persists.

Stani's just staring at him. All pale-blue bloodshot eyes squinting with distrust. But then Tom gets sick of the groveling and walks toward the door.

"On your father's honor?" Stani asks as Tom reaches the door.

"No." Tom's not wanting to bring his father into this . . . into anything in his life. "On my uncle's. On Joe's. You knew him?"

Stani nods with a sigh. "Yeah, I knew Joe."

The guitar playing begins again. It's slow and she's thinking too hard. He can imagine the look on Francesca's face while she concentrates on the chords. She picks a Waifs song—a good one for learning because it's just one or two chords and it's slow.

"I can hazard a guess, but I'll never know
Why you put these walls up, I can't get through
It's as though you want to be lonely and blue."

Francesca Spinelli's voice can do anything, and singing alongside her always made Tom sound better than he was. Justine was the same. One of those musical geniuses. Except she chose the accordion, or as she'd say, it chose her, and it's not exactly the conservatorium's choice musical instrument. When they were in Year Twelve, the three of them formed a band and called themselves The Fey. Tom was purely into writing their own material. Originals or nothing. Francesca didn't mind dabbling with a cover once or twice. Justine was neutral. They ended up with a mixed bag that they always believed made them unique, and for the first year of uni, they played gigs around each other's campuses, constantly hiring and firing drummers until they decided they'd stick to just the three of them. They were different from the others in their group. Tom and Francesca, especially, had a bit of a lazy streak, courtesy of natural ability. They just liked playing music with absolutely no ambition of going anywhere with it and it was Justine who took care of business and was in charge. By the end of their first year of uni, Siobhan Sullivan was working three jobs, saving to go to London, and Jimmy Hailler was nursing his sick grandfather. Tara Finke was stuck with three music fanatics who dragged her to every gig they had.

Just listening to Francesca's voice makes Tom think of those

50

nights he'd camp out at her place and they'd be practicing in her bedroom and Tara would fall asleep on the bed still holding her study notes.

"We're going to be famous one day and you'll tell people we used to put you to sleep," he teased at the time when the looks between them changed into something intense. They had enjoyed some kind of clumsy antagonistic attraction since they had first met in Year Eleven. Tara Finke dealt with it by ignoring him. Tom slept with other girls. But it had always been there, scrutinized by Francesca and Justine. The same two staring at him now from the back-room door.

"Seems like Tom here will be washing plates," Stani tells the girls. "In the kitchen with Ned."

Still nothing from the two except a bit of irritated surprise on their faces.

Justine is the first to break the silence.

"If his friends come in, I'm calling the police," she tells her uncle.

"And he gets the lockup shift," Francesca says.

They speak like they're in charge, and judging from Stani's shrug, maybe they are.

He remembers the times they'd walk toward him in the playground with that same look on their faces, but double in number with Siobhan and Tara. "It's the four horsewomen of the apocalypse," Jimmy Hailler would say. "They're going to make us do something we don't want to do."

"We're not going to give in," Tom would say.

But they did. Always. "Think of the alternatives," Jimmy said. "They love us. Imagine if they hated us."

There's no need for imagining here.

Francesca walks away, taking out her phone and texting. He knows who it's to and what she's saying. *The dickhead of our lives is back.*

He gives himself four weeks to pay off the debt and never walk into this place again.

chapter six

To: mackee_joe@yahoo.co.uk
From: georgiefinch@hotmail.com
Date: 16 July 2007

I practice my response, Joe. Because it's what everyone wants to ask. I can see it in their eyes. How did I let this thing with Sam happen? And this is how I try to respond: That he was hiding in wait, one street away, hovering on the perimeters of my world, still hanging out with Dom and the others. I'd know. Because I'd smell him the moment I'd walk into anyone's house. I was like a wolf—able to follow his scent through this whole city. It's what happens when you've lived with someone for seven years. But I didn't want anyone to take sides, remember? You did. You never spoke to him again, Joe, but it wasn't the way I wanted things. I just wanted everyone to keep their end of the bargain and never *ever* expect Sam and me to be in the same room or to discuss him or his child in front of me. The Jews tear their clothing when someone in their life dies. I was Jewish the year Sam's child was born. Tearing everything inside of me that wasn't already torn.

But then you got on that train, Joe. And it was Sam who spoke to Foreign Affairs, contacting every person he knew in London to try to work out what they knew in those first couple of days. It was Sam who booked my flight because we all felt hopeless waiting for you to come home to us, and it was Sam who traveled with me. In London it was Sam who went to every hospital, hanging up photographs of you in waiting rooms and outside Tube stations. Sam who told me and your beautiful Ana Vanquez that there was no body to take home. No evidence of you except your cash card being used that morning to buy a weekly ticket at the Tube station. It was Sam who had to listen to the words over and over again, *"I can't go home without my brother's body. Don't ask me to do that to my mother."*

And then he was back in my bed, Joe. I don't know how. I didn't ask him. He didn't ask to come back. It's as though I woke up one morning and Sam was lying there beside me. And he stayed and I couldn't understand why, because I hated everyone around me. Every time anyone opened their mouth I wanted to tell them to shut up because their words were useless. But Sam stayed, and here we are, Joe. Sam and I.

Almost living together, and I'm able to forget.

Except for the Fridays, Saturdays, and Sundays, when he has his son.

chapter seven

Tom works at the Union from five o'clock onward because it's the only time Stani serves food. The menu is limited to sausages and mash, T-bone, and salad. Stani doesn't cater to vegetarians. "Bloody bastards," he mutters when people complain. "Cook in your own homes."

The cook's name is Ned and he's a lanky guy Tom's age, with eyes that swing all over the place nervously, and a height that makes him stoop with awkwardness. He's slightly too cool-looking to be considered goofy, but it's a very fine line that he walks.

Tom's ex-flatmates used to do impersonations of the way Ned would say, "Hi, Sarah," in a puppy-dog fashion, tongue hanging out, and then they'd do an exaggerated circular motion to the other side of the room and say, "Hi, Zac." They didn't know which way he swung sexually, but then again, Zac didn't know himself, so it could have been him projecting.

Once or twice Tom attempts to make conversation, but Ned the Cook seems to have the same problem as Mohsin the Ignorer. With Francesca, Ned the Cook is different. Ned the Introvert becomes Ned the Wit. On Tom's third night working, Ned spends the whole time speaking Latin to Francesca. It was one of the useless subjects she took as part of her history degree, and the two banter and giggle using words ending with *cus, tis,* and *ergo* that make Tom want to commit a felony with a scourer sponge. He makes it clear what he thinks through small snorts of disbelief.

Ned the Cook is doing a double degree in art and education and has a novel in his hand at all times, and the worst thing is that no matter how much Tom wishes it, the bastard doesn't even come across as pretentious.

When Francesca and Justine aren't serving outside or rehearsing in the back room, they're hanging out in the kitchen with Ned and invisible Tom. The only time they don't chat incessantly is when the news comes on and Francesca is listening to it, and then they start up again until Stani calls Francesca up the front and Justine goes back to rehearsal.

Tom takes it for just a week. He has no problem with the girls not talking to him. When it comes to wars of attrition, these girls are the commanders in chief, but Ned the Cook is a different story.

"Do you have a problem with me?" Tom finally asks forcefully.

Ned throws a T-bone on the grill. Doesn't miss a beat.

"I didn't like your friends."

"Really?" Tom feels like playing the cruelty game. "Funny that. Because I heard you had the hots for both my flatmates."

The cook lays the lettuce out on two plates and starts chopping up the onions.

"Yes, I did," he says casually. "In the first minute I met them. Then in the second minute, I decided I wasn't going to be into dudes who treat others like crap only because they can. And then in the third, I actually stopped noticing they were around. I'm easily bored around stupid people."

Tom hadn't worked out that his flatmates bored him until the fifth minute, so he feels slightly inferior to Ned the Cook, who is also able to articulate what the great white whale represents in *Moby-Dick* while cooking a T-bone to a perfect medium-rare.

And that's how Tom spends his nights. Washing up alongside Ned the Cook, who makes a bigger mess than is necessary just to piss him off. On the nights she's rehearsing at the Union, Justine spends half the time whispering to Ned about the latest guy she's in love with, and Francesca journeys into the kitchen every hour to listen to the news. She'll say, "There's been a cyclone in Sri Lanka, Ned," or "Oh, my God, an earthquake in southern Turkey . . . a car bomb in Karachi." Ned just listens patiently and Tom wants to warn him not to nurture her obsessive compulsiveness because it always turns into something devastating. But he can't be bothered.

Most days, when he arrives before the nighttime shifts begin, he can hear the sounds of guitar and accordion from the back room. From what he's picked up in conversation, Justine and Francesca are putting together a compilation for everyone they know overseas so they can post it on their MySpace page. He only knows that because he has to listen to every single one of their conversations without taking part. Six covers. Six originals. For Siobhan Sullivan they choose "London Still" because — surprise, surprise — she's in London still, and one afternoon he hears them practice "The Blower's Daughter" and wonders if that's for Tara. They're still trying to work out one for Jimmy Hailler, who seems to have disappeared, and Wonder-Boy Will, and Francesca's parents, who are in Italy until September. The last one is for Justine's cousin in Poland. He also hears the reason Francesca's learning guitar. It's because the guitarist who replaced Tom in their band told her that all she could do was "sing and look good in a sundress," which is probably more than that tosser could do.

"What about your originals?" Ned the Cook asks her after six minutes of silence listening to the news and a short discussion about the kidnapping of hostages in Mogadishu. Francesca knows all the hostages by name. She switches the radio off the moment the sport report comes on as if there's no one else in the room who may want to hear the outcome of a league player's salary cap appeal.

Tom recognizes the signs. Some afternoons she's flat because most of her world is away. If she's not listening to the news, she spends her days sewing wedding dresses with her grandmother. Sometimes she speaks about the intricacies of the beading and he watches the way her fingers dance and her eyes come to life as she demonstrates. A useless arts degree in the classics, sewing with her grandmother in a room above a Leichhardt haberdashery shop, and pining for her boyfriend. Knowing Francesca's mother, she's probably despairing about the lack of ambition in her daughter's life.

His days are worse. He's either bored to death at work or lying in the attic listening to music. Georgie's pretty moody at the moment and sometimes Sam is around and Tom doesn't really know how to react. He was fourteen when Sam and Georgie fell apart and it was hard on everyone because Sam and Tom's father had become best mates. Tom had never really thought much of him when he was younger. Sam was a bit of a know-it-all back then, working in a wanky law firm. He was a smart-arse, really. These days he's a lawyer with the Industrial Relations Commission. That was the thing with Sam, Tom's mum would argue. Refused to let the Mackees believe they were better than him, Georgie included, but Sam's passions for unions came through knowing the Finches and the Mackees. Perhaps his whole sense of social justice came from knowing them. Despite the way Tom felt about his father these days, he knew Dominic Mackee would bust a gut to make sure some worker wasn't getting taken advantage of. It was the kind of passion that enticed Sam away from a six-digit salary.

Despite the obvious evidence of a fetus in her womb, Tom hasn't worked out if Georgie and Sam are sleeping together. There's too little said between them, not necessarily awkward, but it's like they don't know how to speak to each other. Except Tom can see the obvious in Sam's face. If Sam's not with his kid, he doesn't want to be anywhere except with Georgie. The two strangers are a long way from the Georgie and Sam of Tom's childhood. Back then, they'd bicker and smooch and fight and tease, and Sam would call her his "Georgie girl," and he was "babe" or "Sambo" to her.

Tom watches them some nights while Sam's tapping away at his laptop and Georgie's watching TV. She's a commercial-television slut, obsessed with *Dancing with the Stars* and home-improvement shows. She cries every time someone gets their backyard renovated, and tries to tell Tom the story. Once upon a time he could have imagined Sam being a bastard about it. Nowadays, Sam seems just grateful for being allowed to sit beside her in the lounge room.

"You okay?" he asks her one evening when they're both sitting out back, on the banana chairs Joe bought her one Christmas. Another couple of eyesores, really. Sometimes Tom thinks Joe did it to stir Georgie. The light's on behind them and she's reading and he's nursing a coffee and playing his guitar.

"My friends aren't talking to me," she murmurs.

He shrugs. "Neither are mine.'"

She looks his way and then laughs.

"The girls will come around."

"I'm talking about my ex-flatmates."

He sips his coffee and then gets up and scrapes his banana chair away from her so he can light up.

"Can I ask you something?" he asks, his voice quiet.

He can see she thinks he's going to ask about the baby, but she nods all the same.

"Why do you think he went off the deep end?"

It takes her a moment to understand he's talking about his father.

"You don't think it was losing Joe?" she asks.

He shakes his head. "That was the last straw. But it began earlier. When I was in Year Eleven and I started hanging out here with you and Joe."

She's not speaking. He's scared she won't.

"Was it their marriage?" he asks.

She shakes her head and then she smiles to herself, as if Tom's not there for a moment. "I started the trend of Dominic being the piper. He came out first and I was right behind him, and it's never changed. It's like everyone's used him to suss out the dangers before they take the next step. If Dominic Mackee was doing it, then it was okay. The thing with Dominic is that no matter what the risk, I wanted to follow. And sometimes it meant that I didn't know who I was if I wasn't his twin sister, but I didn't care. Because he never left me hanging. That's what I loved about him. He always looked after me. Meanwhile Bill just went on and on about Dom's duty to me and to the world, and then when Joe was born seven years later, that responsibility was cemented in place. And your father took it seriously, Tom. I remember once, when we were twelve, we wanted to go to the Easter Show on our own and Bill insisted that we take Joe. He drilled it into Dominic that he wasn't to let Joe out of his sight. The lecture went on forever and all we wanted to do was nick off with our friends."

Tom could see that the memory was vivid and painful, but then again, any thought of Joe was.

"And we lost him. Dominic was holding his hand and somehow he lost Joe in the crowd, and it took us and the police three hours to find him. Your father was inconsolable. And I hated Bill for this part of it, because the moment we got home, the belt came off and Dominic got it so bad. Joe and I cried and cried, begging him to stop."

"What did Nanni Grace do?"

"Nothing. The discipline was always Bill's thing and if there was one thing Nanni Grace agreed with, it was that Joe and I were to be looked after. 'You're responsible, Dom. Responsibility, Dominic.' It's all he ever heard, so it's no wonder he ended up captain of his primary and high school and everywhere he's been since. That's not to say he didn't have a bit of a bastard bullying streak, but thank God he used it for good, because he could have been a real prick, you know."

"But never one to Mum and Anabel."

She sighs, wrapping her arms around her body to block out the cold. "He was tough on you," she says, looking over to him.

Tom's shaking his head.

"No, he was," she insists. "He was just like Bill. They both treated their wives like princesses, but their sons were different."

61

"How come Bill didn't treat you like a princess?"

She gives him a droll look and he laughs.

"Come on, Georgie, it's because you don't give people a chance to treat you that way."

"Not true. There are some women who get away with being princesses and I'm not one of them." She looks at him closely. "Did he ever hit you?" she asks quietly.

Tom doesn't speak for a moment.

"Not like you said Bill did to him that time when he lost Joe. Except maybe a bit of shoving around in those last years of high school."

Tom could tell Georgie about the days after his mum and Anabel left, but he preferred not to. He couldn't deal with anyone's judgment of his father, no matter what.

One morning he had asked, "Do you think that's a good idea?" after watching his father pour a glass of scotch.

"Do you have a better one, Tom?"

"Yeah, actually I do, Dominic."

He got a backhand for that. It split his lip and made his head spin.

"Shit," his father muttered, grabbing Tom to see what he had done, but Tom stepped away, tasting blood in his mouth. He watched his father stumble. "Come on, Tommy. Just let me look at it."

It began a pattern between him and his father. And on the very day Tom woke up hoping that he didn't have to go through that ritual of watching his father down a scotch just to get him through the morning, or that he didn't have to stick his father's head under a shower spray and sober him up for a meeting between the Labor Council and industry bosses, that he didn't have to kid himself that a mug of black coffee would work a miracle—on that very day that Tom woke up wishing it would all go away, it did.

Georgie's stare pierces into him, jolting him back to the present.

"You know you'd make your mum happy if you rang her," Georgie says.

"I was pretty cut when she walked out on him," he says, relieved to be thinking of something else.

"She didn't walk out on him, Tom. She took Anabel to Brisbane so Anabel wouldn't have to see him at his worst. She did that for Dom, not for herself. It was a horrific year and Dom just crashed. It was the hardest decision she's ever had to make. But she didn't leave him and she didn't leave you, Tom. She wanted you to come up with her. She begged you to."

"So what about before? When I was in Year Eleven and things were just beginning to get bad?" he asks again, not wanting to remember the look in his mother's eyes when he wouldn't say good-bye a year ago.

She shrugs. "Who knows? I think when Jacinta had to go back to work, it killed them both for a while."

"I thought she wanted to work."

"Anabel was only eight, and your mother had worked all through your primary years, so I really think she wanted to be home for Anabel. Pick her up from school, turn up to sports carnivals, be a real at-home mum. I think Dominic felt he failed her by not being able to support you all on a single wage, but your parents were mort-gaged to the hilt and interest rates were ridiculous. Plus his job was always so full-on and he had little to show for it, especially when the government came down hard on the unions."

"So he regretted dropping out of uni?" he asks.

63

"Why ask that?" she snaps. "So you can blame yourself and say you being born stuffed up their lives? Well, it didn't, and once he got into the union, he never looked back. It was like he was born for that job. There were no regrets, Tom. A bit of guilt from Jacinta because she thinks your father missed out on something, and a bit of guilt from him because he thinks she missed out on something." She smiles. "But there was nothing wrong with their marriage. I could be a fool for believing this one hundred percent, but there was never anyone for Dominic but Jacinta and vice versa. They knew they'd get through the shitty part."

"But they didn't," he argues.

"They're not divorced, Tom. That marriage is not over."

"Georgie, they've been living apart for more than a year and we don't have a clue where he is."

And there it is. A look that tells him everything and nothing. All of a sudden he's pissed off. Not quite sure who with, but somehow Georgie gets in the way.

"Where is he?"

She sighs, getting up from her chair. "Let's not do this now."

"You have no right to keep it from my mother. You've always thought you were more important than her when it comes to him, but you aren't," he says angrily.

She stops walking. Can't hide the hurt.

"Where did that come from?" she asks angrily. "I would never keep anything about Dominic from your mother, and he would never be in contact with me before being in contact with her. Sisters and daughters come second in this family, Tom. They always have. So if you want to find out anything about your father, pick up the phone and speak to your mother."

"I didn't mean to—"

"Yes, you did," she says, cutting him off. She's crying and it makes him feel like a piece of shit.

"Georgie, I'm sorry!" he shouts as she disappears inside, but all he hears is the sound of her footsteps and the slamming of her door.

He goes for a walk and finds himself two blocks away in Temple Street, outside the house he grew up in. It's a semi, much smaller than Georgie's, with a tiny garden path and a bit of lawn and a border for planting roses. His father was a stickler for keeping it perfect. At the moment, they rent it out and everything's dead.

It's a bad place for memories. Some of the best moments of his life happened here and some of the worst. It's where his father broke the news that Joe was probably dead. Tom remembers Dominic standing on this very veranda, waiting for him, saying, "Tom . . . Oh, God, Tom."

He crouches down to where a dead stem is buried in cracked dirt and crumbles the soil inside his fist.

"I called police!" He hears a voice from next door.

He peers around the hedge and smiles. The light's on and he can see their tiny neighbor, clutching her quilted dressing gown around her.

"Hey, Mrs. Liu. It's me, Thomas. Thomas Mackee."

Her face registers shock and then joy. "*Oh*. Oh. Thomas. Very sorry."

She steps onto the lawn, and he climbs over the hedge and into her garden, bobbing down to kiss her cheek. When he was at school, she used to walk up the main drag of Stanmore with a white mask over her mouth as if the SARS virus was in the neighborhood.

Sometimes his father would have to go up to the shops with her to translate. It's not as if Dominic knew how to speak Mandarin, but somehow both Mrs. Liu and the person behind the counter seemed happier when his dad was patiently repeating what the other had to say.

Tom answers the questions about his mum and Anabel, and when she asks after his father, he tells her the truth and says he has no idea where he is. Then she invites him in and he wants to say yes, so that he can see his family's kitchen from her living room. But he can't stand the idea of seeing another Tom sitting at the table. Another Anabel resting her face in her hands, elbows on the table, grinning. Another Jacinta and Dominic doing the sums about whether they could afford a new fridge. People spoke within the walls of their home. His parents genuinely liked each other. They liked their kids. Love's easy. It kind of comes with the territory. But liking is another story.

"When Jacinta and Dominic come home, Tom?" Mrs. Liu asks, tears in her eyes. "People in your house," she continues, leaning forward to whisper. *"Dirty. Very dirty."*

That was another thing his father didn't take into account when he allowed everything to fall apart. That neighbors like Mrs. Liu were left lonely, living next door to dirty people.

They talk for a while. Small talk, really. It reminds him of his father coming out here every night to water the plants, back before the water restrictions. "He's always had a thing for old women," his mother would joke. She'd call him the patron saint of the lonely. He could sit outside and spend hours chatting with anyone who just wanted to talk. "Even five minutes of your time can make someone's day," he'd tell Tom and Anabel.

Tom was beginning to understand the five minutes a lot more these days.

Later, when he's back at Georgie's, he finds her in the kitchen making a cup of tea. He thinks of those nights after Joe died, when Nanni Grace and Pop Bill returned to Albury, which was hours and hours away. In his own home, he remembers how his mum would sit on his bed at night, encouraging him to talk about how he was feeling, and the way Anabel would huddle onto his father's lap and whisper for him not to be sad. He remembers the murmuring from his parents' bedroom, always the murmuring. But had they forgotten about Georgie alone in this house? Were her friends there for her? Did they sleep alongside her? Is that how Sam came back into her life? Tom needs to know. Who kept one of their own from the mind-numbing solitude during those nights of hell? And because he can't stand it any longer, because sometimes he thinks everything inside him will crack, he walks to where Georgie has her back to him at the sink and wraps his arm around her and they stand there for a long while, their bodies shuddering from the exhaustion of this dry retching of emotion.

chapter eight

When Georgie approaches the Union, her nephew's standing outside, having a smoke during his break. He looks lonely out here on his own. When he sees her, he stubs out his cigarette and gives her a hug, but already there's an irritated look on his face.

"Don't complain about the food."

"What a ridiculous thing to say," she says. "Why would I complain about the food? I love the fact that Stani's finally introduced it."

"I'm warning you."

When she follows him inside, her eyes go straight up to the blackboard menu and then back at him, with irritation.

"Why introduce food if he's only going to offer two plates?"

"Georgie, don't."

"I'm just saying . . ."

"Go for the T-bone. You'll love it."

He's pushing her—no, actually he's shoving her—toward the table near the door, and then Francesca Spinelli is there saying, "Georgie!"

Georgie tries to move around Tom and fails. It's like he's blocking her, but Francesca manages to push him aside.

"Oh. My. God. You're pregnant!"

For a moment, Georgie is stunned. Tom's muttering while Francesca is grinning from ear to ear. "You look gooooorgeous."

There's hugging all around, and before Georgie can stop herself, before she even wants to, she's talking trimesters and morning sickness and the joy of her growing bust size and how she's carrying it all at the front, which could mean a boy, and she's saying aloud every single thing she was frightened to even feel. To this girl who used to hang out in her attic with her friends and Tom, playing music and arguing and calling him a dickbrain and every other suffix or prefix you could stick *dick* to. And there it was. A memory of a time when Tom was at his happiest and the girls were the key.

Francesca kisses her with the promise of returning on her break and then she's gone and Georgie sits at the table, the greatest of relief overcoming her. As if she's been holding her breath for so long.

She's having a baby. Months or days don't count anymore. It's all about weeks now. Twenty weeks. Too late to change her mind. Too early to feel safe, but close enough.

"How bloody rude was that?" Tom says with disgust, staring at the bar where Francesca's serving. "I mean, what if you had a fat gut and a bigger arse because you'd put on weight?"

"Oh, what a silver-tongued devil my nephew's turned out to be."

Lucia and her sister, Bernadette, are twenty-five minutes late. "Don't be critical," Lucia protests.

Georgie shrugs. "I would never get away with being twenty-five minutes late," she says.

"Kids . . ."

"Give you an excuse to be late."

"You have no idea. . . ."

"And it also gives you permission to say the words, 'you have no idea,'" Bernadette says. "She was supposed to pick me up half an hour earlier."

Lucia looks disgruntled, but then she spots the blackboard. "Since when have they had food here?"

"Six months. But only two choices."

Tom comes out of the kitchen, and Georgie beckons him over again. He leans over to kiss Lucia and Bernadette.

"Why is there no vegetarian dish?" Georgie asks.

He shrugs. "I think the boss wants to do things slowly."

Georgie sees Stani, and her hand goes up in a beckoning wave before Tom grabs it.

"Don't call him over and tell him off about the menu," he warns.

"Don't tell me what to do, Tom. It's ridiculous that there's no vegetarian dish."

"More ridiculous that you're *not* a vegetarian. Sam's been cooking protein all week."

This seems to interest Lucia and her sister, who exchange a quick look that doesn't go unnoticed by Georgie.

When he walks away, Lucia stares after him. "I don't remember him looking that much like Dom. It's freaky. How's he doing?"

"Him or Dom?"

"Both."

Georgie shrugs. "They all need to be together. They've never been good without one another."

Lucia's doing that probing stare thing. It's part of her arsenal. Wearing Georgie down emotionally with an empathetic stare and then trying to sort out her life.

"So Sam's cooking for you?"

70

Georgie doesn't respond.

"No one's being critical, Georgie."

"Well, that pisses me off," Georgie says angrily. "Seven years ago it was all fire and brimstone and everyone telling me to forget about him, and now . . . now I should give it a go. Would you, Lucia? Would you take Abe back?"

Lucia doesn't respond for a long while and then sighs. "I don't know what I'd do, Georgie. Probably what you did. Lose my mind a bit. Be angry forever. But things aren't exactly the way you put it."

No one ever dares say the words to Georgie, but she knows they want to. That it wasn't behind her back. They were having a break, called by her. Because back then Sam was a bear with a sore head for so long, the time came when she said, "I want you to go, Sam. I want you to just work out what you want, because sometimes I don't think it's me."

"You've got it wrong," he had said with a sigh, getting into bed.

But she insisted on it. There was no talk of it being long-term or forever. In her heart she felt she was giving him the room he needed to work out whatever it was that was weighing him down. There was never any talk of them going out with others. Of having drinks on Friday night after work and sleeping with a colleague. Of starting a relationship, a five-minute relationship, that meant absolutely nothing to him. There was never any talk of Georgie finding out through the inner-west gossip network about the affair, or three months later finding out about the pregnancy. People said Sam's hair went straight to gray after that bit of information, but nothing beat what it did to Georgie.

"I would not forgive him for *the suit*," Bernadette says.

The suit. The title for the mother of Sam's child. Lucia had known *the suit* when they both worked with Sam years ago, and somehow Sam's son and Lucia's son, Daniel, have ended up at the same primary school, in the same class.

"How can you stand seeing her at Saint Michael's, Lucia?" Bernadette says.

Lucia doesn't like Bernadette's tone. It's written all over her face. "So I have to take Daniel out of school? Bernie, I have Sam's kid at my house most weekends. Through Sam, not *the suit*. I can't just turn around and ignore her when we're doing tuckshop."

"You do tuckshop with her?" Georgie asks, horrified.

"Well, if it makes you feel better," Lucia says, "she's having problems."

Georgie bites her tongue. "So everyone imagines that I want her to be miserable."

"Why not? I want her suffering like you'd never believe," Bernadette snaps.

"I think she's having issues with the guy she's been dating for a while." Lucia leans forward. "I think they're very serious and he prefers it when Callum's not around."

"I can't believe she would tell you that," her sister says angrily. "You're one of Georgie and Sam's best friends. She has no right using you as a confidant."

"She didn't confide in me," Lucia argues. "She told Kate Blaxland while they were heating up the chicken tenderloins the other day."

"Because she knew you were listening," Bernadette argues back.

Georgie doesn't know whether she can handle a full-on argument between the sisters. Despite how distasteful she finds the topic, she decides to join the conversation to avoid the conflict.

"I can't believe any of you are shocked that the boyfriend prefers

72

it when the kid's not around," she says quietly.

"Well, if he loved her . . ."

"That's *bullshit*. You can't measure someone's love based on how they feel about your child."

"And I love the way she gets to do the tuckshop because Sam's paying her enough child maintenance so she only has to work two days," Bernadette says bitterly.

Lucia's nodding. "She gets her hair straightened every week and the suit has been replaced by expensive Pilates gear."

Georgie doesn't want to hear any more. Regardless of how she feels, Sam's kid seems happy and well adjusted, so they must be doing something right.

Francesca Spinelli and Tom bring them their food and stay for a moment. Lucia and Bernadette know Francesca's family, and they chat for a while, the young girl's arm around both their shoulders. Georgie feels like a pushy parent, desperate for Tom to hang out with her again. Francesca speaks about her parents traveling through Italy and how her *nonna*'s moved into their house so someone can be at home for Francesca's younger brother at night.

"Her *nonna*'s the best seamstress in Leichhardt," Lucia tells them.

Francesca nods in agreement. "I'm kind of her apprentice this year. I do most of the beading, and I'm beginning to do patterns as well. I made this," she says pointing to her dress, perfect for her figure and coloring, all full breasts and rich olive skin. "And most of Justine's clothes."

"How beautiful is that?" Georgie says, feeling emotional. "Making wedding dresses with your grandmother."

"I've got grime to scrub from the wall," Tom mutters, standing up and walking away.

73

Boredom becomes a killer. It makes him do things he would never contemplate. Like read every online newspaper from back to front. He hates the blogs the most, but he becomes hooked. The sports ones are the worst, and although he'd rather die than admit to Georgie that ex–league stars can't string a sentence together because of all the battering they've taken around the head, he finds himself clicking his tongue with frustration at the way they can ruin the language.

Beside him, Mohsin the Ignorer chuckles at something on his own screen.

"What?" Tom asks, getting sick of the ignoring.

Nothing. In the movies, the Mohsin guy would turn to him and say, "Oh, just something I am reading that amuses me, my friend." The Mohsin in the movies would use the words *my friend* a lot. But circumstance stops Mohsin from saying those words. Some history that has nothing to do with Tom. He can imagine the story. It's probably one of those tragic ones where Mohsin's father was placed under house arrest in his country and then imprisoned and killed for something he wrote. The family probably had to travel across the world in a leaky boat and his mother probably spent time in

Villawood detention center with her kids, trying to keep them sane. Regardless, it didn't give Mohsin the right to ignore anyone who wanted to be friendly, especially someone who would understand the humor of what some sports commentators get away with. But nothing from Mohsin the Ignorer.

When Tom's done reading the *Sydney Morning Herald, The Age, The Guardian,* and the *New York Times* from top to toe, he starts reading his mobile-phone statement online. The curiosity of his low phone credit on the night he ended up in hospital doesn't become an issue until tedium makes it one. What he notices are the international numbers. The country code of the first one is 44 and the second is 670. The phone calls were made at 10:47 p.m. and 10:49 p.m.—sometime after his dive off the table. One of his ex-flatmates and their hangers-on must have taken his phone while he was flat on his face bleeding and rung two overseas numbers. How low can people get? It was probably their dickhead drummer, who was into some Swedish chick he met on the Internet. So Tom goes to the Google search and looks up international phone codes. Not Sweden. The first belongs to the UK, the second to . . .

He chokes. His reaction must be loud, because everyone turns to look at him, except Mohsin the Ignorer. Tom's eyes are fixed on the screen, and after a moment he fumbles through his backpack for his mobile, realizing that he left it back home being recharged. The countdown to three o'clock becomes an excruciating waiting game, and then he breaks speed records racing to the station, jumping turnstiles, taking the stairs up to the platform two at a time, and practically throwing himself into the train. He sprints out of Stanmore station so fast that one of the slacker skateboarders tries to race him.

Back in Georgie's attic, he yanks the phone out of the socket and begins scrolling down the names under dialed calls, praying to anyone who will listen. God. Baby Jesus. Saint Thomas the doubter. Saint Whoever, patron saint of losers. Praying, *Please, please, don't let it be true.*

The first name shatters him.

The second makes his head spin.

He hears the clumps of footsteps on the stairs, and then Georgie pokes her head in.

"What?" she asks, alarmed.

He can't speak because his tongue gets stuck in the roof of his mouth.

"Tom? You screamed."

"No," he says listlessly.

"You screamed. And swore. Like this. *Fuuuuuuuuuuuuck.*"

He tries to recover for a moment and stares at her. "Stubbed my toe. Painful."

She squints with total disdain. "More painful than childbirth?"

"Oh, so now everything's going to compete with that one," he mutters. "I've got to go."

He passes her and flies down the stairs and out of the house.

He can only get his head around one thing at a time.

That on the night he dived off that table, he rang Tara Finke in Timor.

And he can't remember a single word of the conversation.

He walks straight to the back room of the pub, where Francesca and Justine are rehearsing.

"You're not on tonight," Justine says, almost as an accusation.

76

Ned the Cook walks in with some food he's prepared for the girls and stops suddenly when he sees Tom.

"He's not on tonight," he says. Accusation in his voice.

It's clear to Tom that he won't be receiving employee-of-the-month badge at the Union.

He sits at the table they've taken possession of, and no one says a word for a moment. Francesca puts her guitar to the side discreetly. He doesn't know how he's going to broach this subject without drawing attention to the fact that he is in desperate need of information only she can give.

"I never thanked you for coming to the hospital that night."

Francesca stares at him. She's not buying it, he can tell. She looks over at Justine and even has the audacity to shrug in front of him as if to say, *I don't know what his game is.*

"No, I really appreciate it," he says.

Still no words. Not even from Justine, with her rosy cheeks and perkiness. She's a walking advertisement for clean living and an overabundance of endorphins. Except now, when she's looking at Tom.

"Ah . . . how did you know I was there?" he asks casually, trying to avoid Francesca's eyes because they're armed with bullets. He knows that if she really wants to play games with him, it could take hours to get information.

"Tara rang us," Francesca says.

Unless she loves the idea of pain being swift and vicious.

"You rang her and she rang Frankie," Justine explains.

In the words of his grandma Agnes, *Jesus, Mary, and Joseph!*

"Wonder how that happened," he said, trying to sound blasé. "Didn't even know her number worked over there."

"Well, you rang her that night."

Ned hands Francesca the sandwich. "Bit extreme," he says. "Isn't she in Dili?"

"No, actually in *Same*," Francesca explains to Ned. "Up in the mountains. *Same*," she repeats, in case he didn't get the pronunciation of the word in the first place.

"*Same,*" Ned says, making himself comfortable.

"This is kind of personal," Tom says, looking at him. "She's a mutual friend of ours." He waves a hand between him and the girls. "Probably won't interest you."

Ned the Cook is going nowhere.

Francesca sighs. "Look, Thomas, why don't you write to her? She's a long way from home and accepts letters from anyone. Plus she's a great letter writer. She brings Same to life for us. She'll respond, Tom. She's never been petty and I actually think you both need closure."

Justine leans forward. "I think she's finally gotten over the *one-and-a-half-night stand*."

When Justine says those words, she whispers them.

Tom can't believe Tara spoke to anyone about those two nights.

"Send her a text message. She loves getting them." Justine says this as if she's reluctantly giving out information. Even Ned seems keen. So with nothing to lose, Tom takes out his phone and keys in the words.

Dear Finke,
How are things, babe?
LOL,
Tom

He looks impressed with himself, and the girls look impressed back.

"The whole *one-and-a-half-night stand* really upset her," Ned explains, pissing Tom off when he whispers the words.

"That's pretty personal, and I don't think she'd appreciate you knowing about . . . stuff."

"When she was here in March, we bonded while exchanging stories about our first time," Ned explains. "We came to the conclusion that they were pretty similar situations."

"Why? Because they were both with guys?" Tom asks.

"No. They were both with fuckwits."

Ned's having fun.

"She's got a boyfriend, Thomas. He's a peacekeeper over there, and I think that all is forgiven and forgotten," Francesca says. "She's a lot calmer than she used to be. Very Zen-like."

The phone alerts him to a message, and the girls clap with excitement. For a second, it's like old times. He feels a bit of a rush, and his heart is hammering in the way it used to hammer back in the days when Tara Finke would walk toward him just before class began. Back then she'd piss him off in an instant, but the adrenaline would still keep running for the rest of the day.

"Read it to us," Justine says.

Dear Thomas,
LOL? Laugh out loud? I'm in East Timor, dickhead! How much laughing do you think we do per day around here?
And don't call me babe.
Tara

The girls look a bit crestfallen, which surprises him, really.

"Let me read it again," Justine the Positive says, taking his phone from him. "Because Tara says they do heaps of laughing over there."

She concentrates hard as she studies the screen. "Look. She uses your name. *Thomas,* she calls you. Usually it's . . ."

She looks at Francesca, who quickly shakes her head to silence her. He can imagine what Tara Finke usually calls him.

"Send her another," Justine pleads.

"Not on your life," he mutters, walking out of the room and out of the pub.

He's had worse from Tara in their time. He probably deserves worse after what he did to her.

"Tom," Francesca calls out from the front step of the pub when he's halfway down the street. There's worry in her voice, and he knows she's seen something in his expression. She's seen the sickness he's feeling inside. But it's not as if he can tell her the truth or that it will make sense to her when it doesn't even make sense to him.

How can he explain that the international code 670 isn't the issue? The 44 is. The U.K.

Because five minutes before he rang Tara Finke, he had made a call to London.

To his dead uncle.

Georgie's not home when he gets there, so he sits in the backyard with his guitar and alternates between playing it and taking out his phone and scrolling down to the dialed number beginning with the 44 prefix. He itches to ring it. Wants to hear the voice.

Georgie pokes her head outside later.

"It's freezing out here, Tom."

He nods and keeps on strumming, and she sits down on the banana chair beside him. He has a strange need to be held. A hug would be great. He'd even go back to the flat and grovel to Sarah. Not just for the sex, but to lie beside someone. Francesca had always been annoyingly tactile when talking and Justine was a hand holder and Siobhan Sullivan was draped over him at all times. And Tara. Especially that night in her parents' house when she stood in front of him and let him wrap her up in his arms.

"On the night I got my stitches," he tells Georgie, "I rang . . . Joe's number."

He knows what's going to happen. She'll ring his mother or arrange for a counselor or something drastic like that.

She keeps her eyes on him. He doesn't know what can of worms he's opened up with this one, but she's silent for a while.

"I write him letters," she says calmly.

"What?"

She nods. "I write him letters."

"Where do you send them?"

"To his e-mail address."

"What do you write about?"

She shrugs. "I went for an ultrasound today and I've got photos, so I'll probably write to him about how it felt."

"So you don't think I'm crazy?"

"You were concussed, Tom. By the sounds of things, you hadn't slept for three nights, and don't pretend that you were just smoking dope, because I know you took speed and God knows what else. Believe me, my nephew doesn't turn up on my doorstep with ten stitches in his head without me going to that hospital to find out what happened."

81

He nods, almost to himself.

"So I don't think there was anything strange about you ringing him or thinking that you could talk to him."

"Who's still paying for the account? His voice is still there. *'Joe here. You know the drill. Leave a message.'* Remember, he used that East End accent just to make us laugh."

He sees it on her face, even in this half-light. Of course Georgie knows the message is still there. How many times has she rung Joe's number to listen to it over the past two years?

"Does it help?" he asks. "The e-mailing."

She nods. "A tiny bit. It's strange. You're writing a letter to someone who's never going to read it, so it kind of frees you up a bit."

"Why not just write in a journal?"

She shakes her head. "I need an audience. Someone who knows me well. Someone I'm used to talking to, who I don't have to set up foundations with."

"Have you told . . . written to him about the baby?"

She nods.

"Do you want to see a photo of it?" she asks.

"The baby? It's not one of those blobs that you pretend has features and form, is it?" he asks.

She laughs again, but he can see on her face that she has a fragile hold on her emotions.

"Play it something."

"What do you want me to play?" he says with a sigh, not really in the mood but not wanting to say no to her at the moment.

"Something that makes me feel."

He plays a Lyle Lovett song because he knows she's seen him in concert with his parents. It's a song about a boat and pony on the ocean, the only Lyle Lovett he ever bothered to learn. Ever since he was fifteen, he had been determined not to be too influenced by his parents' taste in anything, although he had a secret obsession with the bands Devo and Big Audio Dynamite because of them, and he still listens to the Cure.

Sam arrives, dressed from work. He's holding fish and chips, and a beer.

"Come and have something to eat," he says quietly to Georgie. Tom notices that he does that a lot. Speaks quietly. It's almost as if Sam believes that if he raises his voice, she'll notice that he's around and then she'll remember the past and tell him to get lost. So these days, Sam speaks quietly. Tom feels awkward observing them. Although they handle silence between them well, it becomes awkward when another person is put into the equation.

"She went for an ultrasound," Tom explains, "and is trying to show me a photo of the alien."

Wrong thing to say. Sam looks cut. Georgie looks sad.

"You didn't mention you had an appointment," Sam says. "I would have come."

She doesn't say anything.

"Is it okay?" he asks.

"Perfect."

Somehow Sam doesn't dare ask for the photo.

"Pass the snapshot over," Tom says.

Georgie takes it out of her book and hands it to Sam, who stares at it and then hands it to Tom.

"Can you see its little nose and eyes and legs?" she asks.

83

"Wow. Yeah. That's . . . that's amazing, Georgie," Tom lies.

She looks relieved and swings her legs over the chair. "I'll get the plates," she says. He gets a sense that she's going inside to cry.

When she's gone, Tom dares to look at Sam and then the ultrasound photo again. "You've fathered the elephant man. Someone has to tell her."

Sam is laughing as he reaches out for the photo to get another look, this time reveling in the freedom of Georgie not being around.

"Could be the elephant woman," he murmurs, staring at it.

"Poppy, at the pharmacy, reckons it's a boy, but Georgie says she feels in her heart that it's a girl."

"Why? What did she say?"

"I switched off after she mentioned breast pads and nipple creams."

Georgie comes out with the plates and hands them to Sam, who begins to divvy up the food. "You can have the photo," she says, seeing it in Sam's hand. "I've got a few. You too, Tom."

He asks Sam about his work. Not because he's interested, but because he won't be able to sit alongside them without talk. He's scared that if no one speaks, the sadness in the air will suffocate them. Sam works with the Industrial Relations Commission and has that same manic look in his eyes as Tom's father did when he used to get hot and bothered about a campaign. The fish and chips are good, and in a way, so is the conversation. Sam and Georgie even have a mini argument about bully union leaders and lazy workers at one of the major car manufacturers, and for a moment there's nothing more normal than Sam telling Georgie she doesn't know what the hell she's talking about. Not so quiet.

"If productivity is down, Sam, someone's obviously not doing their job," she says. "All I'm saying is that there are two sides to the story. Dom would agree."

"Not in this case, Georgie!" Sam says.

"Would your father agree?" she asks Tom. Tom doesn't want to have an opinion, although he's certain that there's no way that his father would be critical of a trade union.

"Dominic would agree with Sam," he says, not so much reluctant to side with Sam, but more so not to talk about his father.

Georgie leans forward in her chair to stare at Tom in a you-have-betrayed-blood-kin-beyond-comprehension stare.

"Don't involve me in your arguments and then look at me like that when I don't side with you," he says, taking a drag of his cigarette.

"And stop smoking around me because that passive smoke is traveling this way and gagging my unborn child," she says back.

"For fuck's sake," Tom mutters, getting up and taking his beer and guitar with him.

Later, lying in bed, he thinks of the words that have come to haunt him this past week. *Talk to me, Thomas.* They were spoken in a sleepy voice. He had awoken her, wherever she was in Timor. Same, Francesca said. Was she lying beside the peacekeeper? *Just talk.* He had heard the same tone in her voice on one of those nights they had slept in each other's arms. The best week he could remember. It was after the never-ending eye contact and hand holding and three-hour nightly phone conversations where they couldn't stop talking. Everything about Tara Finke triggered a reaction inside him. Like that time she walked in with the foil colors in her hair and he was rehearsing with the girls and he started strumming the guitar, crooning, "Danke Schoen," because he knew she liked it from watching *Ferris Bueller's Day Off* so many times with him, and then she was smiling and laughing, and yes, Uncle Joe, it was time to STD.

"Plans?" she had asked, but she was talking to Francesca and Justine because whenever things flared up between them, Tara did a whole lot of avoiding.

"Will and I are going to Sallo's party down at Cockle Bay, so come with us," Francesca said.

"She's not dressed for it," Tom had pointed out. Tara was wearing a skirt over jeans and some high-neck black skivvy that flattened her even more than she was, but it wasn't nightclub stuff and he was cheering in silence.

"Come to my gig," Justine said, locking the case of her accordion. "It's just a bit of a jam session with some of the guys at the Con."

"Will I be the only one who's not a musical genius?" Tara asked.

"Probably," Tom answered for Justine. "And it'll make you feel inferior and then depressed, and then you'll want to slit your wrists and you don't want to be caught dead wearing a skirt over jeans. I mean, what is that look, Finke? Really? On the other hand, I'm cleaning my stuff out of Georgie's attic 'cause Joe's coming home, so you may as well come with me."

He said it with a shrug, as though he was pretty blasé.

"Oh, the choices," she sighed, unraveling herself from her satchel and putting it down on the floor. "I've got to go to the loo."

He had watched her walk away, and the skirt rode up her jeans and sat where he wanted it to sit. Although there was no flesh showing, his body had already kick-started into something completely out of his control. He felt Justine and Francesca come up beside him

86

and he put an arm around both of them, humming "Danke Schoen" until he realized they weren't just standing around waiting. They were staring up at him.

He looked from one to the other. "What?" he asked, on the defensive. "*What?*"

"What are you doing?" Francesca asked.

"Thomas?" This came from Justine, who usually protected him from the wrath of the other girls.

His hands fell to his side.

"What did I do now?"

"Do you want us to fill you in on something, Tom?" Francesca, Queen of Rhetorical Questions, asked, because she was going to fill him in whether he wanted to be filled in or not. "You know how Siobhan gave Tara a mobile phone for her birthday? Well, we set it up for her so that every time one of us rings, a particular tune comes on. Have you heard of Tom Petty and the Heartbreakers, Tom? Because when you ring her, the tune to 'Stop Draggin' My Heart Around' comes on."

Now he was really pissed off. "*Back,*" he had said, looking at Justine. "*Off,*" he said to Francesca.

"I'm texting Siobhan."

He looked at them both with disbelief. "As if I'm scared of Siobhan."

Francesca got out her phone, and in desperation he had grabbed it from her.

"Please, Frankie. I'm begging. Don't text Siobhan."

Tara walked back into the hall and Francesca managed to pry her phone out of his fingers by giving him one of those pinches where she got a grip on the hair on his arm and twisted.

He grabbed his guitar and jumped off the stage, then picked up Tara's satchel and steered her toward the door.

"I haven't said good-bye to them," she said, trying to get her satchel from him. He slung it over his neck.

"Tara says bye," he had called over his shoulder.

And that began the week when advice came flying from Joe across the seas on how not to stuff things up.

Tom needs the guru to provide him with the words to make things right now. But he knows he'll never hear them again and he stumbles to the toilet, spewing out the ache of loneliness churning itself inside of him.

chapter ten

They go to Lucia and Abe's for a barbecue celebrating Abe's forty-second birthday. A small gathering in the Charbel household means at least forty people were about to converge on them. Georgie is designated the task of straightening her goddaughter's hair and allows Bella to straighten hers haphazardly in return.

When the guys walk into the kitchen to get the meat for the barbecue and Bernadette arrives with the cake, Georgie knows this is her last chance before she loses her nerve.

"I'd like to make an announcement before everyone else arrives," she says. For a moment there's silence.

"What's with the hair?" Jonesy asks.

"Jonesy," Lucia says, shushing him.

For a second, Georgie's eyes meet Sam's and there's a flicker around his mouth and a softness in his eyes.

"I'm having a baby," she says firmly.

There's a moment's silence.

"Oh. My. God!" Lucia says, feigning surprise. "Who would have guessed."

Abe laughs and he reaches over to hug Georgie.

"I'm twenty-two weeks and it's due in November," she says, holding on to Abe because she wants desperately to hold on to someone and Abe's the closest thing she has to her brother.

She looks at Sam. "Close your ears if you don't want to know what I suspect to be the sex of your child," she says, and he blocks his ears.

"It's Sam's?" Jonesy asks, surprised, just as he gets a message.

"Where have you been, Jonesy?" Bernadette says. "In La-La Land?"

"Contrary to popular belief, I think it has no penis," Georgie whispers to them while Lucia covers Sam's ears.

Jonesy looks up from his text messaging, shocked. "Poor little guy."

After everyone's eaten and the men are outside playing cards in the tiny courtyard, Abe's mother dangles a necklace over Georgie's belly to see if it's a boy or a girl. As she sits surrounded by the women and her goddaughters, who watch with the widest of eyes, she is suddenly overcome with emotion. Leila sees it on her face and takes it gently between her hands. "She misses her mama, don't you, Georgietta?" the older woman says.

"What's it going to be, Tata?" Bella asks. "The baby?"

There is a certainty on the older woman's face. "A boy. It's all at the front and there's no change in the face."

Later, Lucia piles Georgie up with leftovers while Sam lights up a cigarette, waiting in the dark on the front lawn.

"I hope you're not smoking in front of her," Lucia says to him.

"Yeah, I lie in bed and puff in her face, Lucia," he says, irritated.

"I hope he's joking."

"He's joking," Georgie says with a yawn, kissing her and then Abe.

When they've pulled away from the curb and waved to everyone, Sam puts on the heater to warm up the car for the short drive home.

"Can you feel that?" he asks.

They place their hands in front of the heat at the same time and both pull back.

"Bella came out and said it was a boy," Sam says.

Georgie laughs for a moment. "The odds are fifty to one. I reckon it's a girl."

Silence again.

"My mother wants to visit," he says.

"Tell her to visit," she says quietly, leaning her head against the window frame and closing her eyes. Sometimes in the past when they'd come home from Dominic and Jacinta's or Lucia and Abe's, they'd make love with a lack of inhibition born of too much alcohol and too few issues in their lives. These days their lovemaking is instigated in silence. No words. No teasing. He had once been verbal during sex. Had to articulate. Swore. Cursed. Prayed. All words entwined in every thrust. "Shhh," she'd laugh, in case they'd wake up Joe, who lived in the attic during those days. But he couldn't keep it contained, so she'd cover his mouth with her hand and she'd see it all there in his eyes. All of it.

She wants to cover his mouth now. Cover the silence and watch his eyes for a sign. But they've become strangers, guarded with each other.

●　　●　　●

91

The next day, Lucia and her sister come over and Georgie has to stop them from wanting to talk babies. Her announcement the day before has reopened the floodgates of communication, which is both a relief and a curse, really. Then they get to talking about Bernadette's decision to try Internet dating, and all three of them end up hunched over Georgie's laptop when Tom walks in.

"Is that my wifebeater?" he asks.

"I don't like the derogatory term, thank you. It's a undershirt."

"Yeah. My undershirt, Georgie," he says. "With a spencer underneath it. Looks ridiculous."

"Shucks, Tom, because I'm really going for the fashionable look these days."

"Buy yourself maternity stuff, Georgie," he mutters.

She feels him peer over their shoulder to see what has glued them to the screen of the laptop.

"Internet dating?"

"People are meeting the loves of their lives this way," Bernadette explains.

"*BabyI'myourman69*?" he asks, reading the name on the screen. "I hope you girls don't think that sixty-nine represents the year he was born."

Lucia laughs. "If the munchkin, whose face I used to wash, tries to explain to us what a sixty-niner is, I'm going to report myself to child protection."

Georgie's not listening. She's too busy following what's on the screen in front of her with her finger. "But look at what this one wrote: 'If you're in your late thirties, I suppose your biological clock is ticking and midnight is just around the corner. So hey, baby, baby.' He's ready. He wants kids."

"His own, Georgie," Bernadette points out. "And we're looking for me, not you."

"And you're not in your late thirties," Tom points out while he fiddles through the cabinets, looking for food.

"Okay, what about this one? *Itsnoworneverer.*"

She finds it difficult pronouncing the name.

"It's now or never," Tom explains, back over their shoulders.

Georgie reads it carefully. "This guy chose the 'Don't want any of my own, but yours are okay' option for kids." She feels optimistic.

"What a surprise that there isn't the option, 'Don't want any of my own, but it's okay for you to be fat with someone else's child,' " Tom says.

Georgie can't get over how cynical her nephew's become.

Tom leans forward and taps the screen with determination. "Look at his taste in music, girls. You can't go out with someone who listens to 'anything from the '70s, '80s, or '90s.' That's what he's written. He has to be more discerning than that. And he's a swinging voter. Sam would never let a swinging voter bring up his child."

Georgie stares at him, unimpressed. "So now we're a Sam fan, are we?"

"At least he's always been specific about his musical tastes."

She turns to Bernadette and Lucia, not believing what she's hearing.

"So who would you choose, Bernie? The faithful guy who listens to '70s, '80s, and '90s music and swings in his voting, or the unfaithful guy who's into the Clash and the Waterboys and still believes the Labor Party are the true believers?"

"They're my choices?" Bernadette asks, dismayed. "Can't I have another one?"

"What does Sam say about this?" Tom asks, eating the cereal from the box with his hands.

"Sam and I aren't together."

He points to her belly.

"So you're giving birth to the Messiah, are you?"

"Why is Sam an issue all of a sudden?" she says angrily.

"Georgie, you're sleeping with the guy!" Lucia says, laughing with exasperation, looking at Tom. "She's sleeping with him, isn't she?"

He stares at them, mid-mouthful. "Please," he says after he's swallowed. "It's bad enough that the middle-aged are having sex, without thinking of my aunt doing it. And I don't know why someone just doesn't tell Sam to use a condom instead of impregnating the women of the inner-west."

Georgie stares at him, stunned, and then she bursts out laughing.

"Middle-aged? What a little dickhead," Lucia says.

chapter eleven

To: taramarie@yahoo.com
From: anabelsbrother@hotmail.com
Date: 25 July 2007

Dear Finke,

Okay, so you're cranky. I can imagine that if you are reading this now, you look cranky. That crease on your forehead and that stare that can slice the bejesus out of anyone. How is life there? Truly asking. Life here is pretty shitty. Mind-numbing at times, to be honest. Don't know why I'm even telling you, but Georgie reckons she writes to Joe and sends the letters to his in-box, and that somehow getting things off her chest helps. (She actually has a chest these days, courtesy of a pregnancy.)

This, by the way, is not helping, but I have nothing else to do, so at least it relieves the monotony. I'm working in a hideously boring data-entry place a couple of hours a day, and I'm sure that Francesca and Justine have told you I'm the dish-pig at the Union alongside your new bestie, Ned. I tend to keep to my corner while the troika bond.

Anyway, I'm just going through the motions these days and wake up each day to the same scenario. I can't begin to tell you how hard it is filling up seven lots of twenty-four hours without the assistance of illicit substances. TV sometimes helps, but Georgie has the most pitiful collection of boxed-set DVDs. I've covered *Sex and the City* (season three is my favorite), as well as *Will and Grace* and *The West Wing*. Every time we have an issue, she brings it back to *The West Wing*. Georgie thinks she's C.J., who was the press secretary.

Best be going. Don't want to o.d. on a good thing.

Cheers,

Tom

There is nothing in his in-box the next day. Part of him is relieved. He can imagine her seeing his name and pressing the delete button, and that thought gives him the freedom to hit the keys again. It becomes part of his way of filling up those seven twenty-fours. Between working alongside Mohsin the Ignorer, lying on ugly banana chairs in Georgie's backyard at night, chatting to Sam, who seems to come by more frequently, or working from five to ten at the Union, his life becomes consumed by the number displayed alongside his in-box. Most times there will be an e-mail from Anabel and one from a mate he met at uni, who sends him the most ridiculous stuff on YouTube or attachments with a plethora of tits or other types of nudity. But Tom decides it's going to be his mission to keep on writing to Tara Finke. He's going to aim for the record. He'll stop at ninety-nine unanswered e-mails. He's going to wear her down.

To:	taramarie@yahoo.com
From:	anabelsbrother@hotmail.com
Date:	27 July 2007

Dear Finke,

I can now type fifty words a minute without looking at the keys. As I type, I'm actually looking at the guy on my right-hand side, who persists in speaking to me although I can't understand a single word that comes out of his mouth. He has a very thick Irish brogue and I feel like Marjorie Dawes in the *Little Britain* fat-busters sketch, who can't understand the simplest of words because the other woman has an accent.

On my left is Mohsin the Ignorer and I don't know why it gets to me that he doesn't talk, but it does. I think he's a racist and that makes me sound petty, but that's the way I'm calling it. Except there's something that makes me want to talk to him, which could have a lot to do with the fact that I don't talk to many people these days except for Georgie and Sam and my sister on the Net. Did you know Anabel was living in Brisbane with my mum? Shit, not seeing that kid kills me and some days I feel like just stealing Georgie's car and driving up to be with them. I haven't spoken to my mother in eleven months, you know. She sends me a text message a couple of times a week and I know she speaks to Georgie almost every second day. I don't have the guts to go there, because I'm ashamed. I called her something pretty bad when she left my dad. Don't worry, because I won't repeat it in this e-mail. I know how you feel about that word. But I'll never forget the look on her face.

Except there seems to be other stuff to stress over, like the whole thing with Georgie having this baby. Not even when the Sam betrayal happened or when Joe died did she seem this bad. I think a nervous breakdown is coming and it's coming fast, and I have front-row seats to it all. Not that I'll be able to stop it, because I would have no idea how, but in a strange way Sam seems to help. When he's around, she's less highly strung and anxious, and somehow she allows him over a lot more because I'm there. It's like I'm the buffer, so I'm going to allow myself to get buffed for the sake of Georgie's sanity.

Write back.

See ya,

Tom

He takes to getting to work at the Union earlier each day. Most of it is about boredom, but usually whoever arrives first has dibs on the MP3 player the moment the day shift clocks off at five. Lately Francesca's been going through the I-miss-Will compilation he burned for her and it's a whole lot of Bloc Party and Augie March and not quite Tom's thing, and then there's what he calls Ned the Cook's emo music and Justine's Monsieur Camembert, and worse still, Stani's talkback.

Today Francesca is in even earlier than Tom, taking advantage of the quiet time until the five o'clock crowd comes in. She's practicing guitar in the back room and he hears a few of the words but doesn't recognize them and figures that it's one of her own.

"Change it to a minor," he tells her from the doorway.

She pauses for a moment but does what he says. Although she's got a good ear for music, her bends are dodgy and he stays to listen.

"You bend like a girl."

He walks over and changes the placement of her three fingers on the neck of the guitar.

"And cut your nails."

"I love my nails," he hears her mutter as he walks out.

●　　●　　●

98

To: tomsister@hotmail.com
From: anabelsbrother@hotmail.com
Date: 30 July 2007

Dear H-anibal,

Yes, for the billionth time, Georgie is very excited about you coming for the Christmas holidays. Don't say she didn't tell you on the phone last night a thousand times, because I heard her. Tell J-Lo she finally told Nanni G and Bill about the baby and I get a sense Nanni G wants to come up earlier because she rings almost every second night.

And no, I don't think it's uncool for a girl to play the trumpet. Can you stop listening to Trixie the Antichrist and Ginger the Ninja? If you give up playing just because you're measuring yourself up against someone else's cool meter, then I'll be pretty disappointed, Anabel Georgia.

Love, Tom

P.S. And may I remind you that I don't care if Luca Spinelli is only one and a half years older than you. He's in Year Ten. You're in Year Eight. What kind of a pervert is he, thinking he can send you a playlist to remember Sydney by? Is he your counselor or something? Have you left Sydney for good and are never coming back? Nip this in the bud or I'm telling J-Lo and Dominic.

He travels home by bus most days, because the trip is ten minutes longer and most of his time is spent trying to avoid being on his own or trying to not look like he's on his own. MP3 players are perfect because the sight of someone walking the streets listening to music means something totally different from someone staring into blank space. It's the joy of smoking for him. Isolation doesn't have to be explained when you're leaning against a brick wall with a cigarette in your hand. Rolling your own is better. It takes more time, and Tom has all the time to spare.

And what keeps him going is the number one next to his in-box when he clicks on the address *anabelsbrother,* or when he takes over the ranking of the footy-tipping competition at work from a guy who left and susses out that Mohsin the Ignorer is at the top, with Tom catching up, or when he listens to Francesca Spinelli trying to get a chord right, or to Justine whispering to Ned the Cook about the next installment of her love for a guy called Ben who plays a violin and doesn't know she exists. Or it's Georgie's voice calling out to him from her bedroom as he climbs the stairs to the attic every night. Sometimes when he comes home and he aches for the sound of something more than a "Hey, Tommy," he lies on her bed and they keep each other company. They talk about Anabel and how much they both miss her and Great-Aunt Margie, Tom Finch's sister, who's a nun way out west. And it always comes down to Tom Finch and the veterans and how every time the phone rings, they think it's the government giving them the news that even after forty years none of them is prepared for. And they talk about Joe. Of the time when Tom was in Year Eleven and he half moved in with them. Because it's hard not to talk about Joe, with the ugly armchairs and banana chairs and LP collections and photographs constantly reminding them.

"He was crazy mad for your father, you know," Georgie tells him one time. "And Dom would have done anything for him. When you were born, Joe was in Year Nine boarding at Saint Sebastian's, and your dad used to ring up and impersonate Bill to get him out of school most weekends. Anytime Joe wanted to be picked up or taken somewhere, Dom would do it."

She's quiet for a moment. Tom wonders if they're thinking the same thing. Dom would pick up Joe anytime, but not that final time. Not Joe's body from London.

"Once when Joe was at uni, he ended up in the lockup at Stanmore police station because he and his dickhead friends got drunk and stole a street sign. So he rings your father and he starts making up the lyrics to Paul Kelly's 'How to Make Gravy.' But instead of singing, *'Hello Dan, it's Joe here,'* he sang, *'Hello Dom, it's Joe here.'*"

"Then he sang about every member of the family. Your auntie Margie Finch coming down from Queensland and your mum's family coming from the coast, and he was bellowing out, 'Who's going to make the jelly?' instead of the 'gravy.'"

Tom can't help chuckling, no matter how many times he's heard that story.

"He reckons even the cops were killing themselves laughing," she says.

"He taught me the chords to that song, you know," Tom says. "'It's a love story, Tommy,' he told me. 'It's a love story between Dan and Joe and every member of their family.'"

He turns on his side to face her, leaning on his elbow.

"Remember when we used to come downstairs and get you to choose who did the best Joe Satriani?"

"Oh, bloody Joe Satriani," she said.

"And that time you couldn't stand it anymore and you bunked in with Anabel down at our place and Joe got me out of bed in the middle of the night and we played Satriani's 'If I Could Fly' under her window so you'd think you were having a nightmare."

The bed shakes for a long time from their silent laughter.

"Be honest. Who did the best Joe Satriani?" he asks.

Before she can answer, she grabs his hand and presses it against her stomach and he's about to tell her he doesn't want to feel the baby, but her hand is trembling. Next minute he's laughing and saying, "Oh, shit. *Shit*," and she's pressing his fingers in deeper and he's saying, "You'll hurt it, Georgie."

Other times they just listen to each other's music.

"What's this one?" she asks one night while they're sharing earphones.

"We've all been changed
From what we were
Our broken hearts
Smashed on the floor"

" 'Smokers Outside the Hospital Doors,' " he tells her, turning it up louder.

Georgie makes him listen to stuff that she doesn't play when she's out in the real world. There's a whole lot of Regina Spektor, who sings about a guy called Samson being her sweetest downfall. Tom becomes a closet fan and listens to it secretly in his attic. He wonders if it's the type of stuff Tara would have written if she had to write music about their relationship.

Other times the door's shut and he wonders if Sam's in there.

Every other moment of his day is a reminder of Tara Finke. When he watches his fingers tap at the keyboard, he remembers her thing about hands. Her own, others, everyone's. It was one of the paradoxes about the very practical Tara Finke. Decides to extend her studies where she'll have her hands in dirt, but has an obsession with manicures. Her school backpack was always sure to contain a manicure set and papaya hand cream. She rubbed it onto his hands one day in Year Eleven, feeling the texture of his fingertips, callused by the strings of his guitar, and his palms, rough from woodwork.

"Productive, despite your lazy streak," she had said, inspecting them.

Some days he e-mails her stuff he knows she'll find funny, like a "Vote Pedro" link because they both had a *Napoleon Dynamite* obsession. No one else in the group got it. Tom's favorite impersonation was of Napoleon Dynamite running away, all arms and legs flailing. "It's not even funny," they'd say, but Tara Finke would be crying with laughter every single time. Back then, they'd send each other links all the time, trying to come up with the smartest. His favorite was "Survivors of childhood subjugation to watching *The Bill*." Both Tom and Tara Finke belonged to a one-television household, a strange type of abuse at the hands of parents obsessed with noncommercial television. In most other ways they were different. She didn't do toilet humor; he loved it. She hated epic fantasy; he hated anything with big Victorian frocks, no matter how much cleavage. Once she made him watch *Pride and Prejudice* and for ages he would reword Mr. Bingley's apology to Jane Bennet, saying, "I've been an inexplicable fool," for anything from losing his keys to burping out loud. Her reply to anything she wanted to do was Jane Bennet's response to Bingley's marriage proposal: "A thousand times yes."

One afternoon in his in-box he sees her name: *taramarie*. The Nazi who collects footy tips every Friday afternoon tells him he has thirty seconds to hand them in, but he hasn't even started on them yet. His eyes are fixed on the screen, his heart is hammering, and finally, with shaking fingers, he presses the in-box and sees words typed in the most ridiculous font.

Can you tell Frankie and Justine that I've run out of credit on my phone and to check their e-mails instead?
Tara

What. A. Bitch.

"It's only four thirty," Stani says to him one day when he walks into the kitchen and puts on his apron and begins pulling the glasses out of the washer.

He shrugs. Francesca's in the back room practicing and Justine's doing an essay at one of the tables in the main bar, so it's not as if he's the only one who has nowhere else to go.

Ned walks in as well, his face reddening instantly when he sees Stani. Ned is intimidated by anyone who speaks or looks at him, except for Francesca and Justine. And Tom. There's nothing about Tom that intimidates Ned.

"You're early," Stani barks.

Ned nods in agreement and then goes to the freezer to get the meat out.

Whether Ned wants him to or not, Tom begins chopping up the salad items just to keep himself occupied. Francesca's voice travels to where they're working silently.

"Catch the news
One more day
Big wide world
Swallowed whole
Rhythm breaks me
Out of step
Need to shake this
'Less I break

'Cause nothing counts when you're not here
Too much sadness, too much fear"

Ned stops seasoning the meat and closes his eyes for a moment, before walking to the door.

" *'Cause nothing counts unless you're here. / Shake these shackles, I might tear,*" he calls out to her before returning to the sink bench.

"I have an aversion to rhyme," he explains, as if Tom's asked.

Francesca's practicing on the banjo today. Tom likes how it sounds.

"She watched *Shut Up and Sing* and thinks she's one of the Dixie Chicks."

Ned's on a roll. He does that sometimes. Explains stuff out of the blue. It's usually about the girls, and, inspired by Mohsin the Ignorer, Tom pretends he's not interested.

She begins singing again:

"Speak the words
Make no sense

No part working
I'm on hold
Need those hands
Make me whole
Hunger breaks me
I can't breathe

'Cause nothing counts unless you're here
Shake these shackles, I might tear."

Ned grunts with satisfaction. Tom stops chopping and thinks for a moment before walking to the door.

" *'Cause nothing counts unless you're here. / Shackles bind me, I walk free,*" he calls out.

He walks back to the sink. Ned stares at him questioningly, shaking his head. "Doesn't make sense."

"When he's home, she's unbound from the shackles constructed by her loneliness and so she walks free," Tom explains before going back to the chopping.

"Whereas I think that if she doesn't shake the shackles, she is so fragmented and fragile that she's like a piece of . . ."

"Tissue paper?" Tom suggests.

Ned nods. "That can tear."

She tries it again with Tom's chorus.

"I think they've had a mini argument long distance," Ned explains. "She's okay with tattoos in ode to her, but apparently he got pissed with the engineers while they had a day's leave and piercing took place. One to the eyebrow and the other . . . she won't say."

Tom looks at him with disbelief. "Will Trombal? Piercing? In places she won't say?"

Justine walks in and has an anxious little chatter with Ned the Cook in the corner. When Tom walks toward them to empty the scraps from the cutting board, they stop speaking for a moment.

"It's not as if I don't know what you're talking about," he mutters.

"We're not talking about you, if that's what you think, Thomas," Justine says patiently.

He goes back to his chopping but doesn't let it go. "I'll make you a two-trillion-dollar bet I know what it's about."

She stands with her arms folded, waiting. Tom and Justine always used to make bets in the trillions and billions, mostly about music trivia and chords, and Justine could never resist taking up the challenge. There's a hint of a smile on her face.

"Go on," she says.

"You're probably in love with some musician at the Con. And we all know how that's panned out in the past. One whole year of having a secret crush you've told no one about and now you've entered the second year, where you talk about him and do nothing about it. Next year you'll be analyzing the way he says, 'Hi, Justine.' Hopefully by the Beijing Olympics—no, the Olympics they'll one day have in Afghanistan—you'll have exchanged mobile numbers."

She stares at him drolly and then gives Ned the same look.

Francesca walks in at two minutes to five, ready for her shift. And the news. "Why's everyone standing around?" she asks, fiddling with the radio.

"Because Thomas is a smart-arse," Justine says. "He reckons I'm

107

not going to get Ben the Violinist's phone number until Afghanistan has the Olympics."

He's ready for the onslaught. Daring to hurt the feelings of one of the sisterhood was punishable by a death stare. Tara Finke's was the deadliest, but Francesca's was the closest by seconds.

"What timeline did I give it?" Francesca asks.

"2025," Ned informs her. "You said she would probably be taking Ben the Violinist on their first date to your fortieth birthday."

"Mock me all you like, but this guy's not shy. He's just not into me," Justine says. "He doesn't even know I exist."

"His name's Ben," Francesca says to Tom, as if he's asked. "And he's twenty-one and he's a violinist and he's from the Riverina and he has a very, very dry sense of humor and he lives in Waterloo with a bunch of mates, and when he plays the violin, he keeps his eyes closed and this one time he opened them and the first thing he did was catch Justine's eye. And then he winked. So now she says it's their song."

Tom makes a sound as if he's sobbing and he covers his heart with his hand.

"And she just has to build up her courage and let him know how she feels," Francesca says.

It's always been the same with Justine. She was the most comfortable in her own skin of all of them, and since they left school, she was the one with the biggest social life outside their group, totally at ease with guys. Unless she's madly in love with them.

Stani pokes his head in. "Are we on strike?"

Justine follows him out, and Tom walks over to the radio and turns it off in the middle of the second news story, which is about some freight train crashing into a passenger train in California.

108

Francesca switches it back on, staring at him with irritation until he switches it back off again.

"It's nowhere close to where your people are," he tells her quietly. "Seeing you've got the original out of the way, what will the cover song for the Blessed Pierced One be?" he adds.

Francesca looks at him suspiciously and then back to Ned, who looks sheepish and gets back to work.

"How do you know I wrote it for him? It could be for any of them."

"*Need those hands. Make me whole.*"

She makes a face as if she's thinking. "That's my mum."

"My mistake."

"*Hunger breaks me. I can't breathe.* That's Will's line," she says.

"Why? Because he's choking the life out of you?"

She forgets about the news and walks away, but he can tell she's laughing.

"Maybe Snow Patrol," she answers from the door. "You know? 'Set the Fire to the Third Bar' or 'Chasing Cars.' Or something by the Silversun Pickups. He likes them."

"Guitar work will be hard for both."

She shrugs. "Lucky I know a good guitarist or two."

To: taramarie@yahoo.com
From: anabelsbrother@hotmail.com
Date: 1 August 2007

Dear Finke,

Bit surprised because I always took you for a practical Times New Roman font girl, so when you sent me that heartfelt note using the

109

GlooGun font, I said to myself, you never really know someone.

Anyway, I thought you should know, since you were always interested, that there's a chance Tom Finch is coming home soon. There's a lot of talk going on about those old-timer vets and the government finally digging up the seven bodies that were left behind. Don't know if you heard about the two they've already returned, but Tom Finch could be next.

I notice more of his stuff around the place these days and I think it's part of Georgie's preparation to bury him. Things like scapulars and his swag and his books. Although I can't see it being a priority in my father's life at the moment, it was always his obsession. Joe's too, funnily enough, because Joe didn't belong to Tom Finch. But Joe was a history fanatic and he was used to working with evidence and it was one of the things he shared with my father. I know that's why the thing with Joe not being buried properly hit my old man hard.

I've never really wanted to ask my pop Bill a lot of questions in the past because he might have thought I didn't respect him just because he wasn't my dad's father. But Tom Finch has never felt like my grandfather. How can you look at someone whose last photo was taken when he was twenty-one and consider him to be anything more than some poor bastard my age, born on the wrong day? But I love him, you know. Can't explain how I love someone I've never met, but I do.

Just between you and me, I think my father and Georgie have always been a bit hard on Bill. My mum reckons that I've always seen my pop as a mellow older guy, but he'll be the first to admit he was tough on my father. They used to have it out on the front lawn, according to Georgie, back when they were seventeen. "*You're not my fucking father, you bastard,*" my father would yell. But I think Bill loved them all the same, and never favored Joe over the others. Everyone said it killed him when

110

Georgie dropped the Mackee name and sometimes I actually think she regrets the decision and misses it, but I think she was angry at Bill and Nanni Grace twenty years ago for moving down to Albury and taking her little brother with them. It was the only way she could get back at them.

When I saw *Ulysses* on Georgie's bedside table and Tom Finch's name written on it in a scrawl so like my old man's, I felt that I wanted to read it as a preparation for what's about to happen to us all. I understand where the brawny part of my father and I come from — Bill. I'm not saying Bill's not smart, but my old man is a pretty intelligent guy and that kind of intellect came from Tom Finch. I want to turn the pages he turned. But honestly I'm actually finding it hard. I think that the whole world has lied and nobody has read the book completely. It's a conspiracy up there with Roswell.

Wish you'd write.

Love, Tom

Shit! He went to the sent box, praying that somehow the e-mail got rejected. No such luck. Twenty seconds earlier *anabelsbrother* sent *taramarie* a message, not with the word *cheers* or *see ya* or *whenever*. But signing off with the word *love.*

chapter twelve

The grief hits her hard one day. The way it can't be controlled. The way that yesterday can be good and so can the day before, and so can the week and fortnight before that, but then today comes and she's back to zero. How she can't type words into her computer or even press the in-box for her mail. The effort it takes to walk. How words can't form in her mouth and how her blood feels paralyzed. For the first time since she can remember, she finds herself dialing Sam's number but hangs up the moment she hears his voice because too much emotion goes into keeping Sam at an arm's distance.

In front of them is a couple. They're Serbian, and for a moment she panics and thinks they've got a Bosnian translator by mistake. She sees their mouths move but hears nothing.

Her co-worker reaches over and touches her hand. "Why don't you go home, Georgie?" he asks gently after they've left.

She's too listless to even shake her head.

"Georgie," one of the girls from the next desk says, holding the phone in her hand and covering the mouthpiece. "It's your brother."

She picks up the phone in an instant.

"*Joe?*"

She hears a sigh of such depth that she doesn't know if it's hers or his.

"Georgie?"

"Dominic," she whispers.

It's just been e-mails until now. She hasn't heard his voice for almost twelve months. Before that, she'd hear it every day of her life. She'd swear to others that she heard it in the womb for those nine months.

"Where are you?" she asks.

"Central. Can I come and stay with you?"

She wants to weep, but she's too emotionally tired.

"That you even have to ask," she says.

She goes home via Coles at Norton Street Plaza to grab some groceries. It gives her purpose. Purpose is good at the moment. Milk, bread, toilet paper, and the newspaper give her something to do that doesn't require emotion or contemplation. Although she has fewer than eight items, she lines up anywhere, and with a shaky hand she texts Jacinta and then Lucia to tell them that Dominic's home.

"Hi, Georgie!"

On the line in front of her is Sam's kid, Callum. Dressed in his school uniform and smiling shyly up at her. Sam says he goes into infantile mode when Georgie's around. Some kind of six-year-old's crush, where he talks like a baby. He has a cardboard box around his arm and then Georgie sees a hand touch the cardboard box. It's *the suit's* hand. Georgie and *the suit* never cross paths, surprisingly enough. The last time they spoke was at a function where Sam worked about eight years ago. *She* was all smart, tailored, slimline fitted suits and straightened hair. She said "mate" a lot and "matey," mostly to the guys. *The suit* came from the school of thought that whatever you wanted, you went out and got, regardless of whether it belonged to someone else. Grace and Bill's lesson was that you had the right to go and get what you wanted, unless it hurt others. Unless people got stepped on. Unless lives were ruined.

Apart from that, there wasn't much of a difference between Georgie and *the suit,* so no big room for analysis of why Sam had gone out with her, or whatever it's called when people sleep together for a month without actually dating. *The suit* was younger, but not young enough for it to be one of those younger woman things. *The suit* was attractive, but Georgie had never been coy about her own looks. She had inherited them from Grace and felt comfortable with the uniqueness of them. Georgie had never quite felt at ease in *the suit's* presence. Not a premonition that this woman would cause the end of her relationship, but an irritation that whether in the presence of women or men, *the suit* had to prove she knew more about pop culture, more about the latest trends and what was happening on the sports field. That no one was more down-to-earth than her. That no one was more up-to-date. She was the type who hogged the pen and paper at a trivia night. No one was more capable.

"Hi, Georgie."

Georgie doesn't speak until she remembers that Callum is there.

"Leonie," she says quietly. It's hard thinking of her as *the suit* when she's standing there in gym gear.

"Congratulations."

On what? Georgie wants to ask. Are they really going to do this?

Toast this pregnancy? Stand around and discuss what good-looking children Sam produces?

Callum pushes the products across the conveyor belt, looking up at Georgie for her approval. Like he wants her to say that he's the perfect helper. He gets nothing, because Georgie's mind is a blank for a moment. She looks at the cardboard around his arm.

"A robot, are you?" she asks.

He nods as if relieved that she gets it.

She wants the guy behind the cash register to hurry up and stop procrastinating, to make up the price of the unmarked butter. *Come on, Amal. Don't grab the microphone,* she wants to beg him, reading his name tag. But he does and it's a couple more minutes of hell in her life.

"Can we talk, Georgie?"

Please no, Georgie wants to say. *Read on my face that I can hardly breathe at the moment and every time you open your mouth, I can breathe even less.*

"I know this is a long time coming, but I need to say it."

While waiting for the price of the butter at the checkout? *The suit's* workshopped this with her friends. Pick a place where Georgie Finch can't make a scene.

"I thought he was looking for some*one* different, back then. Not some*thing* different. It was never to best you."

When Georgie called a break, she never truly believed Sam wanted to walk away from her, despite some of the issues in their relationship. She knew it was about his job and life in general. That was why she gave him space, so he could sort himself out without taking their relationship hostage. Except she never imagined what it had done to his pride for her to call the shots. Sam had a capacity for coldness. He was passive-aggressive and too many things about Georgie were an issue for him. Her lack of ambition. Her reluctance to give in to him. Someone always has the power in a relationship, he told her once. She had told him in return to stop seeing life as one-upmanship.

The butter gets its price and *the suit* hands over the money, and the moment Callum walks away, to push the trolley back to where it belongs, Georgie speaks.

"Apart from my brother being blown up, talking about this is up there in the top three things that make me feel sick to my stomach, so I'd prefer that you never bring it up again because I'm not here to make you feel good with absolution, Leonie. I never actually got the turn-the-other-cheek lecture in religion. Don't try this again, especially when Callum's around."

The suit doesn't respond. She picks up her groceries and waits for Callum to return, and, clutching her shopping bag, she takes his robot hand and disappears around the corner.

Georgie would like to have been cooler about it. Flicked her hair back in disdain a bit more. Delivered it like maybe Julia Roberts or Reese Witherspoon in a movie, southern accent and all. But she knows her voice was wavering and her hands were trembling and her face was twitching with emotion.

"I can't *believe* it," Lucia says when Georgie rings her from the car park.

"Believe it. And she doesn't even have a proper environmental shopping bag. Still using plastics."

"What. A. Cow."

●　　●　　●

She goes to the Union to speak with Tom. It's five and she knows he would have started by now and she wants him to know about his father before he comes home that night. Doesn't want to spring Dominic on him. Out of all the relationships, the one between her brother Dom and his son is the most fragile, the most heartbreaking. On a good day, she thinks that Jacinta and Dom will make it somehow, and that they shielded Anabel from it. But not Tom. Tom's hero fell off a pedestal way too high and he smashed all over the place. If Georgie hasn't been able to forgive aspects of life with Bill by her age now, she can't imagine how long it will take Tom to forgive his father. Dominic and Tom were inseparable most of Tom's childhood. The betrayal was felt deeply.

When she sees Stani, she points to the back and he nods. She comes around the bar and pokes her head in to where Tom works silently with a guy his age. How did he get to be so quiet? This boy who was born talking and who came from a family that never shut up.

"Tom?"

He hears her voice and swings around quickly, alarm on his face. Fear. Terror. Such despair. She knows that feeling too. Of believing that each time someone says her name, it's to tell her that something bad has happened.

"It's okay," she says with a smile there. A tired one, but she watches his shoulders relax and he swallows hard.

He follows her outside, his trembling arm around her shoulder.

"You okay?" he asks.

She nods, reaching up and kissing his cheek.

"Tom, your father's back."

117

There's a look of disbelief on his face, and she can see he's fighting hard to keep some control.

"Where?"

"He's back at the house, I think."

Tom's shaking his head. "*Why?* Why isn't he up north seeing Mum? What's he doing here when he should be fixing things up with her?"

She puts a gentle hand to his mouth. "It'll be fine. He's been sober for more than half the year, Tom, and he'll be determined—"

He cuts her off. "You didn't live with him," he hisses. "When she left and I was living with him, he was *determined* every day."

She doesn't want to fight Tom. He's too fragile and she doesn't know how it will manifest itself.

"For most of your life, he was a pretty fantastic father and husband, and I think it will be very sad if you remember him for what happened when Jacinta left. I'd hate to think any of us will be judged on a handful of years, Tom."

He's shaking his head. He doesn't want to hear.

"I have to go," she says, taking a deep breath because she doesn't know how she's going to prepare for Dominic. "I'll see you at home tonight. You knock on my door when you come up to bed because I'll be awake until you come home. Do you hear me?"

He pulls away and goes back inside without responding.

Her brother is waiting for her on the front step.

Dominic Finch Mackee.

School captain of Saint Sebastian's, with his stocky swagger that beckoned the world to follow. "He's the bloody pied piper," Bill would complain when Georgie and Joe copied everything he did. Dom, who got his girlfriend pregnant, married her, and dropped out of an honors law degree so Jacinta could finish hers, and never once in twenty years dared express a regret over what could have been. Dom, who made a speech on the Sydney waterfront back in 1998 when the Patrick company sacked their entire workforce in the dead of night as a threat against unionism. Delivered it with his four-year-old daughter in a pram next to him and his thirteen-year-old son by his side. But he could also be Dominic the bastard. He was a drinker, Dom was. Always had been. Enough to make him the life of the party when things were good, and when it got bad, enough to make him a bad-tempered bastard for at least three quarters of the day. So if his son grunted an answer back to his mother in a typical adolescent way, it was a shove up against the wall with enough force to bruise him. Until Tom learned to shove back and ended up spending most of Year Eleven with Georgie and Joe.

He looks thin, not the thickset build he's always had. And there's such a hollowness in his eyes. And he's looking older. They always prided themselves on looking youthful. "Forty's the new thirty," they'd joke. Until heartbreak and grief enter your life, and then forty's the new one hundred.

He stands up and holds her for a while and she feels his body tremble.

"Come on," she says quietly.

"Tommy?"

"He's working at the Union. Won't be home until ten. Let's go in."

Dominic shakes his head, seems like he needs fresh air.

She leaves the groceries on the porch and takes his hand. "Then let's walk."

They cross over to the park and she fights the shivers from this early August night. "I think he's at breaking point," she tells him, as though he's asked. "He came to me four weeks ago with ten stitches in his head."

Silence.

"Drugs. Bit of speed. Heaps of weed. Hanging out with a bunch of dickheads."

She can't see him in the dark, but she knows he's gutted.

"He's working, though," she continues. "With Bob Spinelli's kid and Stani's niece. And that can't be a bad thing."

They sit on the swings for a while, not talking. In the park where they used to hang out on Sundays with Jacinta and Anabel and Lucia and Abe and their kids. Georgie was the picnic instigator. She'd have all the food and picnic gear under control so there'd be no backing out and no excuses about it being too much of a hassle. In summer they'd stay there until the sun came down. Tom and Dominic could kick a ball around for hours and not get bored. Even without Sam, it didn't take much to make her happy. It had been the unspoken deal between her and Jacinta, years back when Dominic's girl came into their lives. It's where his other girlfriends had failed. Share her brothers and Georgie would be loyal for life. Jacinta got that, smart girl. Georgie missed her sister-in-law these days as much as Dominic. She longed for her niece, Anabel, with an anxiety that a phone call every second night couldn't soothe.

They return to the house and Dominic grabs the groceries and follows her to dump the bags in the kitchen and then they settle his things in the front room that doubles as a study. When he sits on the futon, his eyes find hers and for once in their lives they have nothing to say to each other.

"I'll make you something to eat," she says quietly, walking out.

Later that night Georgie hears the front door open, and she comes out of her room and walks down the stairs to where they stand in the corridor staring at each other. Tom and Dominic. Same height. Same bog Irish looks courtesy of Tom Finch. *Say something, Dom,* she wants to shout. *You've always had something to say. Tell him you're sorry you let him down but you're human. Tell him you'll work hard to make this right. You're a union man, Dom. The person who can get dialogue going between two opposing sides.*

But Dominic says nothing and Tom pushes past him and takes the stairs two at a time, as if to get as far away as possible.

chapter thirteen

When Tom gets to work on Monday morning, he notices that despite not getting his footy tips in on time, he's kept his place in the top three. The only person he imagines getting them as accurate as him is Mohsin the Ignorer.

"Mate, did you fill out my footy-tipping sheet?" he asks when he sits down.

Mohsin ignores him and Tom wants to spit chips. When Mohsin the Ignorer finally looks at him, Tom can't hold back.

"What's your fucking problem?"

Mohsin has the audacity to look taken aback and Tom just bars him with his own look and goes back to work.

Like he does most afternoons at the Union before his shift, he stands at the door of the back room, watching Francesca and Justine negotiate their compilation. Each time, they acknowledge him with a nod before going back to the music. Once or twice he suggests a shift in key or a need for more force in a bend, but mostly he just watches as Justine plays her accordion and Francesca works with the lyrics and scribbles down the corrections.

Today Francesca looks up at him again, and he senses it's an invitation to let him come in and listen.

"It's going to be hillbilly," Justine explains, as if he had asked. "Harmonica, accordion, and guitar. Bit like 'Crazy Train,'" she adds, referring to a Waifs piece they used to do.

"We've called it 'I Met You at the Cornerstone on the Highway to Bedlam,'" Francesca says.

He thinks about the title for a moment and nods, kind of liking it, really.

"Go on," he says. "Read me the rest."

"Only if you commit to playing on the compilation."

Francesca has that arrogant air of being in charge. It still amazes him how they could have been misled by her personality in Year Eleven. It's what depression does to a person; it changes them completely.

"You invited me in to listen," he argues.

"It's very confronting to have you listen to my lyrics," she explains. "You'll be critical and you'll snicker. If you're going to be a critical snickerer, I'd prefer that you pay with a bit of guitar playing."

"And harmonica," Justine says, trying the first line in another key. He always loved watching her fingers fly over the little black bass dots. Their best times on stage were when they dueled.

"I'm not good enough to do harmonica and guitar at the same time," he says, still irritated that he's at their mercy.

"Then work on it."

Francesca flicks through her notepad and reads out some of the lyrics.

"I met you at the cornerstone on the highway to bedlam.
Walked with you to the pinnacle, along that ledge to hell,

123

Traveled along the passageway of all things aching,
But would crawl with you if you wanted me to
On the steeple point to hope.

So we can tip the stars and hold the moon,
Graze the sun, but make it . . ."

She glances toward the doorway and whispers *"soon"* to end the chorus in rhyme. It's clear she doesn't want Anti-rhyme Ned to hear.

"I think the chorus could be longer," Tom suggests, "especially if it's going to be hillbilly."

"So we can tip the stars and hold the moon, / Graze the sun, but make it soon. / Come home, Jim, we're waiting here," Justine suggests.

Tom and Francesca are nodding and thinking.

"With three cigarettes and a glass of beer!" Ned taunts mockingly from the kitchen.

The three of them exchange looks. "He's very annoying," Tom says, taking the lyrics from Francesca. He didn't realize the song was for Jimmy, but it makes sense really. Jimmy was all bedlam and hell at times. A curse to be around when you just wanted things to be calm. He never played by the rules, which made things too unpredictable most times. Both Jimmy and Tom had been forced to hang out with each other when they attached themselves to the female force. When he met Tara and these girls, he didn't explain the shit of what was happening at home with his father's drinking and why he spent so much time with Georgie and Joe. He just sat behind them on the bus home in the afternoon and took advantage of the therapy they dished out to Frankie, whose own home life was falling to pieces. Until being with them made more sense than being with his other mates. It kept him sane, really. It wasn't until Jimmy Hailler called him on it, not until the crazy bastard had started sitting with him in woodwork classes, that he actually started talking. Jimmy Hailler was a killer of a listener. The guy understood fragmented people.

"Suggestions?"

Francesca and Justine are standing in front of him. Their lyrics are in his hands, and he doesn't realize until Francesca reaches out to steady the paper, her dark eyes piercing into him, that his hands are shaking.

He thinks for a moment. "Yeah," he says, but his throat feels croaky, so he clears it.

"So we can tip the stars and hold the moon,
Graze the sun, and fate our chances.
But make it soon; our sorrow lingers
And time just seems to slip away."

He shrugs. He doesn't know where to go from there without sounding sentimental.

Justine puts the accordion down. "It's five," she says, looking up at the time.

She walks out and Tom waits as Francesca packs up.

"Where is he?"

"Who?" she asks, looking up.

"Jimmy?"

"Jim," she corrects. She shrugs. "Who knows with Jim?"

"What happened?"

125

"He just nicked off after his granddad died last year."

"His granddad's dead?" Tom is stunned. Jimmy had lived with the old man for years. As far as they were concerned, there was no one else around.

"When?"

She's confused by the question. "November last year."

"So where did he go?"

She shrugs. "Away. Out bush. You know Jim. He was never going to stick around."

"Why did you let him go?" Tom can feel himself getting angrier and angrier, but he can't control it, especially when he sees her expression contains fury beyond anything.

"Jim couldn't cope," Francesca snaps. "Jim went out bush. We don't know where he is. Once in a very blue moon we get an entry on Siobhan's MySpace page. He once sent her a message asking if he could borrow a hundred dollars. She deposited it into his account. Another time he sent my mother flowers for her birthday. What do you want me to say, Thomas? Jim doesn't want to be found just yet. We had the funeral and then he was gone."

"Did anyone turn up?" he asks. "His mother or father?"

She shakes her head. "Just us and our families, and some of the old guys his grandfather knew, Ms. Quinn and Brother Louis and even Mr. Brolin from school."

Everyone but him. He kicks the chair across the room and the music goes flying.

"*Whose decision was it not to tell me?*"

She shakes her head, grabs her stuff, and walks out of the room, pushing past Justine, who stares at Tom from the door, stunned.

"People can hear, Thomas."

126

There's something in her eyes that makes him feel like he's sickened them, like that time when they saw him lose it years ago after a night in a pub on Broadway, when some guy had tried to pick a fight. Tom always did anger well. Hid it well, but showed it even better—courtesy of his father and Joe, who could go off at any given moment. Joe said it was a Bill thing. Nothing about nature there. With the Mackees, it was all nurture.

"I can't believe you didn't tell me about Jimmy's grandfather. I would have been there."

"Frankie . . ."

"I don't care what Francesca decided! I would have been there."

Justine walks toward him, and he can tell that she's angry. She picks up some of the sheet music from the floor.

"Why do you do that, Thomas? Make Frankie the villain? Just say it was me?" she says, pointing to herself. "Just say it was me who said, 'Thomas doesn't give a shit about us'? What would you say?"

Stani is at the door. *"Hey!"* he says, looking directly at Tom. "Keep it down."

What would he say? He'd say, Thomas doesn't give a shit about himself.

"Why don't you go ask your dumb flatmates why you didn't know? Frankie told them to pass on the details. We just thought you didn't care."

He feels knifed. Doesn't know why he stays, but he's in the kitchen putting on his apron.

Ned the Cook is pissed off and makes a mess for him to clean up. The next minute, Tom has him down, grinding Ned's face into the floor, and Francesca is pulling him off, crying, and Stani's there grabbing him, holding him back, his steel bar of an arm across Tom's chest.

"Tom, take a breath. Take a few deep breaths." He hears the accent in Stani's voice that only comes out with emotion. "I've got you. I've got you, Tom."

Ned is bleeding from somewhere on his face and Francesca helps him to his feet.

He's trembling, Tom is. His whole body is shaking, but he can't help it. His eyes are fixed on Ned's bloody face, and when he stops shaking and Stani lets go, he takes off his apron and walks out calmly.

He can sense their surprise when he walks into the house. Both Georgie and his father are in the kitchen, eating soup in silence. Tom takes out a bowl and helps himself, and then sits at the table opposite them.

"Have you rung your mother?" his father asks.

Tom looks up from his soup, the expression on his face filthy.

"*Don't*," he warns.

"She wants . . ."

"*Don't* lecture me on how to treat my mother. Not you. Not after the way you've treated her."

They're the first words Tom's spoken to him. A couple of *don't*s and *not*s.

"Tom . . ." Georgie begins, putting a hand gently on his shoulder.

"And don't lecture me on how to talk to *him*," he snaps, shrugging her hand away. "You're always sticking up for him like he's never done anything wrong."

There's not much to say after that, so everyone goes back to slurping in silence. Tom's determined not to be the one who walks away first. He's not going to give the bastard the satisfaction. Of course, the great Dominic Mackee gets up because he's good at leaving. He takes his plate to the sink and begins to rinse.

"She got her doctorate," his father says with his back to him, washing the plate. "She left a message. Wanted you to know."

And then his father walks out without looking back.

Later in the night, he dials the number with trembling fingers.

"Hello."

"Mum?"

He hears her catch her breath. "Dr. Jacinta Louise Mackee to you, thank you very much," and it's said with a sob and a laugh at the same time. It's the first time he's spoken to her in nine months and it makes him want to cry.

"Are you at Georgie's?" she asks.

"Yeah."

"Have you spoken to your dad?"

"No. Not really."

"Talk to me."

"I just wanted to hear your voice." His voice is cracking. *Keep it together, Tom. Don't be a loser.*

"Then I'll talk to you."

He swallows hard. "Just not about him, okay."

He hears her sigh and it sounds so sad. And then she starts talking. It's what she'd do every morning he could remember when he was a kid. She'd wake him up at six in the morning with a cup of tea and they'd lie in his bed and talk for an hour before she had to get ready for work. It was to make up for the fact that at times she wouldn't see him until six at night. Some mornings they'd read together; other times she'd explain what she did during the day. Tonight she speaks about the doctorate and about Anabel's soccer and trumpet lessons and how Anabel's not really enjoying school, and how sometimes she thinks she's made the wrong decision, but most times knows it's the right one. She talks about Grandma Agnes and his great-grandfather, who's going to turn eighty-five and who told her he feels as if he's closed his eyes for a moment and sixty years passed by. And then she stops for a moment.

"What?" he asks. "What's wrong?"

"I don't know how to do what you asked me, Tom," she says sadly. "I don't know how to talk about our lives without talking about your father. He's in every one of the memories and every one of my decisions."

He closes his eyes and wants to sleep through the next sixty years.

"I've got to go."

"I love you, Tom. He loves you."

Her voice whispering love soothes him. They'd never done that before. Weren't that type of family. Except now he doesn't know what kind of family they are. What word is it that can define them? What would they call his family in the textbooks? Broken? He comes from a broken home. The Mackees can't be put back together again. There are too many pieces of them missing.

chapter fourteen

To: mackee_joe@yahoo.co.uk
From: georgiefinch@hotmail.com
Date: 7 August 2007

I think of Dom and me lying in our bunks in Fort Street, Joe. He'd tell me that our father, Tom Finch, was coming back to us one day. If they hadn't returned a body, it meant he was still alive regardless of what everyone else said. We'd work ourselves up wondering what would happen to your father if Tom Finch returned. What would happen to Bill? What would happen to Mum if she had to choose between both her husbands? It made us hate Bill, you know. We stopped ourselves loving him, Joe, because we couldn't bear the idea of loving Bill like a father and then Tom Finch coming back. And then years later you were born. And I'd want to kill anyone who called you my half brother because there was nothing half about how Dom and I loved you. From the moment I saw you, when I was seven years old, in that incubator, Joe, I started thanking God that my father hadn't come back. Because if he had, you would never have been born.

And now I look at Sam, who would never have gotten on that plane to London with me, who wouldn't even be back in my life again today if it wasn't for you dying. And it's like God's being cruel and saying, "Well, if you want Joe, you can't have Sam back. That's the deal, Georgie." And perhaps I could choose, Joe, but then God makes it worse. "If you want Joe, you can't have this baby."

When Georgie walks out of the station that afternoon, Sam's there. Leaning against the railing on the Main Street side, next to where someone's chained a bike. It takes twenty seconds to walk through the tunnel under the platforms toward where he stands, and she keeps her eyes on him the whole way while he tries to get as much out of his cigarette as he can and then tosses it into the bin as she approaches. Today his son isn't with him. He only gets Callum from Friday to Sunday and although she never gets a sense of his anticipation to be with the boy on Thursdays, she always senses his flatness on Sundays.

Sometimes he forgets the unspoken rules written by their past and he places a hand around her shoulder. It's instinct, intimacy is. Sometimes he lets it linger, while other times he drops his hand by the time they get to the lights on Salisbury Road. But apart from that, words have been removed. Words are intimacy she won't allow and he would not dare ask for. The Georgie and Sam of the present have no past together. No talk of memories. No reminiscing of holidays, or friends and parties.

"Do you want a hot chocolate?" he asks as they walk past Le Chocoreve.

She shakes her head. She thinks of the e-mail she received today from Ana Vanquez, the girl Joe loved in London. They were teachers together in their East London school. Ana teaching her native tongue of Spanish, and Joe teaching English and history.

These days she avoids Ana Vanquez's e-mails and tells herself she'll read them when she feels stronger. She knows what they'll say.

"I'm going to Melbourne for a couple of days for work," he says, watching her closely because he knows the signs. "Why don't you get Bernadette to move in?"

"I've got Tom and Dominic," she says.

"They're not exactly the best of company at the moment, Georgie."

Which is an understatement. Her brother spends most of his time locked away in the study. Sometimes he disappears early in the evening and she thinks it's to go to an AA meeting, but he's not ready to talk about it yet, so she doesn't ask. Apart from his jog every morning and the brief appearance he makes at dinnertime, she's hardly seen him. As a result of Dominic's presence, Tom stays away or confines himself to the attic. She misses their talks. She misses Dominic more now than when he was away.

"I'll get Dom out of the house tonight," Sam says.

"Where?"

He shrugs.

"I don't know. Down to the pub."

She looks at him, horrified. "Don't be ridiculous, Sam. You don't take an alcoholic to the pub."

"He'll have to get used to being normal again, and being normal is all of us down at the pub. I'll get Abe to come down and Jonesy."

"*No,*" she says. He used to make fun of the way she said it. "*No-wa,*" he'd exaggerate.

"And anyway, Tom's down there and it will be uncomfortable for both of them."

"It's not the only pub in Sydney."

"No."

He sighs and she picks up a bit of irritation in the sound.

"What? Are you going to follow him around for the rest of his life now?" he asks. "Make sure he doesn't walk into pubs or linger around bottle shops? Are you that powerful, Georgie? That you can protect your brother from whatever's out there?"

She stares at him, taken aback, and he mutters something under his breath and she can tell he regrets his words.

"Mick Thomas is playing at the Vanguard tonight," he adds quietly. "I'll take him there."

These days he's almost all gray, not the fair-haired guy she once loved and although he tries to keep fit, he has to work at it harder than ever and she knows that irritates him. He never had Dom's charisma or his gift of the gab. There was a distance to him that forced people to work harder at trying to get his attention, but she knew it wasn't game playing for him. Sam had been brought up in a cold household where people had no idea how to communicate with each other. His parents were working-class people who believed in very little, and Sam observed a loveless marriage where the only bonding that took place was in front of the television set at night. Georgie was with Sam when his father had died suddenly at the beginning of their relationship, and there had been no emotion. She had never seen him cry. That Sam and his mother loved each other was obvious. That they loved Sam's boy was even more so, but there were very few words between them. It had been through Georgie, back when they were together, that his mother was able to express her affection toward Sam.

With their friends, though, Sam was different. If they were warm to him, he returned that warmth. It was what Bernadette had once said that she loved about both Sam and Dom and even Abe. "A lot of times you're around men who are so in love with their wives or partners that they don't have anything to offer any other woman in conversation. Especially single women. But Sam and Dom and Abe can be in love with you three and still make a girl feel as if she has some kind of sex appeal. That's nice."

"Dom knows he can look and not touch," Jacinta said.

"Does Sam look?" Lucia had asked.

Georgie thought about it and nodded. "He loves breasts, so sometimes I see the eyes follow a bounce here or there."

But for all the love that Bernadette had seen, here Georgie was walking home with Sam as though they were strangers, and Dominic and Jacinta were living a state apart from each other.

They reach the house and he shuffles through her bag for the keys.

"Do you want me to stay tonight?" he asks.

"Do you want to?"

"Just answer the question, Georgie."

"Why can't you answer mine?"

He unlocks the door and there's the sigh again.

"Tell Dom I'll pick him up at seven."

chapter fifteen

To: taramarie@yahoo.com
From: anabelsbrother@hotmail.com
Date: 10 August 2007

Dear Tara,

My father's back. He's living in Georgie's study and I want to hurt him. God, I do. I want to go in there and pound the shit out of him. Because I stayed that time after my mum left. For him. No matter what, I couldn't bear for him to be on his own after she took Anabel away. She called it tough love. "I'm not nurturing this, Dominic. Fix it and I'll come back." But I couldn't leave him because you have no idea how he felt about Joe and how fucking sad he was that year. Joe wasn't just his brother; they were best friends. I was scared for him those first couple of weeks after she left, honest I was. And then six weeks later he walked out on me and I mightn't have been a kid anymore, but I wasn't ready for all my family to be gone. They can't suffocate you for years and be on your tail and have rules about when to be home and who to be and how impor- tant uni is and then take it away from you and leave you in that house with all those memories. On my own. And I don't give a shit if my mum was begging me to come up and be with her and Anabel, or that Georgie was always trying to get me to come and stay with her. I wanted to stay there and wait for him to come home. And he didn't, and now he won't even look at me, the coward. The great Dominic Finch Mackee and the only thing I can understand him doing is drinking himself to oblivion. I can do oblivion, you know. I can do it better than him. I'd like to see how he likes it if I just disappear from his life without a word. It was okay for him to keep in contact with Georgie and my mum, but not once did he pick up the phone or write to me. Like I was fucking nothing to him. Like I'm nothing to no one.

He presses the send button and his fingers are shaking. Like always, he regrets the pressing of *send*, but he doesn't care. Mohsin the Ignorer is in his way, and he shoves past him and just walks out. Except he can't go home because the enemy is in the house and there is no way he's turning up at the Union. Ned and Stani have probably got the police out after him anyway. But Tom doesn't care. They can go to hell. Everyone can. If Georgie wants her beloved brother staying with her, she can forget about Tom.

He fights the urge to go back to his old flat. He just wants to get wasted and not think so much. Except the more time goes by, the more he despises his ex-flatmates. All they'd be is a reminder of what a soft cock he was all that time he lived with them. How they stole from Stani. How they used to boast about pissing on the toilet seat if they knew it was Justine or Francesca's turn to clean it at work. How they didn't tell him about Jimmy's pop. He remembers the note Jimmy Hailler left in his family's post box two years ago. *Don't know what to say, Mackee, except if I had to wish for anything at the moment, it would be that this hadn't happened to you and yours.* With all the shit in Jimmy Hailler's life, he would have wasted his one and only wish on Tom. Yet one year later, when the only person in Jimmy's life died, Tom was nowhere around. What a piece of shit he was.

He goes back to their old house next door to Mrs. Liu, where some other Tom is living with his dirty family, not knowing that just around the corner is a catastrophic event that's going to change everything. Tom wants to knock on the door and warn the poor bastard. That it's all make-believe what they're doing in there, playing happy families. It's all coming to pieces. Any minute now. He begins pulling out the dead flowers from the potted plants lining the brick balcony, and one smashes on the ground and he hurls the pieces across the front lawn. Then someone calls the cops. Probably thinks he's trying to rob the place. *It's my home,* he wants to shout, and they end up bringing him in, maybe because he throws a punch when one of them puts his hand on his shoulder.

Siobhan Sullivan's father is the head of the cop shop in Newtown and he doesn't say much and writes nothing down.

He looks at the details in front of him and looks back to Tom.

"This where you used to live?" he asks, because he'd know. He knew every single detail about Siobhan's friends. It's why she's in *London still.* So she could escape.

"You want me to take you home, Tom?" he asks.

Tom shakes his head.

"Who are you staying with?"

He doesn't respond. Why can't he just walk off the face of this world without Francesca turning up to hospitals, and Georgie living around the corner and Siobhan Sullivan's father now having a tail on him?

"Are you staying with Georgie Finch, Tom? Are you staying with your aunt?"

He nods. It's not that he doesn't want to talk. He just doesn't have the energy to.

"I'll get one of the boys to drop you off, Tom. How about that? Maybe we can talk tomorrow after you get some sleep. You look like you need some sleep, mate."

When he gets in, the house is quiet, but his father comes out of the study. The cop car would have awoken him.

"What happened?" he asks, and Tom can't see his face in the dark.

"Fuck off," he says, walking up the stairs.

He dreams of his footy team. Someone's chanting the Tigers' theme in his ear, but there's no image. A dream with the sound but no picture. And then he realizes that it's his phone. His hand reaches out to the bedside table and he mutters a hello.

"I don't have much credit left so you're going to have to ring me," he hears a voice say.

"Tara!"

And then she hangs up.

He dives for the light but then remembers that *he* doesn't have credit and he trips out of bed, desperate to get to a phone. He flies down the stairs and bursts into Georgie's room.

"I need your phone."

"Get out, Tom!" he hears Sam say in a strained voice and he steps back outside again, taking deep breaths.

Yes, everyone, he'll say. *Sam and Georgie are having sex these days.* Pretty embarrassing all round, but that doesn't stop him from knocking again.

"I really need the phone."

It hits him hard in the face, and he fumbles to catch it and flies up the stairs again.

He goes back to his mobile, searches for her number, and then begins to dial.

"Hi."

"Hi."

"I just walked in on Georgie and Sam doing the deed."

He doesn't know why he says that. Maybe because the shock of it has just hit him.

"Justine and Frankie want to know why you didn't come into work this week," she says.

"Have you spoken to them?"

"No. They texted. Siobhan too. Something about her father arresting you."

He can't believe these girls. Separated by the Timor Sea and the Indian Ocean and they can still keep each other informed at the speed of lightning.

"I just needed to know you were okay," she says.

"I'm okay."

"Good."

"So how are things?"

"I'm not talking to you, Thomas, so no small talk."

Shit, she's calling him Thomas. But how can such a snippy voice do crazy things to his blood flow?

"Fair enough."

There's silence and then he sighs, because he needs to know.

"When I rang you that night I cut my head open, what did I say?"

"Nothing."

"No, really. I need to know."

He's begging God that he didn't make a fool of himself. Not with her.

"I didn't declare my love for you or anything like that?" he asks in a ridiculous jocular voice.

"No, you didn't."

Relief.

"So I rang and said nothing?"

"Nothing at all, Thomas."

He can sense she's about to say something and it seems like hours rather than seconds.

"Nothing? Are you sure?"

He wants to ask what made her say the words *"Talk to me, Thomas. Talk to me."*

"You cried," she says, her voice so gentle it kills him. Tara Finke doesn't do gentle. Tara Finke does practical, or abrupt, or furious, or passionate. But the gentleness in her voice undoes him.

"Sorry," he mutters. "Shit, I'm sorry."

"Don't be sorry. This will cost you a fortune, so you better go."

Say something, he tells himself. Don't let it end this way.

"Are you going to write or are you going to spend the rest of eternity ignoring my e-mails?" he asks huskily.

"I don't ignore them. I just choose not to respond to them and if you ever write me another one like today's, where you go on about oblivion and stuff, Tom, I swear to God I'll come back there and show you oblivion. And I'll make sure it hurts. Stop feeling so bloody sorry for yourself. You just piss me off, honest you do."

She hangs up.

141

He feels shock at first. Perhaps a bit of anger. He's stunned. But his heart's hammering with hope. In Tara Finke language, that conversation was progress.

If he can still piss her off, then it's a whole lot better than indifference.

chapter sixteen

Georgie's felt it coming for days now, ever since she received the e-mail from Joe's girl. Ever since she discovered that Dominic coming home doesn't mean the end of the pain. She puts the blanket over her head and just wants everything to stop, but Dominic is there, or maybe Tom, and she's trying to explain but then she realizes that it's like one of those hallucinations. It's like she's explained it, but she's in the same spot and she's explained nothing.

"Georgie." She hears Dominic's voice from the door, then knocking and walking in, and she realizes it's Tom who's been with her for a while, asking her if she's okay.

"Georgie, is everything okay with the baby?" her brother asks.

Oh, God, she's forgotten about the baby.

"Georgie, is everything okay with the baby?" he repeats.

She manages a nod and Dominic gently pulls her up. He looks so sad; she can see that in this afternoon light.

"Georgie. You have to get out of bed."

It's the same voice she remembers from her childhood. The one of authority.

"Later." She says it in a whisper.

"She'll get out of bed later," she hears Tom say. "She's fine. Let her sleep."

"No. *Now,* Georgie," Dom says firmly.

She doesn't move. Tom's right. She'll get out of bed later.

"Georgie, I have to go to my AA meeting and I need you to come with me, *now.* I can't do this on my own."

"I'll look after her," Tom's saying, panic in his voice. "She'll get out of bed later. Don't bully her."

She feels Dominic's hands cup her face. "*Please,* Georgie. I need you to come with me. I can't do this on my own."

After the meeting, down at the Stanmore Community Hall, Dom sits with her in the park.

"What happened?" he asks her quietly.

She shakes her head and closes her eyes, and the tears are there.

"Just a bad day." Her voice has no volume, no energy. "Where's Sam?"

She knows she's asked that same question a few times now. She remembers that he's answered, but she can't remember what the answer is.

"In Melbourne for work. Come on, Georgie. What sent you over the edge?"

She can see her house from where they sit. She's left the light on in her room and she wants to go back there and shut the door.

"Did I not go to work today?"

"It's Saturday. You didn't go yesterday. Talk to me, Georgie, or I'll have to take you to Lucia's."

There's panic in his voice.

"I got an e-mail the other day," she says. "From Ana Vanquez."

He thinks for a moment. "Joe's girl?"

She nods.

"And I was happy for her, honest I was, Dom. She had written to me a while back and told me about this lovely man she had met back in Spain and now they're having a . . ."

She can't say the words and he tries to put his arm around her, but she doesn't want it there. Why is it that Sam's the only one who understands that she doesn't want arms placed around her every time she wants to talk? That every time arms are placed around her, she stops talking.

"I just want him back, Dom," she sobs. "Why can't we have him back? Why can't that baby be his? It should be his!"

He nods. At least family members don't use shit clichés.

"She wants me to tell Mummy and Bill . . . but I can't."

"I will."

She lays her head on his shoulder and closes her eyes.

"Can I love my baby if I loved Joe?" she whispers.

"Oh, God, Georgie. Don't even ask that."

They sit for a while and she hears the sprinklers come on illegally in someone's backyard. She reaches over and takes his hand, because he seems to be in another miserable world.

"You and Jacinta? Is it worse than I think it is?" she asks.

He doesn't respond.

"She told me you were in contact six months ago," Georgie continues. "And that she lets you speak to Anabel, but not to her just yet."

He laughs, bitterly.

"I'd been sober for two minutes, and thought I could just drive up there and collect them."

There's more silence and she squeezes his hand.

"Do you know what she said?" he asks.

Georgie shakes her head.

" 'Returning home is my decision to make, Dom,' she said. 'Not yours. And if you come and get me, I'll never forgive you. If you take this decision away from me like you did before, I'll never forgive you for Tom.' "

Georgie watches as he focuses on the merry-go-round in front of them. She shivers. It always looks creepy at night without kids playing on it.

"And I didn't get what she meant," he says. "At first I thought it was about me walking out on Tom six weeks after she took Anabel away. I thought it was about the drinking, but then something told me that it was more than that. And I've spent this whole time trying to work it out. How far back do I go?"

His head is in his hands and sometimes he's muffled and she has to lean closer to hear him.

"And I went all the way back to when we were twenty," he says, his voice still bitter. "Four generations of housing commission and welfare, and Jacinta Louise, the wonder girl, wins a scholarship to Sydney Uni from the western suburbs of Brisbane, and two and a half years in, I get her pregnant."

"Oh, Dom, don't do this," Georgie mutters.

"I remember the look on her parents' faces when they drove down. *Shit*, Georgie. She was one of five girls to make it to Year Eleven at her school, because everyone else got knocked up or were off their faces on drugs by the time they were fourteen. Even the nuns wouldn't let her out of their sight. And I swore to them all, on my family's honor, that I wouldn't let her drop out of uni and that I'd take care of everything. For years people would go on about how I threw it in so my wife could finish her degree. I was Mr. Wonderful."

He shakes his head with disbelief.

"You know what I think, Georgie? That I wanted to throw it in. And worse still, she didn't want all that. Not with a baby on the way. We made the plans, but no one asked Jacinta Louise what she wanted. What if all she wanted was to be at home with her boy?"

He looks at her for the first time, his expression so pained as he rubs his hands over his mouth. "While I was telling her to get the baby on the bottle because it wouldn't work if she was still breast-feeding him. So it makes sense that six months ago, she's crying on the phone, Georgie, and I heard the anger when she said, *'If you take this decision away from me, like you did before, I'll never forgive you for Tom.'*"

Georgie closes her eyes. She wants to be one of those ventriloquist dolls and have someone put the right words in her mouth.

"Okay," she acknowledges. "Maybe. But she's my best friend, Dom, and we've covered every conversation there is to cover over the last twenty-two years. Believe me, I know things about your sex life that I should not know."

He glances at her and she almost laughs at the look of horror.

"But Jacinta's said it to me before. That she was never happier than the time when we all lived in that dump in Camperdown after Tommy was born. And how your uni mates couldn't grasp the fact that you weren't studying law anymore and they spent most of their

147

time with us in that mad house listening to Joy Division and the Pretenders and drinking and having arguments about politics and religion, and how we'd watch *Rage* every Sunday morning and then we'd wrap up Tommy and go to Mass. And if it wasn't for the fact that she hadn't met Anabel Georgia yet, she'd want to go back to those years and not move an inch. Because she had her gorgeous boy and you."

She presses a kiss to his arm. "Jacinta loved that she got to use her brains, Dom, and she loved that Tom and you were inseparable for those years. 'Better than men who don't get to know their kids,' she'd say. Don't take that away from yourself just because of what's happened in the last two years."

He's still stooped over and she puts her arms around his back and leans her head against him. They stay like that for a while.

"So what's the deal with you and Sam?" he asks later.

"So what is the deal with me and Sam?" she asks tiredly. "Are you shocked?"

"Who wouldn't be? It's amazing."

"The baby?"

"No. I just can't get over your boobs."

She laughs and sits up, looking down at them.

"Aren't they fantastic? B cup and growing."

"You don't get to keep them. You know that, don't you, G?"

And then she's laughing some more, because that's the closest she's got to hearing Dominic's real personality. The dry drawl in his voice. The shit-stirrer extraordinaire.

"I'm going to breast-feed this kid until he's in kindergarten."

He pulls her gently to her feet and they cross the road, looking up at the front veranda. "Have you seen the way he looks at me?" Dominic asks quietly. She knows he's talking about his son.

They walk up the steps of the terrace, where Tom sits smoking a cigarette in the dark, putting it out quickly before she gets to him.

"Don't leave butts in my potted plants," she says firmly.

"You've killed them all anyway," he mutters, but she catches the relief in his eyes and holds out a hand to him, which he grips for a moment before she goes inside, their fingers lingering like she'd let them when he was a kid.

chapter seventeen

When Tom can hear her safely in the kitchen, he looks up at his father.

"Is she okay?"

Dominic shrugs. "For the time being."

"Sam rang. He's really pissed that you took her to . . . a meeting."

"What did he say?"

"I recall the letter *c* and the letter *u* and the letter *n* and the letter *t* and lots of *f*s and *k*s. It will filthy up my mouth to repeat the words."

Tom doesn't know why he says that. It's what his mum would say when she had to repeat someone's swearing, and his father would laugh every time. The princess, they would call her. But the princess packed her bags and took Anabel with her and told his father not to come near them until he had been sober long enough not to remember his last drink. "And if you break that rule, I'll file for divorce and you'll have to see your daughter through a court order," she had said. But she still added "my love" to it. So his father stayed away all this time, and now Tom thinks he's doing it all wrong. In the movies, the guy gets sober and goes straight back to reclaim his family, like something out of a Paul Kelly song. He doesn't hide in his sister's house, still avoiding the world.

Sometimes Tom wants to break into his father's room and search it. Does he hide his booze there? Did he get up there tonight at his meeting and say, "Hi, my name's Dominic and I'm an alcoholic and I'll never drink again because I love my family too much to screw up again"?

They walk into the house and his father shuts the door behind them.

"She hasn't eaten all week," Tom says quietly. "She's going to go straight up to her room. Do something."

He doesn't know why he says that either. Why he thinks his father will be able to do anything. But he follows Dominic into the kitchen, just because it's instinctive.

"Can you make us something to eat, Georgie?" he hears his father say.

It's about eleven thirty and he hears the beep of a horn. At first he thinks it's random, but Tom knows that horn well and peers outside the tiny window and sees the Valiant first and then Justine and Francesca jogging on the spot to keep warm. They're dressed up, he can see that. It's what they used to do years ago with Tara and Siobhan. Beep the horn and he'd have to determine in a split second, by the way they were dressed, where they were all off to. One minute's notice. Tonight he has no reason to respond, because their lives aren't like two years ago, but Francesca and Justine aren't budging, so he grabs a pair of jeans and collared shirt.

Five minutes later, he's out of the house, and without a word, Justine and Francesca get back into the car and he hops in after them. They end up in some warehouse nightclub in Rosebery for a schoolmate's twenty-first. He hasn't seen the school crowd since the last of the eighteenth birthdays. The moment they step inside, Justine and Francesca are kidnapped by Anna Nguyen and Eva Rodriguez, off to the dance floor where he knows they'll spend the rest of the night. He ends up out back with some of the guys, smoking. Someone hands him the bottle of Johnnie Walker doing the rounds and he shakes his head. If there's one thing that makes him sick to the stomach, courtesy of Dominic Mackee, it's the smell of whiskey.

"When your uncle died, I felt it here, bro," Shaheen says, thumping his chest.

"Same," Travis says.

It gets too intense and someone brings up football. Tom's relieved to be talking about something that has rules and purpose, and next minute they're arguing and everyone's calling each other pussy and dickhead and boofhead and turd with such affection that it almost brings tears to his eyes. Later, he goes inside and ends up on the dance floor with the girls and it's hazy and sweaty and he doesn't have to think; he just has to feel the bass inside him. It's what he always had with Francesca and Justine. They were uninhibited when it came to music and sometimes the three of them had a tune inside their head that no one else could hear, and tonight it's there between them and they're fucking the space with their bodies.

In the early hours of the morning, a bunch of them drive to Maroubra Beach like they used to when they were at school. The last time they were all here together was after graduation night, with their dates. Tom thought Tara was making a statement because she hadn't asked anyone to be hers. He had been going out with one of the

Year Elevens who seemed keen, but that night he couldn't keep his eyes off Tara Finke and he knew she felt it. They drove around the city with Tom as their designated driver, planning to stay the night on the beach, where there was too much drinking and too much emotion among all of them. Will Trombal and Francesca had been apart because he'd graduated the year before and had been overseas for most of that year. Despite Francesca's rule that they were going to take it slowly, the two couldn't keep their hands off each other. And he remembered the water that night and how warm it felt and Jimmy doing a nudie run along the beach, and then they all stripped down to underwear and even now, looking at how rough the surf is, he can't believe they went in, the others were so tanked. But in the darkness that night he knew exactly where to find Tara. He hadn't realized he was looking until his hand snaked out and grabbed her, their mouths connecting and tongues taking over while his brain was saying, *Danger, danger, Will Robinson.* His mouth had been everywhere, hands with minds of their own . . . fingers . . . his . . . hers . . . scratching, searching, kneading.

"Tom!"

Until his date's voice rang out through the night and Tara pushed him away. And she was crying. His one claim to fame, he thinks. Being able to make Tara Finke cry. All he could say the next day was, "Sorry about last night. *Shit.* What was that?" Like he didn't know, the weak bastard that he was.

He feels someone against his shoulder and it's Francesca calling his name again.

"You're getting your jeans wet," she says, and he walks up the sand with her to where Justine's sitting on the hood of the car under one of the streetlights. This place isn't exactly the best spot to be hanging out on a Saturday night if you're not a local, but it's like they couldn't even be bothered being scared.

He lights a cigarette and sits between them.

"Stani's going to have to find a new dish-pig if you don't come back," Justine says.

"He was actually thinking of promoting you to glassy," Francesca adds.

"Oh, my God. Then what am I going to do about the job offers from Bill Gates and Donald Trump?"

"Tell them the Union's a better gig," Francesca says. "It's where you need to be."

He can't speak because it's like there's something in his throat, but these two have learned the art of silence and they stay there until some shifty-looking guys come along and it's time to go.

And as quietly as they arrived to pick him up, they drive back over the Anzac Bridge and drop him off in front of Georgie's, just as the sun begins to appear.

"You don't have to play," Francesca says, "but we're running out of time for our compilation and we need lyrics. Think about it."

He gets out of the car and waits for them to pull away. His stomach's churning and he realizes that it's a subconscious thing, seeing Francesca and Justine. That he was always used to seeing Tara with them, and he wonders if he thinks of her more often because they're around. He wants to hear her voice again, but he can't bear the idea that she could be lying beside some guy, some pasty-faced soldier.

He turns when he hears a sound behind him and sees that it's his father, preparing for his morning jog. Obsessive-compulsive to a T, Dom Mackee is.

His father looks at him closely as he passes him, and Tom realizes bitterly that the prick has the hide to be assessing whether he's drunk or off his face on drugs. He wishes he was, so he could say, "Because of you."

But neither says a word to each other, and it's his father who puts the earphones in and looks away first.

chapter eighteen

Tom's at her bedroom door the next morning, a look of worry on his face. Georgie winces. She's supposed to be the adult around here and instead, this poor kid's looking after her.

"I'm okay, Tom. I promise," she says, shuffling out of bed.

But he's shaking his head. "Georgie, I'm sorry."

She grabs her dressing gown, which doesn't even reach her sides these days.

"I got so stressed yesterday and freaked out and . . ." he's saying.

She stops and places her hands on his shoulders. "Calm down. It's fine. I'm fine. I'm going to have a shower now and then eat breakfast. And then I'll do the grocery shopping and tonight I'll cook properly. I promise."

It takes a lot of energy to speak, but she doesn't want him to see that.

"I rang Nanni Grace and Bill yesterday because I was worried about you," he says.

She nods. She wants to get that look off Tom's face. "I'll ring them today and tell them I'm okay, Tommy—I promise."

He's pointing outside and then down. Tom was always a pointer. Pointed at his food as a substitute for words.

She hears barking.

"They're downstairs, Georgie. And they brought the dogs. And big suitcases."

Oh, my God.

She's out the bedroom door in a moment. "Mummy!" she calls out from the top of the stairs. The dogs respond to the sound of her voice and she clutches the banister as they come bounding up the stairs.

And there she is. Amazing Grace. A grief-ravaged face, but the beauty and style is still there. No unruly hair for Grace Mackee. She's all sleek bob cut and lipstick.

"Bill. Get the dogs off Georgie!"

"Bruno! Bazzi!"

Lots of bellowing.

Dominic stands behind their parents, at the bottom of the stairs. A bit shell-shocked really. When Georgie reaches them, Grace does that practical thing where she hugs her quickly and pats her on the back without lingering. *Just one second more, Grace,* Georgie wants to say. *Just one second.*

"Bill will get some breakfast."

"Is Bill going to get the dogs, or is Bill going to get breakfast?" Bill asks. Dom gets his drawl from Bill. It's a Burdekin drawl, no matter how many decades he's lived down south. Georgie hugs her stepfather awkwardly and he holds on. Maybe that's why she has resented him all her life. Because he would hold on longer, when she wanted it to come from her mother. He looks worn out. Although still fit and working outdoors fixing tractors in Albury, Joe's death had aged him. Around him the dogs are going insane and everyone's falling over one another with suitcases.

"Do you want the spare room or the study?" Dom asks, and Grace agrees that the spare room is the way to go.

Georgie tries to wash up the plates from the last two days quickly, ashamed at how untidy the house looks. In the past, if she'd known her parents were coming, she would be spring cleaning for a week.

Her mother comes up behind her, holding a small diary. "What do you think, Georgie? Should I change Bill's November checkups to now, seeing we're here?"

"That sounds good, Mum."

"But as long as your father doesn't drive. As soon as we hit Sydney, he was useless. I told him the whole time not to take the Hume Highway. Do you think he listened to me?"

"Organize it with Dom and he can drive you both around."

"He's getting Alzheimer's. I'm sure of it."

"I'm not getting Alzheimer's," Bill says, walking into the kitchen with a box of produce they've brought up from Albury. Dom's behind him with another and begins stacking some of it in the fridge.

"Great," Georgie whispers to her brother as they huddle at the fridge door. "Bill gets Alzheimer's and has an excuse to forget what a bastard he was all those years."

The doorbell rings and she thinks it's the neighbors coming to complain already, so she rushes to answer the door. To Sam.

"Where were you?" she blurts out. She doesn't mean to make it sound like an accusation, but it's out of her mouth before she can stop it.

"I told you I was in Melbourne. Shit, Georgie. Do you ever listen to me?" He's not happy. "Next time I come back to you looking like this, you're moving in with Lucia and Abe."

It's not until the dogs come running toward them that she notices that Callum is with him.

"Hi, Georgie."

"Hi."

And suddenly Grace is there, looking from Georgie to Sam and then the kid.

"Hello, Sam," her mother says quietly.

"Grace." He leans forward to hug her. It's all a bit awkward. There was Sam who was like a son-in-law for seven years, Sam the adulterer who they didn't see for years, Sam the savior who was around for Joe's death, and now Sam the impregnator of their daughter, standing on her front porch with his son by his side.

Grace looks down at the kid.

"You better come inside," she says. "Bill wants the door shut to keep the dogs in."

Sam looks awkward. Georgie, defeated. Once Callum crosses the threshold, she doesn't know what will happen. It changes the rules completely, although she isn't quite sure what the rules are. The kid seems entranced. Usually there's intrigue about Georgie's front door. A whole lot of quiet and the mystery of what's beyond there. But there are dogs barking and people bellowing, and Tom's being a smart-arse and accompanying it all to music, strumming his guitar in a fast Spanish piece. He comes up behind her in the corridor, serenading over his grandmother's shoulder, and then he looks down at Callum as well.

"Tom and Grace, this is Callum," Sam says with a sigh.

The kid giggles at Tom's antics, and the dogs come bounding. Georgie has no choice but to usher them in and shut the door.

chapter nineteen

That day, while planning a getaway in his head from the Mackee/Finch circus, he receives an e-mail from taramarie. Not exactly an e-mail, but a link to the Lenina Crowne Fan Club website.

Like he does most times when he thinks of Tara Finke lately, he smiles. And types. And decides he has nothing to lose.

To: taramarie@yahoo.com
From: anabelsbrother@hotmail.com
Date: 15 August 2007

Dear Finke,

Flattered that you remembered my obsession with Lenina Crowne. So I must have told you that Huxley's *Brave New World* was the porn of my Year Twelve year. Took me ages to work it out that it wasn't her physical description or sexual liberation or curiosity that turned me on, but the voice of the vixen who read the part of Lenina in 12A English every lesson for four weeks.

Tom

To: anabelsbrother@hotmail.com
From: taramarie@yahoo.com
Date: 15 August 2007

Dear Thomas,
The only thing Lenina and I have in common is that we've both defied cultural conventions by dating one guy exclusively for several months. And we've both had misguided attractions to misfits in the past.
Tara Finke

Life just got one trillion times more bearable.

There's nothing like the Mackee clan all under the same roof to help convince Tom to return to work the next night. He'd rather face Stani and Ned the Cook than deal with a harassed Georgie, or a rundown on how the drought is affecting rural areas and a whole lot of Sydney-bashing. Worse still was the conversation Nanni Grace was having in whispers after lunch about how some tablets Bill had taken for depression had affected him having sex. Even Tom's father looked horrified and left the kitchen while Georgie was screwing up her face and looking at Tom, as if she had never heard anything so disgusting. After walking in on Sam and Georgie having sex, Tom was becoming a bit numb to the pain of it all.

The Union is pretty busy and he pushes past some of the regulars who are drinking and smoking on the pavement. "No glasses on the street," he tells them, before walking in. In the kitchen, Ned looks a bit harassed and the plates are stacked up, leaving him with little room.

"Move," Tom says, pushing him away from the sink.

Ned feigns a frightened sound, which Tom ignores. He doesn't know how to deliver an apology. It'll sound contrived now.

Francesca walks in with some dirty plates.

"Are you going to forgive him?" she asks Ned.

Ned stays silent.

"If I told you he can burp the whole of the national anthem, would you be impressed?" she says, dumping the plates next to Tom's pile.

"Impressed only because a burp would replace the word 'girt.' "

She walks out and Tom begins filling up the sink with clean water. Some of it flicks Ned, who feigns the frightened sound again, and Tom stares at him, unamused.

Francesca pokes her head back in. "What if he can recite to you the whole of 'The Love Song of J. Alfred Prufrock'?" she says.

Ned looks at him, half impressed.

"Don't look at me like that," Tom says. "You're not my type."

"The whole thing? Not just the first stanza? Not just the last lines about the mermaids singing? Not just the poxy rhyming line about Michelangelo?"

Tom ignores him.

"I'll make you a bet," Ned says, wiping his hands on his apron and going to his backpack to retrieve his *Norton Anthology*.

"You carry your *Norton* around, you dickwit?" Tom asks.

"I'm an English lit student. I can't believe you even know what one is."

"It's on page 1340," Tom tells him.

Ned looks at him suspiciously and flicks to the page, looking even more suspicious when he proves him right.

Tom begins: " 'Let us go then, you and I . . .' "

• • •

Stani walks in later, glaring at them both.

"*Bloody bastards*. One minute punching each other, next minute reading poetry. What's wrong with everyone this week?"

Tom can tell that Ned is pissed off that he's lost the bet.

"What the hell made you learn that off by heart?" Ned asks. "Didn't you drop out of construction or something?"

Tom sponges up the last of the grime around the sink. "His name's Tom. T. S. Eliot. The only Tom I kind of like. I have a cursed name."

"Try Ned. How many Neds are there in history? Two. Ned Kelly. Neddy Smith. Both crims."

"You forgot Ned Flanders," Tom says.

He spends some of the night serving out front, where a cute girl with an uncomplicated walk flirts with him. She's not a regular, so she's the first person for a long time who doesn't have that hint of sorrow in her eye when he speaks to her. He feels normal for a change, flirting all the way back and enjoying it.

At closing time, when the girls are rehearsing in the back room, he takes the lyrics he's scribbled on a piece of paper from his pocket and hands them to Francesca.

"You play it," she says, holding out her guitar.

He shakes his head. "No, you said you wanted words. You didn't say anything about playing."

"Oh, come on, Tom. At least give us an idea of the melody in your head," Justine says, peering over Francesca's shoulder as she holds out the instrument. He loses the stare-off and grabs it from her. He hasn't played a tune for real in front of anyone but Georgie since he dived off the table.

"Play me something that makes me feel;
This soul inside me is made of steel.
Brain is breathing, but heart's not beating
And, babe, I need you to make things real.

Walk inside me without silence,
Kill the past and change the tense.
Empty gnawing and the ache is soaring;
Take me places that make more sense."

He looks up. Justine and Francesca are nodding. Ned, however, looks stunned.

"I never took you for a rhyming guy."

"It's a song lyric, Ned. Rhyme is important," Francesca explains.

"It's a shame that someone who reads 'Prufrock' writes such shit."

"Fine," Tom says, pissed off, tearing up the song.

"No!" both Francesca and Justine yell, grabbing it from him.

"I like rhyme," Francesca argues. "But I think the line should be *Brain is beating but heart's not breathing.*"

Ned makes a rude sound.

"And what about the music?" Justine says. "It has a great melody."

Ned sighs. "You're right. Very uplifting. Might just go hang myself now."

"Yeah, you just do that, little emo boy," Tom snaps.

"Oh, that was pathetic," Justine says. "As if he looks tortured enough to be emo."

Francesca looks at Tom and tries to keep the torn paper intact. "I loved it. And I know, for you, that counts for nothing, Thomas. But there it is. I *loved* it."

"*Loved?*" he says, imitating her. It was too easy to slip back into high-school idiotic mode.

"And your voice . . . it was a real turn-on. Really sexy," Justine says.

"Hush. I'm blushing."

Ned is still looking pissed off, and Tom figures that it's truly too late for an apology.

"Regardless of how he comes across, Ned, he's very sensitive," Francesca explains. "Stands up for old people on the bus and cries in movies."

"Bullshit," Tom mutters, picking up his backpack, wanting to get as far away from everyone as possible.

"Oh, you do too, you liar," Justine argues.

"You cried in *The Lord of the Rings* when Sam Gamgee sobbed for Mr. Frodo," Francesca says, doing an impersonation. "*Mr. Frodo!*" Tom goes to the greatest of pains not to laugh. "*Mr. Frodo,*" she continues to cry out.

Even Ned's laughing. No one's a bigger show-off than Francesca when she has an audience.

"Ask the girls," Justine says and Francesca is already taking out her phone to text Tara and Siobhan. "*When did Tom cry in a movie?*" she says as she texts.

"Okay, back to business," Justine says. "Put your bag down, Thomas. We've got a song for Will, Frankie's mum, and Jimmy, as well as this one you wrote for Tara. So we just need another two."

Alarm bells ring in his head. "What are you talking about?" He tries to get the torn paper back from Francesca.

"Tara's cover will probably be a Josh Pyke, and the original will be your untitled rhyme song."

"No!" And then for further emphasis. *"No."* This time he is more forceful in trying to grab the words back. "That's not for Tara."

"Well, who's this one going to be for? Frankie's mum and dad? Siobhan?"

"Why not Siobhan? Or your cousin in Poland?"

"I think my cousin's will be a bit of a rock number," Justine says. "They really like tacky eighties stuff there. Very Eurovision." Francesca starts singing "The Final Countdown," and Justine dances along to it. Ned's just shaking his head.

"And you know Siobhan. If she can't dance to it, it doesn't rate for her," Francesca reminds him.

"It's a perfect song for your mother, Frankie," he tries, but he knows he's defeated. "She'll like the sensitivity in the melody."

Francesca makes a snorting sound. "Is it true my father offered you an apprenticeship if you don't go back to uni?" she asks him.

He nods, not knowing where she's going with this, but she'll go some long-winded way, by the look of things.

"Some advice, then. He'll listen to whatever I send my mum and you'll be on the credits. You don't want touchy-feely songs on the résumé in case you decide to take him up on it. I'm not saying you will, but it could happen. So let me tell you something about my father, Thomas. Do you know where he was on the twenty-seventh of February, 1972? At the Led Zeppelin concert. He's told us a million times. We let him think he's got an edge."

Her phone buzzes with a message and she reads it, grinning with satisfaction.

"From Siobhan. *LOTR*." Francesca looks around. "Do I need to tell anyone what film she's referring to?" She clears her throat and reads from the screen. *"He cried when Aragorn kneels at all their feet."*

"Oh, yeah, I forgot the sobs during that part," Justine said.

The phone beeps again and Tom tries to grab it from Francesca, but she holds it above her head and Justine comes to her rescue.

"From Tara."

Justine peers at the screen, as if trying to make sense of it. *"He cried when those two muppets climbed that mountain in New Zealand."*

Ned looks confused and Tom bursts out laughing. That's what it was like with the girls. They have the most inane conversations, to the point of being absurd, but they always make him laugh despite the fact that he doesn't want to.

"Muppets?" Ned asks.

"Hobbits," Tom explains.

"New Zealand?"

"Mount Doom."

"Tom made her watch all three movies one afternoon," Justine says. "I wonder if Tara's ever forgiven you."

The phone beeps again and she reads, *"I want those ten hours of my life back."*

And this time they're all laughing and Stani walks past them, clicking his tongue with disbelief.

"I'm off," Ned says, with a wave, "to hang out with my *little emo friends.*"

After a moment, Tom puts down the guitar and follows him. Outside, the regulars are still hovering as if they miraculously believe Stani's going to reopen for them. "Read the sign," he says, pointing to the one that tells them to respect the neighbors' need for silence. The girl who flirted with him all night hovers by the doorway and they exchange a look. "Wait for me," he finds himself saying.

Ned's already at the corner and he calls out to him. "Ned! Oi, Ned."

"Yeah?"

Tom catches up to him. "Look, I'm sorry."

Ned doesn't say anything.

"About . . . you know . . . punching you."

"And not for the shit lyrics?"

Tom knows he's trying to rile him, but doesn't allow himself to be riled.

"They were very . . . I don't know . . . James Blunt-ish. Was that the sound you were going for?" Ned asks, before waving him off and walking away.

Behind Tom, the girl is waiting. Her name's Rachel and she's from up the coast. She takes him back to where she's staying. The sex is good, but even if it wasn't, he enjoys the feel of skin against skin, of hands to clench, of the uninhibited dance of it all. And despite it being so casual and nothing serious, "because I've got a boyfriend anyway," she lets him stay the night. He tries not to compare the awkwardness of Tara Finke with her. He had tried not to with his flatmate Sarah, or any of the girls he's slept with since that night with Tara. But lying here next to this girl, he can't get it out of his head. The lack of awkwardness that Tara and her peacekeeper will enjoy after months of *exclusivity*.

He doesn't realize until now that it's not just regret he feels about how he walked away from Tara after Joe's death. It's more than regret. If he had the guts, he'd begin with how he made her feel that night in her parents' house. Except he knows that the moment he mentions it, he won't hear from her again, and for the time being, he's like a starving man waiting for the e-mail crumbs she throws his way.

"Out of bed."

He stares up at Bill with horror. First, because it's five thirty in the morning. Second, because Bill is wearing the most hideous jogging shorts. So brief. The type where you can almost see his balls.

Next minute they're out in the street behind his father, who's doing tae kwon do movements in the next-door neighbor's driveway. At least when his father was a man on the verge of a breakdown, he was way cooler.

"You can't jog wearing thongs, you drip," Bill says.

"Let's call them flip-flops, Bill," he says, yawning. "A thong is a G-string. Do you know what a G-string is, Bill?"

Dominic is running ahead of them, belting through the streets in front of Bill, with Tom flip-flopping after them until he gives up on the shoes and takes them off, trying to keep up. The only thing that inspires Tom to pick up speed and almost break the one-hundred-meter sprint record is when he sees his father heading toward Camperdown. There's no way he wants to meet his ex-flatmates coming home from a gig with Bill in those shorts and his father doing Jackie Chan impersonations. Once Tom's redirected them, his father sprints past him and Tom doesn't even try to keep up.

They reach their old place on Temple Street, where Dominic is talking to Mrs. Liu. Tom hears him promise that he'll come around and mow the lawn before he grabs her wheelie bins and tucks them away at the side of her house. Mrs. Liu looks like all her Christmases have come at once. By the time his father is sprinting off again, Tom's lungs are killing him. He hopes they come across a few more lonely people in the neighborhood who'll stop Dominic

Mackee for a bit of a chat in order to save his son from cardiac arrest. Worse still, Bill wants to talk.

"You working?"

"Yeah . . . kinda . . . yeah."

He's going to give up smoking soon. Maybe get one of those patches.

"What are you doing during the day?"

He wonders if he's getting the first signs of emphysema. "Just data crap."

"What type?"

"Data. I don't give it an identity."

Bill stops for a moment to check a stitch.

"When are you going back to uni?"

"I might not."

Tom presses a hand against his hip to make the pain go away wondering if this is the let's-go-for-a-jog-so-I-can-lecture-you-about-your-future trick.

Bill looks at him for a long while.

"If you've got time up your sleeve at Christmas, your auntie Margie Finch needs some help out at Walgett."

The unspoken rule has always been that they do anything for his great-aunt. It was her money that kept Georgie and his father and Tom and Anabel in private schools. She always said it was what her brother, Tom Finch, would have wanted the Finch family money spent on. She rarely asked for anything in return. But the building of the recreation center, run by her order of nuns, has been an issue for years.

"I thought maybe it would be built by now. It's been two years," he mumbles.

"You should know better than that. No one does anything for nothing these days."

Bill sighs. "She's got funding for the bricks and material. She just needs the workers."

He takes off again.

They stop for a rest at one of the cafés and Tom is stuck doing all the talking.

He's never quite understood his father's relationship with Bill. Never *Dad* or *my father*. Always Bill. Bill was old school. As kids, his father and Georgie had convinced each other that Tom Finch would have been the kindest father in the world compared to Bill the tyrant.

He was just as tough on Joe. On one of the nights when Tom lay talking to Georgie, she tried to explain it. "I think Bill had a harsh upbringing. He doesn't talk much about his father and spent a lot of time at Tom Finch's house, according to Great-Auntie Margie Finch. Auntie Margie always said that Bill wanted to be a Finch. We thought he did the next best thing and coveted his family."

Their coffee arrives and they drink it in silence. Dominic has two short blacks before Tom finishes his. Tom understands addiction, but even when he was getting high all that time, it hadn't seemed to attack his system like his father's. And then he's walking home behind both men and he can't help notice how they walk alike for two people with no blood ties. Although there's silence between them, they seem to want to stay side by side. Once in a while Bill makes a comment about a tree. He's a tree freak, Bill is. "Wait till these jacarandas flower," he says in wonder. "Any day now."

Inside, Tom can hear Nanni Grace and Georgie chatting in the kitchen.

"Want to show you something," his father says. Tom doesn't

know whether he's talking to Bill or him, but he follows them into the study.

There are maps all over the place. All over the floor, all over the study table. Vietnam. He'd know the shape of the country in his sleep. He could pin the tail on the donkey of the exact spot his father claimed Tom Finch was left. Behind enemy lines. How could such important words to his family sound so clichéd? But that's what happened to Lance Corporal Tom Finch. His mates knew he was dead. One even crawled through the entangled mass of roots, over and over again, to try to free his body. By that time it was riddled with holes and to remove him would have been suicidal because the attack was coming from all sides. Those poor bastards never got over leaving Tom Finch behind. Tom had met them. They'd told him to his face when he was twelve years old that you never leave your mates behind.

"They've got a portable X-ray machine out there, a navigator, field engineer, forensics. There's seven of them and they swear they've got the location," Dominic says.

Tom is still stunned by the amount of detail around the room.

"They know the body's there," his father is telling them. "All they need to find is contextual evidence. A dog tag. A map."

"Won't it be damaged?" Tom asks.

"Tiny Parker's was found pristine and once they got Peter Gilson's under the right equipment, they confirmed it was his," his father says, referring to the two who had been returned to their families in July.

Both Tom and his father are looking at Bill.

"If they've got it all wrong and we think Tom's coming home . . . for burial . . . and he doesn't . . ." Bill's shaking his head and Tom can see he can't speak. "Don't let me have to put Grace through this all over again, Dom. Not after the way they've fucked things up with Joe."

Tom's father sighs. "Jim Bourke and his guys have done the work for them. This is the real deal. I *know* it. I'd bet my life on it."

Bill is shaking his head, eyes closed. Tom recognizes that look. He's seen it on his own father's face. Too many people to worry about.

"I'm going to go over there when the time comes," Dominic says quietly. "I'm going to bring my father's body home."

Tom feels sick. Bringing a body home. How many families get to hear those words twice in their lifetime?

"You don't even have a passport," Tom mutters.

"I do now," his father says, but it's Bill he looks at. "You're going to have to start preparing Mum. Soon. They've returned Parker and Gilson to their families. I think it could be us any day."

No one says anything for a moment.

"Georgie knows?" Bills asks quietly.

Dominic nods. "But Sam's not happy. Doesn't want this happening now. Doesn't think Georgie's ready for what it all means."

"Are any of us?"

"You are," Dominic says emphatically. "You've been ready for this all our lives. Shit, Bill. Let's bury him. He deserves it. We all fucking do."

It's way too tense. Someone's either going to get into a fight or cry. Neither option is preferable. Tom points questioningly to another sticker.

"If the body was left there, why would they be digging here?" he asks, pointing to another spot.

"Because he would have been . . . disposed of properly because

173

of hygiene. They would have buried him because of their religious beliefs," his father explains.

Bill sighs, standing up, and he looks at Tom. "How much do you know about this?"

Tom rubs his eyes tiredly. "Joe used to write to me about it."

It was Joe's obsession, as much as theirs. Tom didn't know what was worse. Growing up children of a soldier who doesn't come back from war, or growing up the only sibling who didn't belong to Tom Finch. His uncle had always been fascinated with the idea of Georgie and Dominic's father. When he taught Tom guitar as a kid, he told him that Tom Finch had been obsessed with Bob Dylan. "He wrote poetry, you know, Tom Finch did," Joe had told him. "And your pop Bill reckons that on the train they heard 'Like a Rolling Stone' on the trannie when they were traveling down to Sydney from the Burdekin. Before they met Mum. It always reminds Pop Bill of hope, regardless of the lyrics."

Tom loved those stories because Joe seemed to have all the information. Nothing could hold Joe back when he was intrigued, and the recovery of Tom Finch's body became his fixation. He taught history. He worked with evidence, and as far as he was concerned, there was no reason why they couldn't bring Tom Finch home.

Bill was looking dazed.

"Joe was always talking about him and Dominic going to Hanoi together," Tom says.

"*Dominic,* is it?" Bill asks, unimpressed. "We're on first-name terms with your father now, are we?"

"Yeah, we are, Bill. Do you have a problem with that?"

And there's the look. The first one Tom has received from his father in years that reminds him of normalcy. The one that tells him that if he uses that tone with Bill ever again, he'll be seeing stars.

"Don't upset Georgie," Bill mutters to Dominic before walking out. "I'll talk to Grace when we get home."

There's something inside of Tom that makes him want to stay in this room. Look at everything his father's collected. Talk to him about how he feels about Tom Finch. About what it's like having to say the words *disposed of* when talking about the body of the father you never knew. And to talk about Bill, to point out, "Can't you tell that the poor bastard loves you all like crazy?" But he can see that Dominic is cut.

"Go make sure he's okay," his father says gruffly.

To:	taramarie@yahoo.com
From:	anabelsbrother@hotmail.com
Date:	17 August 2007

Dear Finke,

I've been thinking of your comment about what you and Lenina Crowne have in common, and have to argue that exclusivity in a relationship is slightly overrated and tends to cause complacency in one partner and lack of ambition in the other. Take Francesca for example, who's sitting on a useless degree and sewing with her granny while Trombal enjoys a single guy's life away from her, probably getting pissed and having sex with whoever he wants over there. I'm not saying I don't understand exclusivity. But at our age, some may say it's a trap. It'll stop you from doing what you want to do in life, because one person is always going to miss out or feel held back. Just a warning in case you're getting in too deep, exclusively dating one person.

Tom

To: anabelsbrother@hotmail.com
From: taramarie@yahoo.com
Date: 17 August 2007

Dear Tom,

This may be difficult for you to understand. Your longest relationship lasted four weeks and only because for three weeks of it, her low IQ prevented her from understanding that "I don't want to go out with you anymore" actually means "It's over." I'm presuming that the length of that relationship was superseded by the one with your flatmate Sarah What's-Her-Face for no other reason than that you didn't actually have to pick up a phone or make an effort to walk to her place. Was it a holler from your room or hers?

Only in your tiny mind, Tom, does Frankie + Will = complacency. I wouldn't exactly call that relationship an easy one to manage, or remotely one-sided, and don't you dare presume you'd know what Will gets up to over there. He might be an arrogant and introverted cold fish at times, but ask him the question in front of his macho engineering buddies, "Where do you see yourself in ten years time?" and he doesn't miss a beat. "Wherever Frankie is." The same useless Frankie who's still working on her music, and running Stani's pub at night, and whose "sewing with her granny" job actually pays a shitload of money these days, and who'll finish a history degree with honors when she's up to going back next year. If that's complacency, then I can't imagine what category I fit in.

Don't let me have to analyze you, Tom. It will be too predictable and you'll come across as a textbook case. I know you can't handle being described as mediocre.

T

chapter twenty

Her parents don't go home, and it's the uncertainty of what they bring to the equation by being in her home that worries Georgie. It means Sam's around more often during the day, as if the more people in the house, the less he thinks she'll notice him there. Plus he has his son during the week these days, not just weekends. It's not that she minds, which surprises Georgie, but that he never stays at night and she's irritated because she misses his body beside her and Georgie doesn't want to miss Sam.

Today Georgie and Grace are baking while Sam's kid plays with the strings of the guitar Tom has left lying around. Sam's outside making a phone call, work-related by the looks of things from the window. Georgie hands Sam's kid a spoon from the bowl to lick, and he hovers between them like the two spaniels waiting for the next bout of generosity. She stares down at him. Her blue-eyed boy, she'd call Sam when they were a couple. At least she doesn't have to look at some other woman's face every time she looks down at this kid. But it makes her wonder if she's looking at what her own child will look like six years down the track. Will he have Georgie's dark hair and gray eyes, or will he be all Sam? Will he have a shy smile like this little boy?

Tom comes in and puts his arms around Grace from behind.

"Can you tell Bill to get rid of the shorts?" Georgie hears him beg against her ear. "It's been a week of jogging with him. It's abuse by humiliation."

"Can anyone tell Bill to do anything?" Grace asks, kissing her grandson quickly on the cheek. "You smell of cigarettes."

"How come he gets to do that?" Tom says, looking down at the kid who's licking the spoon with abandon. Tom wrestles Callum for it, and the boy giggles, because his crush on Georgie has moved to Tom.

"Show Tom how you can play the guitar," Georgie says.

Tom puts the kid on his lap and grabs the guitar, his arms around him, holding Callum's fingers in place. It reminds her of how Joe taught Tom to play in the kitchen at Northumberland Street. Callum strums a tune and they all clap. The kid's beaming and then Tom puts him down and picks up the guitar, asking for requests. Grace says Elvis.

He plays "Viva Las Vegas" with exaggeration and Sam's kid is laughing. Next minute, Georgie's holding Callum's hands and they're swinging around the kitchen.

"You'll hurt yourself," Grace laughs, because all of a sudden Georgie is fragile in her mother's eyes. If she had known it would have taken a pregnancy to get her mother to notice her she would have got knocked up years ago.

Later, Sam comes inside while Callum is hovering by Georgie's side.

"Sit," Sam orders.

Callum sits. So do the dogs.

Sam begins to set the table, which is only built for six and not seven, and then Dominic comes in and the men begin talking

178

collective bargaining and union stuff. Georgie puts the finishing touches on the cake and Sam's kid is there again, knowing there's one more spoon to lick.

"Callum, sit," Sam says. "You're getting in Georgie's way."

No, not getting in Georgie's way at all, Sam. You are, she wants to say.

They sit crowded around the table and Dom ends up standing by the window to eat.

"We'll have to get a bigger one," Georgie says.

Tom mumbles something about a table.

"What?"

He looks up, his face stiffening under everyone's questioning looks.

"There's the one Dominic made on Temple Street."

No one speaks. Dominic had built that table for Grace, so her children and daughter-in-law and grandchildren and Joe's Ana Vanquez could fit around it perfectly when they all came down to Albury for holidays two years before.

"Well, where the fuck is it?" Bill asks, and Georgie avoids the look Sam's sending her. She knows he doesn't want anyone swearing in front of his kid.

"In storage," Tom says, because it was Tom and his mother and Georgie who had packed up the house that time when Dominic left.

"Then we'll have to get it out someday," Grace says quietly. "So we can all fit."

Georgie takes the next day off to drive Grace and Bill to their check-ups because, according to Grace, "Dominic has things to do." So

Georgie takes them from the skin clinic to the heart specialist to the breast clinic to the podiatrist. In the car she listens to discussions about Dominic looking fuller in the face and the disgraceful Sydney traffic. Grace warns her she's going so fast that she's almost kissing the car in front of her, and Bill tells her about the house for sale on their street in Albury. Bill has always believed that they'll all miraculously decide to move down south and live in the same street happily ever after. Grace reminds Bill that Sam has a son and he would never be interested in moving down south, and Georgie reminds Grace that Sam is not in her life. Bill brings up Roger, the forty-five-year-old divorced optometrist, about five times. Bill hates Sam because when Bill dared to criticize the Labor Party, Sam called the Nationals a bunch of fuckwit whingers and then asked Bill politely not to swear in front of Callum. Bill had called the Greenies a swarm of arseholes, then Tom had asked what arseholes and bees had in common. It's the type of communal stream-of-intellectual-Finch-Mackee-consciousness that used to cause her and Joe to laugh hysterically.

She'd been here before with Joe a couple of years ago. He had reminded Bill that Roger, the optometrist, was a cross-dresser and that Georgie hated sharing anything, let alone her lipstick and shoes, so it was bound to end in a divorce where they'd be fighting over the boob-tube dress she wore to her Year Ten formal and the Jimmy Choo shoes she bought on eBay. That time both siblings had killed themselves laughing so much that Georgie was snorting. Grace had told them both to grow up. She said it to Joe affectionately, and to Georgie disapprovingly, before saying, "How old are you, Georgie?"

By the time Georgie's driving up Crystal Street, her heart is pumping blood at a rate that frightens her and she wants to be home, in her bed in her room, door locked. But one street away from sanctuary, a police booze bus stands in the way—random breath testing.

"Could you count to ten, ma'am?" the cop, who looks approximately fifteen years old, asks. She wants to give him a lecture on how insulting it is to call someone *ma'am*. It makes her feel one hundred years old.

"Have you had a drink today, ma'am?" he continues to ask.

"No, but I'm planning on going home and getting shit-faced. Is that all right with you, Officer?"

"Oh, Georgie," her mother mutters.

When they walk into the kitchen, Dominic looks up from what he's reading. Georgie wants to rant and she does. He sits and listens, and then says quietly, "I could have taken them. You don't have to be a martyr, you know, and do it all yourself."

"It's good to see that the bastard streak still lives within you, Dom," she snaps, shoving past him and her mother along the way. "You said you asked him first," she accuses Grace, who follows her up the stairs, warning her about blood pressure and babies.

"Dominic's not an invalid, Mum."

Grace makes the sound that Georgie knows all too well. She used to call it "the Grace-full sigh of disappointment" but Dominic and Joe had no idea what Georgie was talking about because somehow Grace dared not express her disappointment in front of her sons. The sigh of disappointment was only dished out to Georgie and Bill.

But worse still is the look she's getting now. The Grace-full look of martyrdom.

181

"Tomorrow we'll take a taxi," her mother says. "We don't want to be disturbing anyone."

"But it's okay to disturb me?"

Next look, the Grace-full stare of hurt. The killer of all looks.

Georgie takes a deep breath. "All I'm saying, Mum, is that you're better off without me racing out of work and *being a martyr,*" she yells, so that Dominic can hear her. "Dominic's home—"

"Dominic has enough to worry about," Grace says.

"Don't do that!" Georgie says. "You always do. 'Poor Dominic has Tommy to care for,' and then, 'Oh, that poor Dominic, looking after Tommy and Anabel and Jacinta Louise and trying to juggle everything,' or 'Joe can't be disturbed because Joe is studying,' or 'Leave him; Joe's trying to have a social life.' "

"You're very emotional because of the baby, Georgie."

"No, I'm not!" she shouts with frustration. "All of a sudden, every other thing pales in comparison. I would have preferred you come to visit me when there was no baby. When I was dealing with what Sam did seven years ago, or having to cope with the decision to go to London to bring back Joe's body, or worse still, coming home without it."

Mention of Joe was okay in her family. Mention of what happened to him was a no-no, but Georgie can't stop herself.

"And do you know what else I remember? When Joe died, Mum, all you could say was, 'We have to go home to Albury. Bill's suffering without his boy and he needs to go home.' *Two days* you stayed with me and then you all went home. *All of you.* And left me here, on my own, to fix up everything, because everyone's lives were bigger and their suffering was greater, because they had their own families to take care of and their own lives to put back together.

But it was like I was worth nothing then, and now, all of a sudden because of this baby, everyone thinks Georgie needs help."

"I suffered for you when Sam—"

"No, you didn't. *'You shouldn't have let him go, Georgie. He wouldn't have strayed if you didn't let him go.'* That's what you said to me and those words killed me more than anything."

"Oh, you're a cruel girl, Georgie, to remember that over everything else."

chapter twenty-one

In the kitchen, they can hear everything. Tom is trying to eat, but it's cardboard in his mouth and his father is fixed on the newspaper in front of him while Bill is just staring. At nothing.

"I've got to go to my meeting," Dominic mumbles, standing up.

"I'll go with you." This from Bill.

Somehow it's as if Tom is left with only two options in the world. Stay in the house with Georgie and Nanni Grace tearing each other's hearts out or go to an AA meeting with his father and Bill. The alcoholics win. There's something about a bunch of people clapping just for saying your name and admitting sobriety that works for him.

Tom's heard it too often in the movies to be touched by it. Now it just seems like a cliché. No one can say it with authenticity without it seeming like a joke.

"Hi, my name's Des and I'm an alcoholic."

Big clap. Clap. Clap.

How great would it be if it applied to other things in his life?

"Hi, my name is Tom and I dropped out of uni and spent the last year smoking weed and getting high."

Clap, clap, clap.

"Hi, my name is Tom and I had a one-and-a-half-night stand with one of my best friends and I don't have the guts to ask her how she felt about it."

Clap, clap, clap.

"Hi, my name is Tom and I treated my friends who hung around to pick up the pieces like they were shit."

Clap, clap, clap.

"Hi, my name's Dominic . . ."

Tom's eyes swing up to the front of the hall, where his father is standing. For the first time in a year, he gets to look at him properly. So far he's been passing him by in the corridor back in Georgie's house or sitting around the kitchen table, but he hasn't dared to look his way, in case there is prolonged eye contact.

Tom finds out things he hasn't had the guts to ask. His father hasn't touched a drink for 150 days. Tom makes calculations, and it means Dominic's been sober since March. Nothing momentous about March. No birthdays. No anniversaries. Nothing. He finds out that Dominic took his last drink in Wodonga on the New South Wales–Victoria border, which means that his father was staying with Nanni Grace and Bill at the time. He wonders if it was Bill who bullied his father out of bed every morning to join him on his daily jog.

"I had been on a blinder for a couple of days and I woke up in a park," his father continues. Tom's heard his father make speeches hundreds of times. At home. In a meeting hall of irate builders. At a union rally. But his voice is different this time. Broken. "I remember the humidity and that I stunk and that I still had my wallet on me. This woman was there. A jogger . . . with a look on her face that makes me . . . I don't know . . . Just thinking of it . . . People's compassion has always floored me. Despite all the shit in the world, people's compassion never fails to surprise me. Anyway, she helped me up and she asked for permission to look into my wallet so she could help work out who I was and what to do, and while she was flicking through it, she came across a photo. She asked me who they were. And I looked at the photograph and I pointed to my wife and said, 'That's Jacinta Louise. She's the love of my life,'" he says, and there are tears in his eyes. "Then I pointed to my baby girl and I said, 'That's Anabel. She's in Year Eight and plays a mean trumpet.'"

He stops, and finds Tom in the audience, and their eyes lock. "And then I pointed to my son." There's so much emotion in that one look. It tells Tom that his father stopped drinking because he loved *him* and that he was sorry and maybe for now he has to allow that to be enough. Tom could move on with that knowledge. That Dominic Finch Mackee gave up drinking for his son, Tom.

"And I couldn't remember his name," his father said, his voice hoarse. "I couldn't remember my boy's name. And that was the first day . . ."

Tom doesn't hear the rest. He feels as if someone's just punched him in the gut. He thinks he hears a sound from his grandfather. Thinks he even feels Bill's hand on his shoulder. He wants to be back in the house where Georgie and Nanni Grace are fighting about the fact that once upon a time Dominic couldn't look after his parents and his sister because he was too busy looking after his son.

He doesn't remember much after that except there's a bit of a collection to cover basic costs and then they serve tea, coffee, and biscuits. His father speaks to almost everyone in the hall. They gravitate to him the way people always have. And they all want to meet

Tom. To tell him that even though they've only known Dominic a couple of weeks, they all love him. Does his father do it on purpose? Cause people to have a dependency on him so that when he's gone, it's hard to cope?

The three of them walk home in silence. It's not Tom's night to work, but he splits from them at the corner without a word and goes into the pub. He knows, with a satisfaction born of bitterness, that his father won't follow him into the Union.

"Tom!" Bill calls out. "Mate, let's go home."

Tom holds up a hand and waves him off.

Inside, it's a quiet Monday night crowd.

He walks into the kitchen and smells something different and peers into the saucepan.

"Is this pasta sauce?"

"Frankie's cooking for her brother," Ned informs him. "Her grandmother's out for the night and she's babysitting."

"Only Frankie would take over the pub for her family," he mutters.

"You're not on tonight, you know," Ned says. He doesn't seem so happy either, and he's taking it out on the T-bone and sausages.

"I've just come in to pick up my pay. Do you have a problem with that?" Tom snaps.

Ned stops and stares at him. He knows there's no pay to pick up. They all must know that Tom doesn't get paid.

"You have the look that says you want to hit someone," Ned says. "Should I be cowering?"

"You have the same look."

"People can smell the pasta sauce," Ned complains. "So every

187

time I go out there to hand over the food, I get asked if we're serving vegetarian. Is your gripe bigger than that?"

"Yeah. My father's a cunt."

"I can't help liking mine, nutcase that he is," Ned says. "Do you want an espresso? She brought the percolator as well."

"It's a *caffettiera*," Tom corrects him, looking over to where it sits on the stove.

"Yeah, whatever."

Ned has absolutely no idea what to do with it and pours water and coffee into the top.

"Your father . . . doesn't have issues about your . . . lifestyle?" Tom asks.

Tom gets eye contact beyond Ned's fringe. "I don't have a lifestyle."

"Your sex life?"

"I don't really have a sex life. I'm not into casual sex or one-and-a-half-night stands like you."

"I'm not into one-and-a-half-night stands either," Tom says bluntly, not appreciating the label.

"What about the spitfire from Dili?" There's a smugness in the way Ned says those words.

"What *about* Tara?"

"When she was here at Easter, we spent a lot of time talking. I'd always look forward to her coming to that door. It was the way she'd stand there with her hands on her hips and that face that you'd actually like to iron out."

Tom's taking deep breaths.

"Can I give you some advice, Ned?" he says, grabbing the *caffettiera* out of his hands and tipping out the coffee and water.

"There are a lot of guys out there waiting to find Mr. Self-Righteous-Know-It-All-Who-Swings-Both-Ways. I'd go hunt them down if I were you."

Ned is watching him carefully.

"You don't fit the mold, you know, Tom. You have a bigger problem with the fact that I could be into girls as well as guys. Why is that?"

"I really don't care."

"Yes, you do." Ned points a knowing finger. "I made them a bet that you still think you've got a chance with her. May I remind you she has a boyfriend?"

Tom chooses not to contribute to the conversation anymore. He makes a show of how to put together the *caffettiera* and slams it on the stove.

"You're a dish-pig who left her feeling like shit," Ned continues. "He keeps peace. Wow, what a dilemma. Wonder who I'd pick?"

"For your information, peacekeepers did bugger-all in the Balkans," Tom argues. It's a bit lame, but it's the best he can do. "And like a pasty-faced army grunt is going to put me off if I want to go for her," he adds with bravado.

"They have Brazilian peacekeepers in Timor."

The air whooshes out of Tom. His whole image of Tara's life in Timor does a ninety-degree swing. He feels sick to his stomach.

"Who's Brazilian?" Frankie asks, walking in with a packet of parmesan cheese. "Are you guys talking about Tara's boyfriend?" She takes the saucepan off the stove and throws the pasta into the colander.

"From Brazil," Ned confirms again with a nod, looking at Tom.

"As in from South America?" Tom can't help asking. "Olive skinned and waxed chest?"

189

"Very beautiful people. The women always come first in the Miss Universe pageants," Francesca says.

"No, I think it's Venezuela," Ned explains.

"So what do they do?" Tom asks. "Salsa and speak Spanish all day in Dili?"

"She's actually in Same and it's not Spanish; it's Portuguese," Frankie corrects.

"She didn't correct me," Tom says half to himself.

"She probably didn't want you to feel stupid for not knowing the Brazilians and the East Timorese speak Portuguese," Ned says, handing Francesca the right spoon for the pasta.

"I reckon a lot of people wouldn't know that." Tom's on the defensive now.

"Ask him." Francesca points to her brother as he walks in holding his drumsticks, and somehow Tom can tell that Ned and Francesca are having fun. At his expense.

"Ask me what?" Luca Spinelli asks. The kid is pathetically good-looking and talks with Anabel on MSN, so Tom wants to hate yet another person in the world. Luca Spinelli punches him in the arm as a means of saying hello.

"Go on. What language do the Brazilians speak?" Francesca asks her brother as she pours the sauce onto the pasta in the plate Ned hands her.

Luca grins up at Tom. Tom knew the kid when he was ten and in primary at their school and had always felt slightly protective of him, because of how hard it had been when Francesca's mum was sick.

"You thought it was Spanish, didn't you, Tom?" The kid is laughing at him.

"I'm writing a song, you know. It's called, 'Oh, if I could be as smart as the Spinelli siblings.' " Tom gets out his own fork and twirls some of the pasta from the plate Francesca's holding. She puts it in front of her brother and then Ned is also there, hovering over them with his own fork.

"How spoiled are you?" Tom mutters.

Francesca is kissing her brother. "He's my *tesoro*," she says. "And I'm going to miss him to death."

"Where's he going?" Ned asks, making a grunting sound of satisfaction when he finally gets to taste the food.

"My mother can't live without her baby, so he's going to join them in Italy for the rest of their trip. In eighteen days, Will is flying home for a five-day break and then they'll fly to Singapore, where Will puts Luca on an airplane bound for Italy."

"Wow, seven hours on a flight with Will beside you," Tom says, feigning wistfulness. "Wish it were me."

"Are you off that day?" Ned asks Francesca. "If not, I can do a swap."

"We don't do airports when he's leaving. Will's banned me."

Tom can't believe what he's hearing. "You can't cry at the airport because he says. What? Is he the boss of your emotions or something? He sounds like a tyrant."

"And in eighteen days I'm going to see my boy," she says, grinning like Luca, "and I will forget his tyranny."

When Stani closes up, the lot of them sit around the back room and it's only because Francesca's brother is there, and Tom used to accompany him on guitar when the kid was learning drums, that he agrees to jam.

It's Luca who's teaching Francesca to play guitar, so he chooses a Dylan song because it's easy but long and it'll give her the practice

191

on guitar she needs. Luca sings because she says she doesn't have the energy to do both just yet. Halfway through the song, Tom pulls Francesca up from the chair she's sitting on, by the scruff of her neck, and she gives him a look of sufferance but keeps on going and it feels like the most natural thing in the world to be playing with them.

Justine is playing, too. How Justine could be so uninhibited on stage and then be unable to speak to a musician she likes baffles Tom. She says the violinist is a genius, but Tom thinks *she* is and for a moment their eyes meet and she grins at him because it's what would happen onstage when they used to perform. It was the high Tom couldn't get any other way, no matter how much he tried. He likes the feel of the harmonica burning against his mouth, the way it seems to have its own emotion, wavering. Stani watches them from the door, smoking a cigarette now that the clientele is gone, and somehow Tom gets a feeling that no one has a place to go to tonight.

When they finish, Francesca groans about the ache in her arm and her brother gives her a massage.

"It's like hanging out with the bloody Partridge Family," Ned mutters, eating from a packet of chips. But he doesn't leave and they rehearse the songs they've written, this time with Luca on drums, and before they know it, it's past two.

Tom notices there're a few missed calls from Bill. And a text from Georgie asking where he is.

He doesn't want to tell her. Not to punish her, but because he wants his father to think he's dead on the street somewhere.

He goes back to the Spinellis' with Ned, and even when Francesca shows them the wedding dress she's working on and her brother goes to bed vowing he's not going to school in the morning Tom stays. Ned makes it as far as the explanation of calico.

"I'm yawning," Ned says, leaving.

When Francesca talks beading, Tom puts up a hand.

"Frankie, not the beading. I don't mind the bridezilla stories, or even the ones where your grandmother's a bitch to clients with bad taste, but not the rest."

"Will loves the beading stories."

Will is such a big fat liar.

She's grinning and he knows it's because she's thinking of Saint Trombal, patron saint of the anal-retentive, coming home soon.

"Is it true about the piercing and the *I love Frankie* tat?" he asks.

She rolls her eyes. "I blame the engineers for the piercing. They are such a bad influence. And I wouldn't exactly call it an *I love Frankie* tat," she adds with a laugh.

He makes himself comfortable, trying to shove the dog away, who's hogging most of the couch.

"So aren't you worried that he's being unfaithful over there? Isn't it an issue for you?"

She looks up at him. "That's a pretty personal question."

"What? I've never asked you a personal question before?"

She doesn't reply.

"What would you do if he did the dirty on you?"

He thinks of Georgie and Sam and the way they haven't really recovered from Sam being with someone else, regardless of the circumstances.

"I'd never take him back," she says without hesitation. "If he was unfaithful, I wouldn't. And I love him as much as I love my parents and brother, and you know how I feel about them. Will knows that.

I've told him. That if he's about to do something that will betray us, then to picture my face because it will be the very last time he ever sees it."

There's a look in her eye that tells Tom she's not joking.

"Then how do you know he's not lying to you when he says he hasn't gotten up to anything?" he asks.

She gives a snort. "Have you seen his face?" she asks incredulously. "Everything's stamped all over it. Every emotion he can't articulate, because he's so introverted is all there. Every time he's lied to me, I've worked it out in a nanosecond."

"So he lies to you? And you're okay with that?" he asks with disbelief. It's like he wants Francesca to conjure up every shit thing about Trombal. He doesn't know what he'd do with Trombal-less Francesca, but he always liked it better when the other guy wasn't around.

"What? You've never told a girl you have a family function on when it's really the football?" she asks. "Will doesn't do romance well. He doesn't believe in Valentine's Day, and if my birthday falls on a night when the Dragons are playing, we celebrate the next day."

"Then what *does* he do well?"

She thinks for a moment, and it's as if she's never had to articulate it. "I told him at the beginning of the year that Tara was homesick. Just in passing. And you know, Will and Tara don't really connect, but there they are, living a two-hour flight away from each other. So when he had a weekend free, he flew to Dili with some of the other guys and she met them there from Same. I swear to God, Tom, she went on and on for weeks about how great it was. And whenever Will's home, he'll go with my brother and my dad to a Sydney FC game and Will *hates* soccer, but the idea of my brother and father and Will hanging out together makes me so happy . . . and he's found me the most unbelievable silk material in those tiny villages in Sumatra, and believe me, he hates shopping in market stalls any-where in the world and the guys he works with give him a lot of shit when he does stuff like that."

She looks at Tom. "And if I get a little chemically imbalanced in the head, like we all know I tend to get sometimes, and I don't want my parents or brother knowing, Will's like, 'We'll deal with it.' He's never said, 'Snap out of it,' and he's never said, 'I don't get it,' and he's never said, 'I'll fix it up.' He just says, 'You're not up to going back to uni to finish your Honors this year? Big deal. There's next year. We'll deal with it.'" She nods. "That's what he does well."

Tom doesn't respond. He's never asked about her depression in the past, just knew it was there like a big black blob over her head. In Year Eleven they thought it was a one-off because her mother had been sick, but he had seen it once or twice again. Francesca knew the signs and he could tell she fought it with everything she had inside of her. He didn't want to think of Trombal fighting it with her. He didn't want to like the other guy in that way.

"I'm going to marry him," Francesca says with such certainty that it makes his head spin.

"Bet your mother's jumping for joy," he says dryly.

"She reckons she didn't go to uni and get herself a master's so her daughter could marry her first boyfriend and sit making wedding dresses with her grandmother in Leichhardt like Italian women did fifty years ago," Francesca says. "But my mother keeps on forgetting that she did everything she wanted to do. Married my father. Went to university. Had a family. No one got in her way. All at our age now. And that's what she taught me. To do what I want to do and stop having people telling me that I can't marry Will because I'm too young and I haven't seen the world or taken advantage of the choices out there. Who says we're not going to see the world? Or that I won't want to sew for the rest of my life, or that I won't want to finish my Honors? Who says choice is better in ten years' time when it comes to guys? Just say there are bigger dickheads out there?"

"But you've only had sex with one guy, I'm presuming. Don't you want to try . . . something different?"

Francesca gives him that look again. "Tom, without going into great detail, Will and I are very, *very* compatible in that department. *Very.*"

He looks at her, trying to get his head around Will Trombal having sex.

"*Very,*" she repeats.

"Enough," he mutters. "I'm sick just thinking of it."

She's grinning.

"He feels the same way about you. When he left that next morning, he sent me a text saying, *If that 'insert-C-word-here' moves in while I'm away, I'll kill myself.*"

"He wrote *insert-C-word-here*?"

"No. He used it. Capitals all the way."

She's looking at him as if he's some insect under a microscope, as if she can truly see inside of him.

"Do you remember the first time we really . . . I don't know . . . connected?" she asks. "You made me dance with you in drama class during one of Ortley's ridiculous 'freeing ourselves' sessions."

He nods.

196

"I asked you later why you got me to dance, and you said it was because . . ."

He nods again. "You always looked sad."

"So did you, Tom. That's why I took you up on it. Because back then, even before your uncle died, you looked as sad as I did. Except you were better at hiding it."

He stands up, needing to get away. Sometimes he feels a pull toward Francesca. She was the reason he came into their group. It was her misery that united them, and somehow it ended up being her personality that kept them together when everyone split. She's the one who writes the letters to keep the world informed. She listens to the news every hour to make sure everyone's safe. So tonight he walks away even though she's moved forward to give him a hug. Because he wants to kiss her, and knows she'll hate him for it and that he'll hate himself. He knows it's for all the wrong reasons and that he'll end up thinking of Tara Finke and her Brazilian peacekeeper and Will Trombal and the way he doesn't do romance but eats the space between him and Francesca anytime he's in the room with her.

chapter twenty-two

Georgie is sitting in the kitchen when Tom comes home. It's late, but she can't sleep because her blood is dancing with anxiety over everything.

"Go to bed," Tom says, doing that thing where he opens the fridge and stares at it for ages as if his favorite food is going to somehow appear miraculously.

"You know he's not going to ask for your forgiveness, don't you? But you know it's what he desperately needs, Tommy."

"Don't," he says coolly. "I don't want to talk about him, Georgie."

Bill's at the kitchen door too and she wonders if anyone's asleep tonight.

"If you say a word," Tom says over the fridge door, addressing Bill, "I'm walking out the door and I'm not coming back."

Despite Tom's tone, he walks by, brushing a kiss on Bill's head. Bill makes himself comfortable in front of her and she realizes, all too late, that it's her he's been listening out for and not Tom.

"She doesn't ask Dominic to drive her to appointments, not because she thinks he's busy or whatever she says . . . She doesn't ask Dominic because she wants you to do it. It makes her feel safe to have *you* there," he says quietly.

She doesn't speak and when she can't handle the silence anymore, she stands up.

"You don't seem happy about the baby, Georgie."

It shocks her to hear those words, coming from Bill. Like no one dared to announce her pregnancy, no one has dared to say those words.

"How can I be happy?" she asks with anguish. "To get this baby, my brother had to die. Do you understand?"

"And to get this family, my best friend had to die," he says gruffly. "So aren't we both a sorry pair?"

The next afternoon, she sits out back with Grace and Tom on the banana chairs. Callum's there as well. It takes her a while to work out that the satchel buckle he has around his shoulder and the hat on his head and the cord from Bill's dressing gown that he is using as a whip actually mean he's Indiana Jones. She has no idea where Sam's disappeared to, probably somewhere with Dom. It's a good day for sun, and between her mother wearing Tom's ridiculous sunglasses and Callum whipping the trees with the cord, Georgie is feeling happy for a change. Grace asks Tom about the women in his life and he just grunts.

"I'll organize a novena for you when I get back to Albury," Grace says.

"What are you going to pray for?" he asks. "That I get lucky with the girl I want? And just say I do? We'll end up having sex. Will the novena people at your church like that?"

"Now you're being silly and making fun of me," Grace says. "I always offer novenas for you kids to be happy."

Georgie wants to point out the low success rate of Grace's prayers

199

to the Virgin Mary but doesn't dare. She's trying to work through the fight with her mother the night before and doesn't want anything to break the peace.

"They work for me," Grace says. "Look at Anabel. She could be like some other miserable teenager, but you can't stop her excitement over the phone. And Dom's been sober for six months when some people can't even make one day. And he's living with you, Tommy, and I know that means everything to him. And Georgie's having this baby."

Georgie catches Tom's eye over her mother's head. She can't hold back. "How can you see things in that way, Mum?" she asks gently, frustrated. "When they've been so awful?"

Grace turns to look at her. Georgie can only see her own face in the reflector sunglasses.

"Because if I don't, I wouldn't be getting out of bed every morning, Georgie," her mother says. "And don't any of you forget that no one was happier than Joey when he died. That's better than some people get."

The baby decides to have a bit of a stretch and Georgie grabs Grace's hand and Grace is oohing and aahing, and next minute Indiana Jones junior is standing in front of them, his eyes wide in awe.

"Can I listen?" he asks.

"It doesn't actually speak," Georgie explains, but she holds out a hand and he takes off his hat and leans forward to press his ear to her belly. Tom takes a photo with his phone.

Callum calls out "Hello, hello" to the baby until he gets a bit bored and goes back to his game.

She hears Tom's sigh of exaggeration. "Okay, you can say a novena to help my love life, Nanni G. Her name's *Tara Finke*. F-i-n-k-e. Don't forget the *e*. Everyone does and she gets cranky."

"Spelling's not important," Georgie says.

"Middle name, *Marie*," Tom adds. "I could get brownie points because she was probably named for the Virgin Mary."

"*Marie* is a cheat name for the Virgin Mary," Georgie explains to him. "That's what Sister Patrick told Marie Fitzgerald when we were in primary school. It has to be either *Mary* or *Maria*."

But Grace is shaking her head. "Tara Finke? Didn't you break her heart, Tommy?"

"*No*," he says, irritated. "Who told you that?"

"I'll see what I can do, but I'm sure there are some people out there who organize novenas for Tara Finke's people. To keep Thomas Finch Mackee away from her."

Georgie's forgotten that Dominic and Joe got their ability to shit-stir from Grace. It used to make Georgie giggle uncontrollably when she was younger. She finds herself laughing now. Tom isn't. He asks Grace for his sunglasses back and goes inside.

"Too sensitive, that one," Grace says, putting her scarf across her eyes. "Gets it from Jacinta Louise's side of the family."

chapter twenty-three

Too many things disturb Tom. One is that even people in his grand-parents' town of Albury know what went down between him and Tara. Then there's the whole thing about the peacekeeper being Brazilian. That starts him thinking about what the Brazilian and Tara get up to and what Tom got up to with her and then his head's spinning, not to mention every other part of his body. It doesn't help that he receives an e-mail from Siobhan Sullivan the next day. He'd been waiting for this one. Siobhan and Tara are best friends, despite being polar opposites. The last time Tom had seen Siobhan was one night in Darlinghurst when he was out with his ex-flatmates and she was about to head off to London. Siobhan hadn't held back telling Tom what she thought of him. He couldn't imagine things being any different eighteen months later.

To: anabelsbrother@hotmail.com
From: siobsullivan@yahoo.com
Date: 29 August 2007

Dear Tom,
I have to be honest that when Frankie sent us a text about you working

at the Union I wasn't ready to get excited. Regardless of how gutted you were, you had no right to treat us like shit. But everyone's grown-up now and I'm glad you and Tara are friends. She seems pretty happy with her peacekeeper. He's really lovely, Eduardo is. Very good-looking, judging from the MySpace photo she has of him. He treats her like a queen. Just what she deserves when you think of the bastards she's been in love with in the past.

I'm still working for British Fail, as they love to call the railroad system here. I'm in charge of making sure the trains run on time. I'm seeing a guy who's so decent that I'm worried. Keeping my fingers crossed.
Cheers,
Siobhan
P.S. Just in case you forgot how to read between the lines. Don't. Screw. With. Tara's. Head. I was there after the one-and-a-half-night stand and I will never forgive you for it!

To: siobsullivan@yahoo.com
From: anabelsbrother@hotmail.com
Date: 30 August 2007

Dear Siobhan,
I can imagine what Frankie said when I turned up at the pub and she sent you a text. She's always been so articulate when it comes to me. I'm presuming the words *dick* and *head* were combined.

And so wonderful to hear about your job. I remember your talent in memorizing the timetable of every guy in Year Twelve, so there is no way the trains won't run on time. Personally, I understand the pride one takes in one's job. I've just been promoted to glassy at the Union and these days I'm walking with a spring in my step as a result.

And finally, thank you for the rundown on Tara. Strangely, the peace-keeper never comes up in the copious amount of e-mails we write each other, or the heart-to-heart telephone conversations we have, or the witty text messages we exchange. And I'd prefer you stick to the singular when it comes to the guys she's gone out with. I pride myself on being the only bastard she's been in love with.

Tom

Siobhan's mention of the one-and-a-half-night stand pisses him off, but it triggers major regrets and memories. Of the night when he took Tara back to Georgie's attic to clear out his stuff for Joe's arrival. *Don't go back there.* He's learned to give himself instructions from a self-help program. The *Learn to Listen to Yourself* program of healing. Georgie suggested it. Worked for her when she was getting over the Sam betrayal seven years ago. Although when he thinks about it, she's now pregnant to Sam, so the results aren't exactly for life.

Don't go back there. Don't go back there.

He goes back there because he can't forget what those foils had done to her hair.

"Foils, fool," she had said, wiggling her fingers to a little kid who was sitting opposite them on the bus. Somewhere back in Year Twelve the insults became signs of affection.

She had been tired and leaned her head on his shoulder, which was the resting place for all their heads, but when Justine and Siobhan and Francesca used his body so shamelessly, he had never felt the need to turn his head and press his mouth against their hair.

"I've finally decided about what I'm going to study," she said. "Permaculture."

"Hmm, Permaculture."

She looked at him. "You don't even know what it means."

"Yeah, I do. It's a hair thing. Like the foils."

"You're a dick." But she laughed all the same. "It works perfectly with cultural studies. There's a component of overseas study, so I'm going to look at how we can create a sustainable urban environment."

"Huh?"

He had felt her watching him and when he shifted his eyes to look down into hers, she had been staring intently.

"Do you know what I'm talking about, Thomas?"

He sighed. He had known exactly what she was talking about. He didn't mind the sustainable, or the urban, or the environment. It was the word *overseas* he hadn't cared to dwell on.

A bunch of gigglers vacated the back seat at Central Station, and Tom grabbed both their stuff and led.

"And I owe it all to your great-aunt Margie," she said, settling into the corner.

Oh, yeah, thank you, Great-Auntie Margie. Love your work.

"She introduced me to one of the nuns. You remember her? Sister Susan. She's one of the Josephite nuns. When she spoke about East Timor at the Town Hall a couple of years back? Well, we've been e-mailing and she reckons I should go over to Timor as part of my studies."

He hadn't responded. Just looked past her, outside the window, as if construction on Broadway was mesmerising.

"You're not interested in what I'm doing," she said, her voice flat.

He moved away from her, so he could look at her properly.

"No, I'm not interested," he had said, pissed off.

205

Her face went pink instantly. She was in retreat and it was going to take him forever to force her back into advance. That was Tara Finke for you. The moment she stopped making speeches and proving a point, the rhetoric went flying out the window and she was all awkwardness, stuck to a wall of vulnerability built over the years. Tom could get her off that wall.

"You're going overseas for how long?" he asked.

"Forget it. You're not interested, remember?"

Then it was her turn to be peering outside. Glebe Point Road had never looked so exciting. He couldn't keep his eyes off her and he knew she felt it, no matter how hard she was looking out that window. Because her face had deepened in color until he actually thought she was going to cry.

"What part of you going overseas, for probably more than a year, would you like me to be excited about?" he snapped. There was no turning back now. She looked up and he had seen it in her eyes. She was getting what he was trying to say. Her face was flushed again. An awkward flush.

"Go out to Campbelltown, Tara. They've got a bigger need for ecological design out there."

She smiled. "You *do* know what it means, you moron."

He leaned closer, his mouth an inch away from hers. "Not working against nature," he said, "working with nature."

She was looking at his mouth and then up at his eyes.

"That's what *permaculture* means," he said with a grin.

She laughed and leaned her head back against him.

"I've never even been on a plane, you know. The only place I've been to is my grandparents' house at the Entrance."

"A very underestimated part of the world, the Entrance is."

Each time the bus door opened, he had felt a blast of cold air. When she shivered, he put his arm around her. He should have kissed her a moment before when the time was right.

"So you e-mail my great-aunt?"

"She reckons you and your dad are going out to Walgett to build something out there," she said.

"Did she, now? I can think of a thousand better ways of spending my holidays, but you know my father. Gets anal about things, so it's going to be Tom and Dom's excellent adventures in Walgett."

"Fun times?"

"Reckons he's going to convince my uncle Joe to come along while he's out here from London, which'll mean that my step-pop's going to want to come too and it'll be the Mackee men building the world, while trying not to get into punch-ups after a couple of schooners."

He grinned. He hadn't realized he kind of liked the sound of that.

By the time they got off at Stanmore, they'd tackled everything from the United Nations to Brangelina, and it was while doing *Little Britain* impersonations with Tara wheezing from laughter that he stopped and leaned down to kiss her. Her satchel was a barrier between them and when he tried to put an arm around her, his guitar case battered her side and she almost went flying out onto the road. He had only one free hand to hold her, and it just seemed to be his mouth pressing down on hers and Tara on tiptoes trying to reach him. And by the time they had reached Georgie's house, they'd stopped four times and he just wanted to get her into the house and up in the attic, where his junk could stay another day. It was late and he figured that Georgie was sleeping, but as they tiptoed up the stairs, she came out of her room.

"Yes, we are cleaning out the Messiah's room," he had said casually. Georgie pointed to her cheek and he kissed her and although she said nothing, there was that close scrutiny of hers, which kind of said everything.

He mumbled something about going upstairs and continued as if every part of him wasn't trembling, and as if his head wasn't yelling, *Georgie knows you want to have sex with Tara Finke tonight under her roof!* Tara stayed behind and he could hear them talk about her mum, who had just left the Red Cross to work for the Cancer Council and about a job vacancy that Georgie should look into. But then Tara was there in the attic and he shut the door behind her.

"What's that?" she had asked, looking down at the LP in his hands, and he knew she was nervous and stalling.

"Slade. I'm going to paste it up on the wall so my dickhead uncle sees it the moment he walks in and stops going on about me losing it."

His stuff was scattered all over the floor.

"You're such a slob."

But then they were kissing again and he was unbuttoning her jeans and she was shaking.

"Stop shaking," he whispered.

"Georgie knows. I can tell she knows. And I've never noticed how beautiful she is. All dark hair and white skin. No freckles. How did she get to have that color skin with no freckles?"

"You're babbling, Finke."

And she was wearing too many clothes. Jeans, skirt, and probably, under it all, tights.

He bent and pulled down her jeans first. "How short is this skirt?" he said with wonder. No tights.

"It's why I wear the jeans. Siobhan gave it to me."

"How white are these legs?" he said with more wonder. Goose-bumped to the hilt. He ran his fingers over them. When he stood up again, he pulled off his sweater. She was still shaking.

"You've got to stop shaking, Tara," he had said gently. "It's just me."

"I can't do this if Georgie's downstairs. Tom. It'll be like having my mother there."

He had tried to take off her top, but she was shaking her head emphatically. "With the light off."

"No light off," he argued. "I want to see you."

And he saw a bit of fear on her face and he didn't want that between them, so he reached over and switched off the light and then took her hand.

"We'll lie down. I promise. We won't do anything you don't want to do."

Please, please, say we can do anything you want to do.

"It's just if Georgie wasn't downstairs . . ."

And he was holding her to him and then they were underneath the blankets and she was trembling and he wanted it to stop and for her to go back to being Tara in charge and bossy, so he wouldn't have to deal with this vulnerability. The skirt was still on, but it barely covered her and he pressed his knee between her legs.

"Come on, baby girl," he had whispered.

She stiffened. "Don't call me baby girl!"

"Okay, honey." He imagined the look on her face but couldn't

209

see it in the dark. "No? Bunny? Sweet cheeks? Babe? Darlin' chicky babe? Munchkin? Poppet?"

And she was doing that wheezing laugh again.

"Doll? Treasure?"

"Enough."

"Petal."

He kissed her again because he couldn't stop.

"Okay," he sighed. "I've just got to go somewhere. I'll be back in a minute."

"Where?" she had asked, alarmed. And then he was crawling under the sheets and he was peeling her undies from her. He loved that they were lace and cotton and he loved the smell of her and he wanted to be all poetic, but in an instant he forgot Joe's poem about Japan except the part about *"you are the bell, and I am the tongue of the bell, ringing you,"* and a new sound entered his life, like when he was a kid and he first heard the sound of horse hooves clip-clopping and he asked his mother in wonder, "What's that sound, because I've never heard it before?" At that moment he was hearing the sound Tara Finke made because of what *he* was doing to her and it was a good sound, a great one, and he had no idea why he was thinking of horses and stuff, but he wanted to hear that type of music for the rest of his life.

When he was up beside her again and when he thought he was going to burst from wanting, he rested on his elbows looking down at her.

"Am I heavy?"

"No. Yes."

"I thought you were getting all religious on me with your 'Oh, Gods.'"

He lay back and she rested her head on his chest and then she looked up at him and he could feel her breath on his Adam's apple.

"Tell me if I'm doing it wrong," she had whispered and he felt her hand crawl down his boxers and he wanted to warn her, because she was not prepared for what was about to happen. And then she started *talking*.

"My mum and dad . . ."

"No, no, no, no, no," he had gasped. "You can't bring up your mum and dad while your hand is down there, Finke."

"They're going to the Entrance next weekend," she said. "Such an underestimated place. And I can't go because I've got exams. So there'll be no one else in the house. No one downstairs."

And her tongue came out and licked his throat.

And then he got all religious on her. Very quickly.

Later, when they were almost asleep, he had called out to her.

"Finke?"

"Yeah?"

"We'll make a good team. You plant. I build."

To:	taramarie@yahoo.com
From:	anabelsbrother@hotmail.com
Date:	30 August 2007

Dear Tara,

It's been very remiss of me not to ask about your boyfriend. I can't imagine him not being your intellectual equal and I'm presuming that you talk books and film and music and politics and that there's a passion to your conversations, despite the fact that you disagree on heaps of things and that he makes you laugh until you make that wheezing sound and that when you're really cranky with him, he knows how to snap you out of it and that when you turn into a bit of wallflower, because sometimes you're a bit awkward with people, he makes sure you're never out there on your own.

I can imagine him being *that* type of a guy.
Love, Tom

To: anabelsbrother@hotmail.com
From: taramarie@yahoo.com
Date: 30 August 2007

Dear Tom,
I'd prefer not to talk about the guy I'm seeing. No offense, but it's a private thing. Except to say that he doesn't have to prove how smart he is 24/7, which I find very refreshing. We always see eye to eye and he's not too intense. And dare I say it, for someone like me, who's never gone for appearances, judging by the one guy I've been attracted to in the past, I can't get over how good-looking he is. A six-pack up close is a very attractive thing and I would strongly recommend it. But enough of my superficiality. How's life with you, Tom?
TF

Oh, she's good. He is so impressed with her aim for the jugular.

To: taramarie@yahoo.com
From: anabelsbrother@hotmail.com
Date: 30 August 2007

Dear Tara,

Okay, then, while you're at it. Give me the textbook reading of Thomas Finch Mackee that will convey my mediocrity. I promise I can handle it.

T

Despite how hard he tries, he can't get the images of the other guy out of his mind. The next night while he's carving out the sirloin at the pub, he's using the chopping board with fury. Ned reaches over at one stage and removes the knife from his grip wordlessly and hands him the lettuce to wash.

"Ned?" he says after a while. "Oi, Ned?"

"What?"

"If someone says to you that the guy they're going out with doesn't have to prove how smart he is, what's your response?"

"That he's dumb."

"And if he has a six-pack?"

"Dumb jock."

"Not too intense."

"Dumb jock with no personality."

"And they see eye to eye?"

Ned pauses. "With the spitfire from Dili?"

"*Same*," Tom corrects him.

Ned holds up a hand to where Tara would reach him in height.

"Dumb jock with no personality and short-man syndrome."

"Thanks, Ned."

"Anytime."

chapter twenty-four

It's a madhouse the next night, with visitors coming and going for Grace and Bill, who are heading home the next day. Later, when the guests are gone, Georgie tries to organize dinner. Tom returns from the corner shop with the stuff she sent him to buy and he's carrying Sam's kid on his shoulder like a fireman carrying a hose.

"Can you do something to help around here?" she asks, irritated.

"Can't, because I'm lifting a few weights before dinner," he says, holding Callum above his head as if he's a barbell.

Callum is delirious with laughter. It's a frightening type of delirium. The type that will send Sam over the edge.

"Tom, did you give him lollies?" Georgie asks suspiciously.

"No." She can tell he's lying, pretending to be outraged that she could suggest such a thing. "Maybe one. Or two."

Georgie hears Sam walk into the house while Bill is swearing about the force of the water coming through her pipes and how Sydney people waste water.

"Bill," she says patiently, "Sam has a problem with us swearing in front of his son, so let's hold back tonight." She puts a finger to her lips.

"And I have a problem with Sam fucking up my daughter's life. So let's just call it even."

"Bill," Grace warns.

"I heard Sam say the C-word the other day, anyway," Tom says, sitting down in front of the kid.

"What's the C-word?" the kid asks just as Sam walks in.

"Can't . . . say."

Sam gives Tom a dirty look.

"If we finish eating everything on our plate, we're going to Norton Street for gelato," Georgie says brightly.

"Cool," Tom says, liking the sound of it.

"Cool," Callum repeats.

By the time dinner is served, Callum is off the Richter scale, Bill's only alteration to his swearing is to change the word to *frickin'* and use it more often, and Sam is livid. He tells Callum to "settle down" constantly, pointing to the kid's untouched food, and Georgie's insides begin to churn. It's like being ten all over again, when Bill would go off because of the noise and mayhem.

"Eat," Sam says firmly, and it takes her a moment to realize it's not directed at her.

Callum looks down at his plate and shakes his head.

"I can't fit in any more," he whimpers. Sam doesn't cope with the whimpering.

His stare goes on forever until the kid puts the food in his mouth but then spits it out, crying, and next minute Sam grabs him and takes him to the corner. "Now stand there until you're ready to eat!"

He sits back down and Georgie is staring at him, shaking her head. He has a look on his face that she hasn't seen for years. In the old days he'd deliver it and it'd make her squirm inside. A look

215

that made her feel small. That's what Sam was able to do back then. Make her feel insignificant. *What would you know, Georgie? Yeah, like you're the expert, Georgie.*

"I can't do this," she says, looking over to where the kid stands. "It's like sitting through the last five minutes of *Blair Witch* when they're forced to face the wall and die."

Wrong thing to say, but then again she knows it is. Maybe deep down she wants to pick a fight, wants to provoke him so then he can grab *her* and put her in the corner as well and she can fight him back. Anything but what he dishes out to her these days. Silence and tiptoeing and unspoken rules and unsaid future plans.

It's a filthy look she's receiving. It belongs to the passive-aggressive hall of fame. She'd prefer her family any day, all rage and fury and getting it out in the open. Fewer lacerations in the long run.

"Sam, remove him from the corner," she says firmly.

There's silence now. Sam goes to say something, but then it seems he changes his mind. Except Georgie knows the weight of the words he's swallowed.

"Say it," she says quietly.

"What?" he asks.

"What you were about to say."

"Georgie," Grace warns, "let's just finish eating and clear the plates, so we can all go for a walk."

"No," she says, shaking her head and looking straight at Sam. "He was going to say that this is none of my business. That it's *his* son. Say it, Sam. Have the guts to say it."

Sam pushes his chair back, grabs Callum, and walks out, slamming the door behind him.

Georgie collects the plates off the table with shaking hands and then Dom's at the sink taking them from her. "Fix this thing up with Sam, Georgie. Fix it now, or you never will," he says.

The front door of Sam's house is open and she walks in and can hear the crying from the kid's room but she knows it's not her right to go in. She finds Sam in the kitchen, where he's standing with his back to her, hands clenching the sink.

"Do you want out?" she asks.

He turns to face her. There's a look of bitterness of his face and she can't help feeling that the bottom is going to fall out of her world again.

"Out of what, Georgie? What are we in?"

"Why do I have to answer that?" she asks. "Why can't you?"

"Because words are a weapon with you. I'm scared to even open my mouth."

It's a controlled fury she sees in his eyes, built up over time.

"Okay, then, let's talk about your son's behavior tonight," she says. "He's a kid. Juiced up on sugar, courtesy of Tom, the village idiot. I'm not telling you how to raise him, Sam. I'm just saying that sometimes there has to be a difference in the way you punish him for not eating his food and for when he does something pretty dire. Because I'm warning you, I'm not into the pulling-the-arm-out-of-a-kid's-socket routine and then sticking him against the wall. So you'll have to find a different set of rules for ours."

There's silence for a moment and she takes a deep breath, almost relieved that she spoke, no matter how damaging the words can be.

"You never use his name," he says. "And I know I have no right to ask anything from you when it comes to him. I know it takes an extraordinary person to love Callum under the circumstances, Georgie . . ."

"But you make me feel a little less than ordinary!" she blurts out. "You place yourself between us. You're an interloper and you make things polite and careful. When I'm forced into being polite and careful, Sam, I find that gene inside of me passed down from Grace. The distant one."

He's shaking his head.

"Does it help that I enjoy his company a lot more when you're not around?" she says, not able to stop herself. "Because that way, you aren't watching me as though I'm going to turn into some kind of demon."

"That's ridiculous, Georgie."

"Don't call me ridiculous. And for your information? That look? The one you gave me in my kitchen? Well, I got that look a lot during the last year we were together. The one that said *a bit* less, Georgie. *A bit* more decorum, please. *A bit* less emotion. Our lives could be *a bit* tidier. Perhaps there's someone *a bit* better out there!"

"You read most of it wrong!" he shouts.

"What part?" she shouts back.

There's more crying from Callum's room and then a knock on the front door.

"We're scaring your son," she mutters, walking up the corridor to where she can see the outline of Tom at the screen door.

"Nanni G wants . . ." and Tom does "gelato" in very poor sign language, so Callum won't hear.

Outside, she can see Grace and Bill and Dominic sitting on the brick fence waiting. Her family. How did they shrink to this size?

She hears Sam come up behind her, switching on the porch light.

"And you did that all wrong, back at my house," she says, quietly to him, because she's not finished yet. "We promised Callum gelato and if you take that from him, he'll think I broke the promise. I don't want to be the bad guy here, Sam."

In defense of her family, they know how to bounce back from an awkward moment with alacrity. It was what Jacinta had complained about for years. One minute tearing each other apart, next minute everyone back to normal like nothing happened. They walk through Petersham and pick up Sam's mum along the way and arrange to meet Lucia and Abe and their kids. They can't find a table big enough, so they end up sitting around the fountain at the Italian Forum. Georgie puts an arm around Grace because she's cold and listens to one of her goddaughters tell her about *Hannah Montana* and Sam's kid tell her about *Ben 10 the Alien Hunter*. Bill talks water restrictions and how the government doesn't give a shit about anything outside Sydney, and Dominic bitterly complains about Leichhardt council and what an eyesore the Forum is and Sam goes on about what happens when developers think they're restaurateurs. Their voices are drowned out by the Qantas 747 flying directly over their heads and Grace's hand reaches over and covers the one around her shoulder and Georgie knows what her mother is thinking. Who she's thinking of.

Later, she hovers with Sam on his front step. Tonight she wants more than just, *I might see you at the station on Monday.* But Tom's there at the gate.

"Bill sent me to say, quote, 'You better not be staying at Sam's, because all he does is give you high blood pressure,' unquote, and then Nanni Grace said, quote, 'Oh, Bill,' unquote."

Sam makes a sound of disbelief. "They're blaming me for your high blood pressure?"

"Let's go." Tom says it with force. He's not leaving without her.

A moment later, Dominic jogs by. "At this time of the night?" she asks.

Tom takes Georgie's hand and leads her away, but he turns back to Sam for a moment.

"I'm sorry about the packet of snakes I gave Callum," he mumbles. "And the lime ice-block. And the Redskin."

Georgie pinches him hard for lying to her, but as they walk back toward her house and she watches Dom do his fist thrusts in the distance, she can't help laughing until she's forced to stop because she can hardly walk.

"He's OCD," Tom says.

"Don't be ridiculous. He's just a bit obsessive . . . in a compulsive sort of way."

"Between my OCD father and you, I can't understand why I'm not in the nuthouse."

And she keeps on laughing until her stomach aches and her bladder feels weak. It's the third time she's laughed this week. But it feels better than crying.

chapter twenty-five

Tom doesn't realize until he wakes up on the morning of his mother's birthday that he honestly believed his father would go to her. That he was counting on it. Praying for it subconsciously. Birthdays were big for his mum and every single year his father would come home feigning indifference and then spring something ridiculously extravagant on her.

"We can't afford it," she'd say.

"We can afford it. Tom and Anabel can just go without food for a week," he'd say.

It was usually a fancy restaurant. His father was a foodie. Looked like a steak and chips guy. Yet another contradiction.

But this year, his father stays closed up in Georgie's study and Tom feels it in his gut. That if Dominic doesn't return to Jacinta Louise today, he never will.

He works alongside Ned, who's complaining about five assignments and exams coming up and Francesca, who's counting down the days before Trombal gets home. He finally rings his mother during his break while he's having a smoke out back. Asks if she's had a good day and he can hear her lie when she says yes. He tries to mumble *I love you* and *Happy Birthday* but Ned's emptying the garbage beside him, listening to every word. Francesca doesn't say much, but he feels her watching him with those big empathetic eyes and he even stays longer to scrub the stove until it sparkles so he doesn't have to chat with them for their nightly postmortem on the pavement, which usually consists of Francesca believing that Stani's going to let them play one Sunday afternoon if the old-timers call in sick. Or disappear. He's worried that if the regular band members are mysteriously killed, he'll have to point a finger at Justine and Francesca.

When he does leave, waving off Stani who always has that intense I'm-watching-you look on his face, Tom makes it as far as the end of the street before he realizes he's being trailed.

"We're going to Brisvegas," Francesca says from the passenger window. "You coming?"

He can hardly see her in the dark. "You're going to Brisbane?" he asks with disbelief, without stopping. He's not in the mood for Francesca and her crap tonight. "What are you going on about?"

"We leave now and we'll get there by eight in the morning, stay a couple of hours and then head back at lunchtime and get back here tomorrow night."

He stops walking, well and truly pissed off.

"Don't be ridiculous."

"You mean *ridicolos*," Francesca says, imitating Stani. "We can drive through the Gold Coast. It's a metropolis. I've been dying to get there for years."

"The same Gold Coast you called a cesspit and boycotted for Schoolies? And we got stuck at Siobhan's cousin's flat at Engadine like the biggest losers around."

"And I've regretted it ever since, so let's drive through the Gold Coast." The way Francesca can feign sincerity is amazing.

The car engine stops and he hears the door opening from the driver's seat.

"Tom, get in the car," Justine says firmly. "We're going to Brisbane. I'm taking the first two hours, then Frankie, and then you and then Ned. Every two hours. Stop. Revive. Survive."

"Ned? What the hell has he been telling you?"

"Get in the car. Now."

They have a standoff. The two horsewomen of the apocalypse still win, despite their dwindling numbers.

He gets in and slams the door, glaring at Ned, who shrugs.

"Don't you have five exams or something?" Tom accuses.

"Some people clean the fridge to avoid studying. I go to Brisbane."

"I've got a plan so we don't fight over the music," Justine tells them. "Everyone gets their MP3s ready and they choose two songs each and we plug in when it's our turn."

"That's fair," Francesca says. She turns to face the back and nods. "Fair?"

"Frankie will choose the two shittiest songs each time, just to piss us off," Tom mutters.

There's a sound of disgust from the front seat. "What a thing to say, Tom. Since when have I been that petty, huh?" She turns to Justine. "Can you believe he said that? Can you?"

"Say you're sorry, Tom," Justine says.

He says he's sorry and Francesca plays Avril Lavigne's "Sk8er Boi." She and Justine are killing themselves laughing because they know the rhyme will almost kill Ned and the tune will make Tom vomit. It's a bit of death by music, really. Justine does the show

223

tunes. It doesn't get worse than "Jesus Christ Superstar" for Tom. Who would have thought to put music to a crucifixion? Worse still is the passion that Mary Magdalene and the good woman of Galilee in the front seat are putting into the singing. The girls know every single word and who gets to sing what. Ned is staring at Tom in horror. They haven't even reached the north coast turn-off yet. "Pick something that will make them hurt," Ned says. "Be vicious." Tom thinks hard and can only come up with "I Don't Want to Miss a Thing" and the caterwauling makes even him sick. Ned won't be part of the bad-taste competition because he claims there's only good-taste music in his MP3 player. He plays Sigur Rós, which Francesca explains is a form of government torture in some non-Icelandic nations. And that's how they get to Brisbane.

When they reach the outskirts, early the next morning, Francesca stops by a roadside fruit vendor.

"Flowers, Tom."

She looks at him through the rearview mirror.

"The tulips are great at this time of the year," she says. "My mum loves them."

And then he's standing at her office door, looking at his mother for the first time in almost a year. His father would say she was all cornflower-blue eyes and attitude. Not feisty, because she didn't lose her cool. Just attitude. Half the size of Dominic in his robust days, she always complained that she could get lost in the Amazonian world of the Finch and Mackees. Big people. Big personalities. "If your father ever wanted to prove I wasn't the mother of his children, they'd just have to look at both of you and laugh me out of court," she'd say. The last time Tom had seen her was when she came to pack up the house after his father disappeared. To beg Tom to come up north. He was stoned out of his brain that day, staring right through her the whole time. But he wasn't stoned enough to forget the look on her face. He'll take that look to his grave.

She glances up from her work as if to ask a colleague a question and he gives her the best smile he can, because she deserves it. And then she's crying. Just crying and crying like everyone in his life does these days. He walks around her desk and hugs her. Vows there'll never be a reason for him to treat her the way he has. Because he doesn't want her crying like this ever again. It's a different cry from the one when Joe died, and Tom knows it's all about him.

Later, they go down to the cafeteria.

"Why doesn't he come up to get you?" he asks.

"Because I've told him not to."

"If he had the balls, he'd come anyway."

She's silent for a moment and shakes her head.

"You don't understand, Tom."

"Then explain it to me, Mum," he says, frustrated. "Because I don't get it. Did he screw around behind your back or something? Did he hit you? *Fuck,* did he hit you?"

"No," she says. "*No.*"

She waves to someone over his head, with a forced smile. "I've always let him—*no,*" she corrects herself vehemently—"*asked* him, to make the decisions. The ones I couldn't make. From the moment you were born, I've said, 'You make the decision, Dom. Because I can't. It's too painful and I might make the wrong one.' And that wasn't fair to him because he had to make some pretty shitty ones,

225

Tom. I just need to know that I've made this next one for all the right reasons. I can't go back without forgiving him."

"He hasn't had a drink in more than half a year. And Bill and he are really good together these days, especially talking about Grandpa Tom Finch coming home, and I've even heard him talk about Joe with Georgie sometimes." He lies about that one. His father never talks about Joe.

She's shaking her head. "This isn't about his drinking, or Joe, or Bill, or Tom Finch, or this marriage, even." She looks so intense, but it's the fierceness of love. How could two people who are in love as much as his parents contemplate a life without the other?

"This is about his son. He left *you*, Tom, and we almost lost you. I don't know whether I can forgive him for that, and I know he can't forgive himself."

He feels like he can't breathe and he's covering his head because he just wants to yell, but it's the Department of Foreign Affairs and Trade, and he'll probably have security on him in a moment.

She takes his hand, kissing it. "But he can't do that without your help. He can't do that with your silence. You need to find a way, Tommy. He's broken without you."

"How do you know? You don't even speak to him on the phone."

It was strange to have his parents needing something from him. Something this big. In the past, they needed silence from him if he was making a racket. They needed him to apply himself. *"I need you to be sensible, Tom."* But not this need. Not the need to make everything right.

"I want to see Anabel," he says quietly. He can hardly recognize his voice. "Can you get her out of school? I need to see her. *Please.*"

•　　•　　•

She's beautiful and, *God,* he loves the fact that she still wears a pony-tail and looks like a kid her age. She's running to him and there's nothing graceful about Anabel because the Finch women aren't really that graceful. They're just beautiful and smart and fierce and ridiculously uncool. A bit like Tara.

They take the City Cat up the river and then they get off at Riverside and he buys her an ice cream and they talk about Georgie and the baby for most of the time. It makes him feel bad that he's never expressed excitement about the pregnancy. He's never seen it as anything but Georgie being depressed or not accepting Sam in her life again. But for a moment he sees it through Anabel's eyes and nothing can be more joyous than that baby being born to them all.

"I'm working on J-Lo," she says.

"How?"

"Every Thursday I log on to mycareer.com.au and download any Sydney job she's qualified to do and then I forward it to her."

He thinks for a moment. "Good work, 99."

"And I've heard her ring a few people to ask if they'd be referees if she needs them."

"Can I have a lick of your ice cream?"

"No, you have smoker's tongue."

"You're a mean girl, Anabel Georgia."

She pokes out her tongue and he puts his arm around her.

He knows he's running out of time, and she knows it too because she tucks her arm into his, almost a death grip.

"Tom?"

"Yeah?"

"I miss Daddy."

So do I, he wants to say.

"Grandma Agnes says that he doesn't deserve a second chance," she says.

"Yeah, well Agnes of God should be a bit more forgiving."

"Since he's been . . . sober, he calls me every night."

"What's his take on Evil Trixie?"

She laughs and he's glad to hear it.

"He said that sometimes people get frightened when someone new comes along and threatens the status quo and that I should make sure they feel as if there is nothing to fear."

"Oh, please. What kind of crap advice is that?"

"Trixie and I are now good friends."

"And the situation with Ginger and the social justice committee?"

"Collective bargaining, he reckons. The Ninja and I are negotiating."

He's looking at a miniature Georgie, who sounds like a miniature Dominic.

"I think he's writing to J-Lo," she says.

Tom looks at her. "*Dad?*"

She nods knowingly. "She comes home and she's all, 'Any mail?' " Anabel puts on a sweet falsetto voice that sounds nothing like his mother. "And then she disappears into her room and once I walked in and she was all . . ." Anabel does this thing where she's impersonating a silent coy giggle.

"Don't be bloody ridiculous. He doesn't do letters. And she doesn't . . ." He impersonates her silent coy giggle.

Anabel sighs. It's an Agnes of God sigh down to a T.

"I'm telling you, Tom. Those kids are writing smut to each other."

He's killing himself laughing, but she looks sad for a moment and he knows this is where she starts falling to pieces. The one thing all three of them, four counting Georgie, have in common is making sure that Anabel's okay, and he wants to make everything right.

"He told me about Grandpa Tom Finch and how he might be coming home," she says, her voice wavering.

He nods.

"I told Pop Bill that if Grandpa Tom Finch comes home, I'm going to play his trumpet. To welcome him, you know. Do you think he'd like that, Tom?"

Tom doesn't know whether she's talking about Pop Bill or Grandpa Tom Finch.

"I think he'd love it." He doesn't even know how those words have come out.

She looks up at him. "I think Bill cried when I told him I would. I wish everyone would stop crying, Tom. Uncle Joe would be so angry about it." But she's crying herself now. "He'd be so angry at us, Tom, for crying so much when all he did was laugh."

It's silent in the car and he doesn't realize until they reach Byron that he hasn't said a word the whole time. They change drivers at Lennox Head and sit on the beach for a while, just watching the surfers. It's cold, but he doesn't want to move. It reminds him too much of that time with Tara Finke at Maroubra on the night of graduation.

Because back then there was the promise of the next day when he drove back to Georgie's and they all got together. All the

229

Mackees and their friends to say "Hooray," as Bill and Auntie Margie Finch, and the rest of those who came from the Burdekin, would say. "Hooray" to Joe, who was off to London to a teaching job. And Dominic stood on Georgie's table while everyone told him to get down. "No, no, no. I'm making a speech here." And he did. One of those speeches that only Dominic Finch Mackee could make. Full of guts and emotion and humor. Tom remembers grabbing his uncle and saying, "I kissed the psycho Tara Finke last night. Can you believe it?"

Joe had looked stunned in that comic way of his. "Because you were pissed or because you wanted to?"

"You know I don't drink."

Then Joe grabbed his face, grinning. "You wanted to. I can see it in your eyes, you cheeky bastard."

And that look of joy, that look of total euphoria, is the last image he has of Joe.

He starts crying and he can't stop. He doesn't know where it comes from, this grief. How it blindsides you. But Justine's hand comes across to clutch his, like she'll never let go, and Francesca's holding him, murmuring his name over and over again and he just wants to go back to the moment when he was in that water. At that near-perfect moment in his life when Tara Finke was in his arms. Because if he could go there, he could start from scratch and make everything in his life right.

"Are you going to be okay about your exams?" he asks Ned in the car, because the silence between Lennox and Coffs gets too much after a while.

Ned waves him off. "First one's *Moby-Dick*head. I'll just go on

about the sperm scene and apply a feminist reading. They love that.
Do you want a chewie?"

"Yeah, why not."

When they drop him off home late that night, he finds both his father
and Georgie in the kitchen. Waiting, it seems.

"If it's Dominic you want to punish, then at least have the decency
to phone me," Georgie says coldly.

"As if my mother hasn't rung you both."

"*His mother,*" Georgie says, looking at his father. "She doesn't
belong to us anymore. Did you know that, Dom?" Georgie stands
up and walks to the sink to rinse her cup.

"I'm going to bed before I say something I might regret."

But his father doesn't move. He just sits there and looks at Tom,
and there's an expression on his face that Tom can't quite place. In
front of him is the *Herald*. Tom knows his father would have read it
line by line; it was always his way. Lots of grunting, lots of "You've
got to be bloody joking." He'd even read the page that told when the
sun set and rose, and if the family was ever away, it was his father's
obsession that they all see a sunrise or sunset together.

Once, just before Tom's final exams in Year Twelve, the four
of them went to Mudgee for the long weekend. Work and study
seemed to have taken over their lives and his dad said it was all
going too fast and they needed to regroup. The first thing they
noticed as they drove into the property was a red vinyl sofa sitting
on a grassy incline, overlooking the country highway in the
distance.

Tom remembers how his dad's eyes were fixed on it the whole
time they were there.

"I'm going to watch the sun rise tomorrow from the hill," Dominic announced on their last night, looking up from the local paper. "Says here it'll rise at 5:47 in the morning."

"Enjoy," Tom's mum murmured, not looking up from the novel she was reading. It's what she claimed you had to do when Dominic got an idea. Not look him in the eye.

"But you've got to wonder why someone would put a sofa up there," his dad continued.

"I'm not wondering at all." Tom kept his eyes on the page. He had been rereading *Brave New World,* hoping miraculously that he'd discover something new that would help him blitz his HSC exam.

"Gang, when are we going to get a chance to see a sunrise together again?" his dad had argued.

"We're not the waking-up-at-five-in-the-morning type of family, Dom," his mum said patiently. "We're the sleeping-in-until-nine-o'clock type."

"Love that kind of family," Tom said.

"I'll come with you, Daddy," Anabel reassured him.

" 'Course you will, Beautiful, and then we can spend the trip home trying to describe the perfect sunrise to these philistines."

"And you can spend the rest of the week blowing her nose when she gets a cold," his mum said.

"Nah, I'll leave that to Tom for not keeping his sister warm on that sofa."

There was silence after that and Tom thought he and his mum had won the round. But it only lasted a minute.

"Don't you wonder—?"

"*No,*" Tom and his mother answered.

"Just say up on the hill is the meaning of life and someone knew it and they wanted everyone else to enjoy it. So they put a red vinyl sofa up there."

His mother had made a snorting sound.

"Aren't you even curious, Tom?" he asked.

Tom finally put his book down. He wanted to give his response all the effort in the world. "I'm *not* getting up at 5:46 in the morning. I'm not. *Not*. Do you understand the word *not*? It's called the negative in many cultures. I'll say it again. *Not*."

He looked his father in the eye.

At 5:45 the next morning, he stood on the incline beside the two snuggled up on the sofa. His father was grinning.

"Come on. Cuddle up, Tom," Anabel said.

"Big boy," Tom muttered, shivering. "No cuddles." There was enough blanket next to his dad to keep warm and he yanked as much around him as he could. The meaning of life had better come soon, he thought, or he was getting back into bed. They heard a sound behind them and his dad chuckled.

"Knew you'd join us, darlin'," Dominic said, patting his lap so Anabel could sit on his knee and he could make room for Tom's mum.

"Because you stole my blanket, you bastard," she said, curling up beside him.

His dad made sure the girls were covered, leaving Tom exposed.

"Cuddles?" Tom begged. Anabel giggled.

The sunrise wasn't much after all. It was too cloudy. But they stayed there for ages, just the four of them, and Tom remembers how silent they were most of the time. How someone spoke once in a while about

233

work, or Sydney, or just stuff. How Anabel fell asleep in his father's lap and he pressed a kiss to her head because Dominic always said he'd never see anything more beautiful than his girls. How his mother had touched his dad's cheek. "What did you do to yourself?"

"Nicked myself shaving," he murmured.

Tom thought they must have looked strange from the highway, sitting on that incline on the red vinyl sofa, but nobody cared. Then his dad yawned, stretching his arms out wide and hitting Tom on the face. On purpose. Sometimes it pissed Tom off when his father did that. "He's just playing with you, Tom," his mum would say when Tom looked like he was going to have a go. But that day he didn't mind. He was too content and he wondered how it could be that no matter how much he loved his mum and Joe and Pop Bill and Nanni Grace and Georgie, that nobody would have got him on that sofa at 5:46 in the morning. Except his dad. And that was the problem with Dominic Mackee. That he could promise the meaning of life with just a look in his eye and a tone to his voice. Tom would have followed the bastard anywhere.

Except here they are in Georgie's kitchen. In a different kind of silence from the one on that hill in Mudgee. And in this silence he knows he's finished with being the Tom of books and rhymes. Tom Sawyer was a weak shit compared to Huck Finn. Thomas the apostle didn't have enough faith in his friends to believe the unbelievable; Uncle Tom was a white man's tool, a disappointment to his people. Worse still, he doesn't know how to follow the piper anymore because it's a path Tom has lost faith in. And the piper knows it. Tom can see it in his father's eyes now. And the more he stares, the clearer it becomes. He wonders if that guy who put explosives in his backpack and blew up Joe's train imagined that two years later, on the other side of the world, his anger would come to this. That the piper didn't know who to be anymore, because he wasn't Joe's brother, or Tom and Anabel's dad, or Jacinta Louise's husband.

It made Tom want to weep all over again.

His mobile rings after midnight. No *hello* or *how are you* or *this is what I'm responding to.* Just straight into the conversation as if she's sure he'll know what she's talking about.

"It all comes back to your family," Tara explains. "On one hand, you're frightened to commit to anyone because you're probably thinking you'll get her pregnant, like your father got your mother pregnant, and then one of you is going to have to give up something. On the other hand, you don't want to move away from your security base because each time a family member has, something awful and tragic happened, like with Tom Finch and then Joe. So your way of dealing with the first is through casual relationships where you don't let anyone hang around long enough, and your way of dealing with the second is not moving out of your comfort zone. Think about it. You moved four blocks away when you went to live with those dickheads and now you're back at Georgie's. Two blocks from home. You could draw a line around the parameters of your world, Tom, and I'm presuming that every girl you've slept with lives within that grid."

He sits up for a moment.

"Is this one of those cheering-me-up phone calls that you specialize in, where you tell me to get on with my life?" he asks, torn between excitement and anger and trying to work out how far back he had asked for the character analysis.

"Sorry." He hears the apology in her voice. She must have picked up on the anger in his tone. "Look, I'll speak to you another—"

"*No.* No, don't hang up. What time is it there?" he asks.

"Two hours behind you."

There's silence for a moment.

"So you think I'm a coward who sticks to my comfort zones?"

He hears her sigh. "No. I didn't say that."

"You did."

"No, I didn't, Tom. I said you stick to your comfort zones. Not that you're a coward."

"Doesn't it mean the same thing to you?" he asks.

"No. I think the worst thing that ever happened to me was leaving home," she says honestly.

"Why?"

"Because I miss it like you'd never believe, and then I go away from this place and I miss here too. I'm scared I'm going to spend the rest of my life in a state of yearning, regardless of where I am."

He gets comfortable. He wants to hear her voice in his ear. In the dark. In this attic. In his bed. He wants to hear it for as long as he can.

"What do you miss most?" he asks.

"Winter," she says.

He chuckles. She does too.

"Only you'd say that, Finke."

"You would too if you didn't get to experience one."

If he had the guts, he'd ask her about that night in her parents' house. It was in winter. He remembers how cold she felt. If he had the guts, he'd ask what she remembers.

"I love it getting dark early in Sydney and I love snuggling under

236

my blanket and wearing tights and boots and sitting with you guys somewhere in Newtown or at Bar Italia and having a latte or lying in front of the heater watching DVDs."

"Then when you come home, I'm organizing a winter's day for you."

More silence. *Rein it in, Tom,* he tells himself. *Don't scare her away. You've wooed her this way before and then you walked away.*

"I miss you," he says, failing to take his own advice.

She doesn't respond.

"Why does it take forever between e-mails?" he asks.

"I don't have regular access to the Internet, but I've made a deal with the Portuguese teachers and they let me use it up at their house."

"Then give me a landline and I'll ring you."

"They decided to skip that technology and went straight to mobiles," she explains. "But it only costs me forty cents a minute to ring."

"How much does it cost me?"

"I don't know. Work it out. Go to sleep."

Logical Tom begs emotional stupid dickhead Tom not to ask the question.

"Are you alone?" he asks quietly.

He hears her breathing so close to his ear.

"Yes."

"Good," he says, his voice croaky. "I'll sleep like a baby."

chapter twenty-six

They're sitting in Lucia's kitchen poring over brochures of holiday destinations for Christmas. Caravan parks down the South Coast are the only option for Lucia, who won't unleash her children onto a resort. The subject moves to Georgie's body, post-baby, in a cossie, and then maternity bras. Once in a while Lucia will stand up and hammer at the window, bellowing to her kids in the backyard to stop killing each other and Georgie reconsiders whether she wants to be part of that mayhem for the new year.

"I'll take you shopping Saturday for maternity bras," Lucia says.

Georgie can't take her eyes away from the bushland surrounding the caravan park in the brochure. "I've already been," she murmurs, having an Azaria Chamberlain moment where her baby gets kidnapped by either members of the savage animal kingdom or pedophiles who hang out in caravan parks. She tries to put it at the back of her mind as part of a twelve-point plan she's devised after accompanying Dom to his AA meetings.

"With who?" Lucia asks.

"One of the ladies from my work."

She doesn't realize that Lucia's angry until she hasn't spoken for a while.

"What did I do?" Georgie asks.

"My counselor says some people don't want to be happy."

The caravan park and its promise of potential harm to her unborn child is pushed aside.

"You have a counselor?" Georgie asks. "Why would you need a counselor, Lucia?"

Lucia's look has an edge. Like those martial arts movies where there are quick slicing sounds and the person stands there for a moment before crumbling into pieces.

"Why would I need a counselor?"

"Yes," Georgie says patiently, "why would you need a counselor? You're happy with your life. You've got a great family. . . ."

The look she receives is one of such anger that Georgie wonders what part of the last hour she missed. What part of the last two years has she missed?

"I'm going to a counselor because sometimes I'm pretty depressed. It's what happens when your best friend is dealing with acute grief. My counselor tells me that I overstress. My best friend getting pregnant to her ex-partner, stresses me. Dominic, who is like a brother to me, going AWOL for over a year, stresses me. His marriage to Jacinta, the world's most enviable marriage, I have to add, falls apart and it stresses me. Jacinta living in another state, miserable out of her brain, stresses me. Another friend—yes, Georgie, Joe was our friend too—well his death doesn't just stress me, it devastates me. Not being able to offer my best friend any comfort, doesn't just stress or devastate me; it kills me. That's why I need a counselor."

Lucia's crying. There's a hopelessness to it all and it leaves Georgie speechless. Worse still, the kids are at the glass door, staring at them as if they don't recognize who anyone is anymore.

"I know this sounds cruel, Georgie," Lucia says, "but grieving people are selfish. They won't let you comfort them and they say you don't understand and they make you feel *useless* when all your life you've been functional to them. And you couldn't even ask me to take you maternity bra shopping?"

Anything Georgie says now will seem contrived, so she says nothing, just sits there while Lucia goes to the glass door and has a quiet word with the kids before they disappear outside again.

"Do you want me to be honest?" Lucia asks.

"What?" Georgie asks, frightened. "The counselor spiel wasn't honesty?"

Lucia gives her a don't-push-it look.

"Georgie, you were a write-off when Joe died. You still are. You won't let any of us in. It's as if everything we say seems inappropriate or dumb. This one time, Sam and Abe and Jonesy and Abe's sisters were at my place, and we were all trying to work out how to deal with what you and Dominic were going through. And all I can remember is Jonesy. We always laugh at what an idiot he is and how he's always text messaging and how young he is in the head. But I remember him that day, sitting around my kitchen table. He just broke down and said, 'I don't know what to say. I don't know what to say to make Georgie better, and I want to.' And out of everyone's reaction, his gets to me the most when I remember it."

Georgie's too tired to cry anymore. "There's nothing you could have said," she says quietly. "I promise you, Lucia. There's *nothing* at all you can say to make us feel better."

"I *know,*" Lucia says. "And Sam got that, Georgie. He understood your silence and he got how you wanted to talk sometimes and not be interrupted, and he got how some days you didn't want to talk at all. For those little moments of calm he's brought you, I will forgive him for anything."

Georgie thinks for a moment.

"If you like, I'll make a list . . . of all the things I should be doing . . . with your help," she says with a bit of humility. "You can be in total charge," she adds, knowing that she just sold her soul to the devil.

She can tell that Lucia is coming around to the idea and watches as she shuffles through a kitchen drawer, taking a pen and paper out. "I'm scribing," Lucia says firmly.

Georgie curses herself for teaching Lucia the art of list-making. Now she makes lists of the schools she'd like to send her kids to if they had x amount of money and then a list of the ones they can afford. She makes lists of jobs she'd love if she wasn't doing the following things, and then she makes a lists of those following things, and her lists become hybrid and feral. In the end, they make Lucia paranoid about all the things she's supposed to be doing that she doesn't have time for because she's making lists.

"What's the first subheading?" Georgie asks.

Lucia clicks the pen into action. "Sam."

She volunteers to go to Callum's soccer game because it's part of Lucia's idea of normality.

"Football," the kid corrects as they cross the road toward the playing field. Sam reaches out to take her hand, and she lets him because it's on her list to allow him to show affection without getting snippy.

"Football is rugby league as far as I'm concerned," she says to

241

Sam after he gives the most inane advice to his son about how to kick the ball.

Once they hit the park, Callum's running awkwardly in his shin pads and soccer boots toward the crowd waiting around the field, and when he finds his teammates, they hug each other and walk around with their arms wrapped around one another's shoulders.

The suit is here with her boyfriend. He's a pleasant-enough-looking guy in a north-shore-rugby kind of way, and Georgie can tell he knows the history of the situation because he's trying his best to fill in the spaces with chatter rather than awkward silence.

"Hi, Georgie."

"Leonie."

A very chirpy soccer/football coach runs around the field with Callum and his team, and then the game begins. Callum isn't much of a soccer/football player and runs to the sideline constantly to confer with Sam or his mother, negotiating time out, because the last place he seems to want to be is on the field. *The suit* deals with it by saying, "Sweetie, off you go. Two more minutes," while Sam huffs and puffs as if his masculinity is being put to the test by his son's ability to play the game. Because Georgie keeps the list in her pocket that states rule number five is to refrain from negativity toward Sam, she swallows her irritation. So what if the kid wants to spend all his time hugging his teammates as well as some of the opposition? At one stage, Callum sits with one of them at the goalpost, deep in conversation. Georgie would love to know what two six-year-olds are talking about with such intensity.

"Last game of the season, Callum. Try to kick the ball," Sam says firmly once they get ready to go into the second half.

"It might even go in." This from his mother. "Wouldn't that be great, sweetie?"

"Ice cream for the one who gets the ball closest to the goalpost," the boyfriend says.

Everyone seems to look at Georgie for her encouragement, even Callum.

"Tom says he wants a photo of you running," she tries.

"But you don't have a camera."

She holds up her phone.

Chest puffed out, the kid sprints up and down the field, miles away from the action of the game and she can't help smiling, can't help seeing for the first time, not Sam's kid with another woman, but the older brother of her unborn child. The closest he comes to the ball is when someone kicks it to his head accidently and then it's over for Callum. Nothing's getting him back on that field. He has a bit of a cry and his mother zips up his jacket. "He didn't do it on purpose, sweetie. He didn't do it on purpose."

Later, Georgie exchanges good-byes with them politely and she feels Leonie watching her as Georgie shakes hands with Callum, who will get dropped off at Sam's later tonight. It's an intense look and Georgie realizes the truth. *The suit's* not *threatened* by Georgie. *The suit* is *frightened* by her. Although there are things about her that Georgie hates, she understands the need to want your own looked after. She learned that from loving Joe and Tom and Anabel and Lucia's kids and even the children of strangers who walk into her office every day. Georgie crouches at the kid's level and shows him the photo she took of him on her phone. "I look like I'm fast," he says with wonder.

"I'll put it in the baby's room for when he's born," she hears herself promising. "So I'll know he's safe."

She feels like the whore of birthing class. She wonders what stories they tell about her in their homes. She's already been to the class with Tom and Dominic.

"Why's everyone looking?" Sam asks.

He can't keep his hands off her stomach and she realizes that he's been dying to touch her there, to allow his fingers to linger.

"What are we going to call him?"

"What makes you think it's a him?" she asks.

"Tom said the woman at the pharmacy says it's a him because you're carrying it all at the front. And didn't Abe's mum say it was because of the chain?"

She cranes her neck to look back at him, amused.

"You? Believe that stuff?"

"I think it's a boy. Shit, just say it's a girl. Just say it's a little Georgie?"

She laughs and his arms tighten around her and her heart's beating fast. Not because of the breathing methods or her blood pressure; her heart's beating fast because Sam's teasing her. She hasn't heard that tone for years. And then they don't go straight home. They go to a Thai place on King Street and they're talking about everything, in the middle of Sam saying, "No MSG. No MSG," pointing to Georgie's stomach. Their conversation seems strange at times, because years ago when she was with Sam and he spoke about work, it would be about people in his office cheating about their call sheets or how they were tossers, and it would be about insurance litigation and how much he hated his job and how much he hated the people. Now they're talking about the James Hardie campaign the year before and there's a fire in him as he speaks about how they'll get rid of the new industrial relations laws and if they can get these fuckers out of Canberra in November, there'll be dancing in the streets. He's giddy beyond comprehension about the possibility of a new government, spewing out his fury at the culture of greed and social indifference under a leader who traded on the fact that people stopped thinking, a government that carefully nurtured an alarmist culture. She tells him about the DNA funding by the Danish government in the Balkans and the anti-mortem data project and how sometimes when she can't get her clients talking about what happened over there she'll get a map of the country, an appropriate map for their world, and pinpoint where they last lived, where their family went missing. Sometimes they would be reluctant to talk, but when they saw the map they would point to a place and say, "There. My village," and that's how their dialogue would begin. With a sense of place.

They're outside her house and they stand there awkwardly and he's touching her face, her hair, his eyes taking in every feature, every dark circle, every crow's-foot, every frown line. "You're beautiful," he says.

And she does something she hasn't done for seven years. Georgie kisses him. Funny how they can procreate, and wrap their bodies around each other, how she can feel his mouth against her neck and breast in those quick moments of lovemaking when he knows he can get away with it, but nothing seems as intimate, nothing makes her feel more vulnerable than pressing her lips against his. She hears it in the way he whispers her name, *Georgie,* like a prayer, and she thinks of what his mother once said, that it's a miracle. These people who don't believe in miracles. Her name is whispered like a miracle and the force of his mouth hurts her, but Georgie doesn't care. They're like two kids pashing on their parents' front porch as though they've got nothing to lose when they've got absolutely everything to lose.

"Come home with me . . . please. *Please.*"

There's a new sound. The sound of Sam pleading. The sound of Sam broken.

She holds his face between her hands. She knows that Callum's mother is dropping him off soon and although she's willing to change all the rules, she's not ready for that one yet. Not with the boy sleeping in the other room.

chapter twenty-seven

To: anabelsbrother@hotmail.com
From: taramarie@yahoo.com
Date: 6 September 2007

Dear Tom,

The official crazy season of the Oz elections has well and truly reached us over here. I'm a bit torn really, because everyone's organizing get-togethers to either celebrate or commiserate, which will be heaps of fun, but rumor has it that my dad is flying me home for the Finke Family Election Party, which is usually a night when people who don't drink get blotto drunk and there's a lot of wailing and gnashing of teeth and screaming at the television set. My view is that the polls have been consistent for too long, but if I express such optimism over the phone to my father, he shuts me down. We have all been forbidden to celebrate until Kevin Rudd is delivering a victory speech. My father reckons Howard's been the perfect leader for generation Y, apolitical and shallow, and it's no wonder we worship Britney and Paris Hilton. I have to remind him that he's talking about my generation and I take great offense to such a comparison (although I wish people would lay off Britney).

Strangely enough, politics don't dominate here with us foreigners. I suppose it's because everyone's just trying to get on with their job without doing a song and dance about it. That's not to say that there aren't the cliquey NGO crowd and some of the foreign media who think they are so bolshie and down to earth. A bit nauseating really. But the majority are a truly fantastic lot and I know I will never, ever meet such a mix of people again. I even go to church because it seems to mean something here. And I go to salsa classes with a bunch of teachers and nurses when I'm in Dili, although the instructor did tell me to sit down and have a rest at one stage. Someone later described me as resembling a weapon of mass destruction on the dance floor. You know what I'm like when it comes to rhythm.

I kind of lied in that first text message. We do a lot of laughing out loud. I think of those little sullen-faced Year Sevens back in high school and here are these people who have such a great spirit and so little. This guy, we call him Gomez, looks like he swallowed a piano. Big white teeth and a smile that just goes on and on.

Anyway, I better go. Did I hear a rumor that you were thinking of going back to construction? I remember those times we'd hang out in woodwork after school and you'd wear that apron and your goggles. You looked so serious and grown-up, so meticulous with your drawing and the way you'd explain the process and I'd look at your hands and think, *Shit, they can do anything*. Like Frankie's Will. Don't you love the fact that he builds bridges? I mean, who can say that? Really?

Speak soon.

Love,

T

He remembers those words a week later when Stani has two workmen looking at the floorboards, ushering them out of the kitchen, muttering "bloody bastard" over and over again.

"Frankie's almost convinced Stani to have a live-music gig one night," Justine explains to Ned and Tom just as she's leaving for a recital.

"What band?" Tom asks absently, trying to listen to what the workmen are saying.

"Whoever registers for the night. Each band plays four songs. Two covers. Two originals."

"What about the regular band?" he asks.

"Leave them to us."

Ned looks at Tom suspiciously. "The heavenly creatures are going to kill the old-timers. You know that, don't you?"

Stani walks back in, muttering more behind the two guys, one who's scribbling in his invoice book. Francesca is trailing him.

"Stani, have you given any more—"

"No," he snaps, following the workmen into the toilet area.

"We've almost got him," she says with conviction.

He comes back into the kitchen with the quote in his hand. Tom reaches over and takes it, reading the amount.

"They've got to be joking."

Francesca looks over his shoulder at the amount and whistles. "It's a builder's market, my father says."

He thinks of Tara's e-mail. Every word she mutters or writes to him is a reminder of what he lost and what he needs to get back, somehow. But there's too much to fix up and he doesn't know how to go about doing it. He pictures himself spending the rest of his days entering data beside Mohsin the Ignorer and being a dish-pig, living with Georgie, who can't make a decision about her own future. Or his father, who could end up in Georgie's study for the rest of his life.

"Give me money for the materials and I'll lay them," he finds himself saying. "They've got great timber down on Old Lilyfield Road."

Stani reacts to Tom's suggestion in the same way he reacts to Francesca's. With total disregard.

"He came third in the state for woodwork," Francesca explains. "We actually had to be proud of him for a whole week. Tough times."

Stani is doing that thing where he thinks while staring straight at you and Tom's left almost sweating from the intensity of it.

"Tomorrow. Take the checkbook."

Ned comes along as well and they drive down in Francesca's father's ute minus Francesca, who's gone to pick up Will Trombal from the airport. At the lumberyard, they trail one of the owners who is pointing to different variations surrounding them.

"What do you reckon?" he asks Ned. "The Kauri or the Baltic?"

Ned nods like he understands what the old guy and Tom are talking about.

"Ned?"

"Were you speaking English?"

But it makes Tom feel normal and the old guy senses his interest and takes him to some brushbox he's got lying around. For building furniture.

"How much is that worth?" Tom asks, his eyes almost caressing it.

"I'll have to check," the guys say. When the sale of the floorboards is finished and they load the timber onto the ute, the old guy points back into the shed where the brushbox is, already walking away so Tom and Ned have no choice but to follow.

"You were salivating," Ned tells him.

Tom laughs. "My father's a carpenter. It's a Jesus thing. You understand?"

Ned points to himself. "Buddhist."

Inside, they stop in front of the timber again and he wants to lean down and take in its smell.

"I hear your father's back," the guy says in a neutral voice.

Tom stares at him. The resemblance must be too obvious. At the AA meetings or at the IR rallies, or anywhere he goes where his father's world exists, there's always a double take.

"Tell him Bert said hi."

"Will do," he says casually. "Let's go," he says to Ned.

"I owe your father some money for something he did for me once. Take it. Sort of quid pro quo."

"Maybe you should work that out with him," Tom says coldly.

The guy shakes his head.

"He wouldn't take it and I don't like owing."

Some other customer comes along and the guy's attention is elsewhere.

"Take it," Ned says.

Tom looks at him, shaking his head. "It's bloody expensive, you know. He's making it seem as if it's not, but it is."

"Then whatever your father did for him must have meant a lot," Ned says.

Despite the voice in his head that says he doesn't want anything that's owed to his father, Tom can't wait to get his hands on it.

"Just take it. Hit your old man over the head with it. You're dying to."

They go back to Georgie's place, lugging the timber in with them through the house and into the back. On his way in, Tom sees the mail poking out of the box and grabs it as they shuffle in.

"What's going on out here?" Georgie asks, stepping out onto the back veranda. She's just started her maternity leave and he wonders if that's going to drive them all crazy.

"Ned. Georgie," he says, pointing to one then the other as a form of introduction.

"What are you making?" she asks. Georgie never acknowledged new people until they'd been in her house a dozen times, and then they were family. With his father, the world was accepted at a hello.

"Something special. For the baby Jesus."

She looks confused for a moment and then he sees it register on her face and she covers her mouth and walks inside.

"You've made her cry," Ned says quietly.

"She cried during the elimination rounds of *Idol* the other night," Tom informs him. "Anything can set her off."

He goes to call out to her because he remembers the mail, but stops when he sees his mother's handwriting. A letter addressed to Dominic Mackee. He's never been home in time to get the mail. He wonders if Anabel was right and his parents are writing to each other or whether this letter is a one-off. Instead of putting it in his father's room or in the kitchen, he keeps it with him. He wants to read his father's reaction.

He sits in the backyard with Ned for the rest of the afternoon, for the most part talking films and music. And then somehow it gets back to Joe.

"You can know someone all your life, like your parents or family, but I'll tell you this, Ned. There's an expression on their face, or a tone in their voice, or a way they walk, that you've never ever seen before. Like they've kept it hidden. Until their brother dies. Or their son. I remember those days and they were like these strangers and I wanted to say, *Who are you people?*"

Ned's not an interrupter. He doesn't offer anything. He just sits and waits.

"And I hated everyone. Every single person in the world. Bush. The Muslims. The Pakis. Blair. Howard. The Israelis. The press. Frankie. Justine. Tara. Siobhan. Jimmy. My parents. Joe. *Bloody Joe.*" He swallows hard. "There were jobs here," he says, trying to keep the anguish out of his voice. "Why go there to teach?"

He doesn't want to break down in front of Ned for the second time in a fortnight, so he stops for a moment.

"And the press were all over us. Every racist in the world came to the surface wanting to use us for their own shit reasons. And others would say, 'Well, you know, those people would have been oppressed by the West, and they would have had a reason.' What reason? What fucking reason is there to fill your backpack with explosives and blow yourself up with a bunch of people who just wanted to go to work that morning?

"And then you just get tired from it all. You go dead, you know, and you don't hate anyone because you don't feel anything. Ah, the joys of mind-numbing drugs."

He looks at Ned and laughs. "Sorry. A bit heavy."

"They used to talk about you a lot," Ned says. "Frankie said you had all waited forever to meet each other and that it was the real thing as friendships went. 'He'll come back to us,' she'd say. I heard every

253

story in the world about every moment you all had and I remember once you came in and they pointed you out. 'That's him. That's *our* Thomas.' I was like, *What the?* No offense, but you didn't really rate as a person when you were hanging out with Sarah or What's-His-Face. And Tara was there, at Easter, and she looked really cut to see you and that's how I heard about the *one-and-a-half-night stand.*"

Tom stares at him, stunned, even going as far as ignoring the whisper of the phrase. "Tara was there once at the Union while I was?"

Ned nods. "You were pretty wasted."

The back door opens behind them and they turn to see his father standing there. His eyes go straight to the timber and he walks over, sliding his fingers over it.

"Ned," Tom mutters. "Dominic."

His father sighs and holds out a hand. "His father," he explains.

"His boss," Ned replies, shaking Dominic's hand.

Tom gives a snort.

"Do you need all of this?" his father asks.

Tom doesn't respond.

"Ernie from the lumberyard said you had to share it," Ned says, feigning innocence, the cheeky bastard.

His father looks confused.

"Bert," Tom corrects, sending Ned a dirty look.

He sees his father's eyes flicker to the bunch of envelopes lying on the lawn.

"Forgot to give Georgie her mail," Tom says, shuffling them together and handing them up. His father takes the bundle and without flicking through them, he picks out Tom's mother's letter and stuffs it in his back pocket. It's as if he would have known her stationery in his dreams.

Francesca insists on meeting them for lunch with Will the next day and they end up in a Vietnamese café in Marrickville. Trombal doesn't make much eye contact and gives Ned a run for his money in the introverted stakes. Francesca has that intense, manic "I want everyone to love each other" look on her face, so Tom's relieved when the menus come and they can all study them without speaking.

"I'm going to go the beef salad," Francesca says.

"It's got coriander," Will says.

"Then I'll go the shitake stir-fry." She looks up at Tom. "Will's coming down to the pub tonight. You can keep each other company, seeing you're not rostered on."

Tom and Will make eye contact finally and the lack of ecstasy in both their stares conveys their feelings about the prospect.

"I . . . have something on," Tom says.

"*You?*" Francesca asks, screwing up her face in disbelief.

He's going to spend the next five days hating her.

After they order, he decides to put some effort into the conversation.

"Tara tells me you've caught up once or twice," he says politely to Trombal.

"Yeah, we did."

Tom would like to explain the rules of dialogue etiquette. One asks a question, the other keeps the conversation going.

"She was homesick, I hear."

Trombal stares him straight in the face.

"No. Her boyfriend was on the other side of the island for a couple of weeks. She was missing him. Thank God the engineers cheered her up."

A declaration of war.

"So do you have anything romantic planned while you're out here?" Ned asks Will when Francesca goes to the ladies'. "She'll like that."

Will Trombal gives Ned a look that says he doesn't appreciate being told what his girlfriend will like.

"Just stuff," he mutters.

Tom decides to step in with some good advice, especially after Francesca's discussion with him about Will not being a romantic.

"Listen, Will. I'd recommend dinner, flowers, and room service for breakfast."

Ned makes a scoffing sound. "Oh, the expert. The way I hear it you don't wait around for breakfast, Tom. So what would you know?"

Ned says, "Listen to me, Will. Frankie's the type of girl who looks good in stuff. Like undies or something. Buy her undies."

Now Tom makes the scoffing sound. "Yeah, the expert on what women look good in," he says. "It's lingerie, dickhead. Not undies."

Will is looking uncomfortable. He's searching over people's heads for Francesca.

"I've got things planned," he tells them in a flat tone.

"Will, you're not exactly Mr. Valentine's Day," Tom says.

"You're going to screw this up," Ned agrees.

Will sighs. He seems a bit doubtful now and looks at both of them.

"Okay," he says, as if he's going to try the idea out on them. "When I came back from overseas five years ago, her father wouldn't let me drive her anywhere. We had to take public transport. Buses, mostly. Bus from Annandale to the city. Bus from Annandale to Central and then the train to Kingsgrove. Bus from Annandale to Concord."

Tom's already shaking his head. Ned has no idea where it's going.

"So I was thinking that I'd try to be romantic . . . you know . . . take her to all the bus benches . . . where we pashed . . . and stuff."

Tom stares at him. Ned even looks impressed just as Francesca returns to them.

"What have you guys been talking about?" she asks.

"Oh, you know," Tom says. "We just gave Will a great idea on how to be romantic."

That night Francesca is back and forth between the bar and their table. She's too hyper. She's a meltdown waiting to happen, already counting down the moments from now to when Trombal leaves.

"He's seen you onstage a thousand times," Tom says, remembering that Trombal was at every single gig they played during their first year at uni.

"But he hasn't heard me play guitar," she says, leaning across the table to show Trombal the list. "Choose any one of them."

"Whatever you want to play, Frankie," Trombal says.

They're looking at each other in a way that suggests that stuff is happening on dimensions Tom has no entry into. Trombal leans over and kisses her. "You choose."

"When you do that so close to people's faces, can you refrain from using tongue contact?" Tom mutters.

Stani taps Francesca on the shoulder and points to the crowd at the counter and she leaves reluctantly.

"So . . . it must get a bit wild over there," Tom says, for no other reason than there is nothing else to say.

Will's attention is focused on the bar, where Francesca's serving and chatting with some locals.

"So, have you been to any of the strip joints? I hear that's what you guys get up to," Tom asks.

This time Will looks at him. There's a whole lot of muscle twitching and holding back. He could not have picked someone more different in Francesca.

"I hang out with engineers," Will says quietly. "What do you think?"

Delivered without a trace of sarcasm. Neutral. Tonight Tom's going to break Will Trombal.

"Does Frankie know about it?"

Tom's tone shows insidious intent.

"We're open with each other."

"Why? Because you get off on telling her about it?"

Will wants out, Tom can tell. Some guy at the bar is chatting up Francesca and he can tell that Trombal's not liking it.

"Tom," he says patiently, "remember that time when you were in Year Seven and I was in Year Eight and your mates decided they would flush my head down the toilet because I was a midget? It ended in tears. Mine, because there's nothing more degrading than having your head down a toilet bowl, and yours, because I don't think you were equipped to embrace the dark side. Tonight will end in tears."

"Mine or yours?" Tom says.

Francesca plonks herself down again. She's giddy beyond sanity. Tom wants her back in normal mode, organizing the troops and listening to the bad news. He wants to remind her that Trombal will be gone in five days. With her younger brother. One more person to worry about. But Trombal is still looking at him. With the answer to his question in his eyes.

Francesca notices the look and there's a bit of panic in her expression.

"What's wrong with you guys?"

Will shakes his head. "Nothing."

"You aren't fighting, are you?"

Will shakes his head again. "We were just talking about football."

"Are you coming Sunday, Tom?" she asks. "Both your teams are playing each other at Leichhardt oval."

Will is eyeing him. There's a *don't even think about it* look on his face.

"I'd love to," Tom says.

They have a drink with Stani and Ned after Stani closes up and they've played Trombal a number in the back room.

"The guitar is a turn-on," Tom hears Will say quietly when they jump off the stage after playing one of their originals.

"Thanks, Will," Tom says.

"But I like your voice best," Will says, ignoring Tom, "and you didn't need anything more than that."

Tom wants to stress to Will that when one is paying their girl-friend a compliment, one should put expression in the voice. It can be useful.

Francesca takes Will's hand and plays with it.

"It was just that stupid guitarist, remember? In the band Justine and I were in when Tom split. And he'd say I was nothing but a good voice—"

"And that you looked sexy in a sundress," Tom says.

"I didn't say sexy," she says, irritated. "Anyway, he'd make us play numbers where there'd be five minutes of him dueling with Justine and all I got to do was twirl my skirt, like June Carter."

"Beautiful woman, June Carter," Stani says.

"Remember how he used to stand up real close to me in the middle of a number?" Justine shudders. "And he had the worst breath and when I told him I wasn't interested, he was . . . just a . . ."

Francesca looks at Will. "What was he, babe?"

Will explains to Tom and Stani and Ned what the guy was, using one syllable.

Tom looks at him with disbelief. "You swear for her? Doesn't that make you feel cheap?"

"He said we were hard work," Justine explains.

"Who?" Tom asks.

"The post-you guitarist," she says.

"If you're comfortable being hard work, so be it," Will says.

Francesca looks at him. "So you think we are hard work?"

Will's shaking his head. "Is this one of those 'Does my bum look big in this' moments?"

"So now you're saying she's got a big bum and is hard work?" Tom asks.

He's watching Will carefully because Wonder Boy is just about to walk into dangerous territory and Tom's loving it.

"It's that you come with . . ."

"Baggage?" Francesca asks.

"Accessories," Will corrects her. "A whole lot of them. And *they* are hard work."

"What he's trying to say is that not everything has to be . . . solved . . . fixed . . . proven?" Tom says.

"Not what I was trying to say at all," Will says coldly.

"It's what they used to do in high school," Tom continues, looking at Ned and Stani. "'Let's try to fix this and fix that' and 'Why can't we do this and that?' rather than just enjoying what was around them."

"Enjoying?" she says with disbelief. "What? The sexism? The lack of choices?"

"Eva Rodriguez never complained once," Tom argues. "Never. I was in homeroom with her in Year Twelve. Never once did she complain. 'I'm in,' she'd say. 'Sound's great.' 'Why not?' 'Hell, yeah.' 'Let's do it.' 'Yeah, baby!'"

"He's got a bit of a point there," Will says. "She was very popular with my year when you girls first arrived."

Tom's relieved that Francesca's attention has shifted away from him.

"Don't give me that look, Frankie," Will says. "You know my tongue was hanging out the moment you walked into that school."

"I know Eva," Francesca says, ignoring the compliment. "Great girl. Smart as, and I can assure you, she has her boyfriend under her boot heels. The pointy ones. I could imagine the conversation. One year in Indonesia to work on a bridge with a bunch of guys? 'Oh, sure, off you go, babe,' I could imagine Eva saying. 'Have fun. Yeah, baby.'"

"She'd stop him from working overseas?" Tom asks.

"Maybe, and if she couldn't, she wouldn't be sticking around."

"So why do you stick around?" Will asks.

"Because I'm not frightened of hard work, Will," Francesca says.

"Did I say I was?" he asks.

Tom thinks this is a good time to step in.

261

"I have to be honest, I can understand Eva not wanting her boyfriend to work overseas," Tom says. "Guys get carried away, regardless of whether they have girlfriends or not."

"Guys only?" Francesca asks. "What about that chick you slept with who had a boyfriend?"

"I told you that in privacy," he mutters, pissed off. "Anyway, it doesn't mean she loves her boyfriend less," he adds. "If you slept with someone else, would it mean you love Frankie less, Will? Like, if you picked up at one of those strip joints you go to over there?"

"Thomas," Justine warns.

"It's okay," Tom says. "Will and Frankie have an open relationship—"

"We do *not* have an open relationship," Francesca says, furious.

"I meant I tell her everything," Will says, teeth almost clenched.

"What I'm saying—" Tom begins.

"Garbage," Stani says, looking at him. "It needs to be taken out."

"It's not—"

"*Now.*"

While he's outside, banished to Garbage Land, he smokes a cigarette, vowing it's the last time he's going to indulge in hypotheticals with his new forced friend, Will. But a part of him feels guilty and he figures that he'll do the right thing and help him out. Maybe give him advice on how to deal with an impending fight with Francesca. With only five days together, his best advice would be to pretend the conversation never happened. There's nothing worse than Francesca wanting to "talk" or "flesh out" the core of the problem.

He walks in and makes it as far as the bathroom, but steps back instantly behind the piled-up boxes of toilet paper, serviettes, and straws. Beyond the boxes, in the kitchen, Francesca sits on the bench. Opposite her, with a lot of space between them, and a lot of silence, Will leans on the preparation bench.

"What do you always say about me?" Tom hears him ask.

She's not answering.

"Frankie?"

"That you use calculus to work out whether we should be together or not," she says.

"I mean when you're trying to compliment me."

She hasn't looked up yet and Trombal waits.

"That you're the smartest guy I know," she says finally in a flat voice.

"Which kind of means less to me these days when I think of the guys you hang out with," Will says.

Bastard.

"Why would the smartest guy you know do something stupid and lose you?" he asks.

She sighs. "Because smart guys have two brains, Will. One in their head and one in their pants."

"Yeah, well both my brains are connected and one is always reminding the other of you."

Francesca doesn't react and even Tom wants her to talk. Or workshop. Or be Francesca in overload. Even he's stressed by her silence.

"I thought we weren't going to drive each other crazy with this type of stuff, Frankie," Will says, frustrated.

"We aren't," she blurts out. "But it's just been the longest year and most of the time I just think of something terrible happening to you over there, Will. But sometimes . . . when you're speaking strip joints with Tom . . . what was that? Bonding?"

"Yeah, like I'd really bond with that *dick*. Hasn't anyone explained to him that there's a big difference between Sumatra and Bangkok?"

"And I'd appreciate if you changed your attitude about my friends."

"I don't have a problem with your friends, except for one. Fuck, how do you think I feel, Frankie? You're either up there onstage with him or in a room with other guys ogling you. You think that doesn't go through my mind when I'm over there? That you might act on the chemistry you have with people who have everything in common with you in the way that I don't? Like Mackee. How can I compete with that? While guys I'm working with are telling me their girlfriends back home are screwing around behind their backs?"

"Okay," she says, determined. "Let's go back to the part where we aren't going to drive each other crazy with this type of stuff."

Tom can see that Will's still fired up.

"Come here," she says.

"No, you come here."

"I said it first."

"Rock paper scissors."

"No. Because you'll do nerdy calculations and work out what I chose the last six times and then you'll win."

Will pushes away from the table and his hand snakes out and he pulls her toward him and Tom figures that Will was always going to go to her first. And here he is. Stuck behind boxes of toilet paper, where he's going to have to sneak back outside and make a song and dance about walking in. Or he can go into the bathroom and flush the toilet and let them know he's there. Especially if he sees skin. It's pervy if he sees skin, although he can see skin now because Will's hand goes up her skirt and it's bunched up around her thighs. So Tom makes the decision to look away the moment, the *very moment*, he sees anything more than that. The moment he sees a glimpse of underwear, he will be officially in Sicko Land and he will be forced to make some kind of noise. Flushing, coughing, heavy footsteps. Talk to himself out loud. The moment he sees anything that in anyway will be considered a sexual act between . . .

"*Stani, the bins are done!*" he yells out.

"What was all that yelling about? *The bins are done. The bins are done,*" Ned says as Stani locks up. The others are already halfway up the street.

Tom doesn't respond. He's over the Frankie-and-Will show and it's only day one.

"Were they making out in our kitchen?" Ned hisses.

"Yes," Tom said with gritted teeth. The kitchen he keeps spotless. Now he's really angry.

Francesca, Will, and Justine stop at the lights.

"We're going down to the Hopetoun to see the Jezebels," Francesca calls out. "Are you guys coming?"

"No," they both snap at the same time.

chapter twenty-eight

He doesn't quite promise Francesca that he'll be kind and hospitable to Will Trombal, but he's already committed to going to the football match with them. Another reason to hate Trombal is for his choice of football teams. The Dragons are an aberration to anyone Tom has ever known, and sitting next to a supporter almost makes him feel like speaking to his father. His father and Tom still do football. Just like they do the AA meetings together. Just like they work in silence in Georgie's backyard on the cradle Tom's making and the rocking chair his father's restoring.

The irony of Francesca coming to a game she has no interest in is that she knows half the people here and spends the whole time socializing instead of getting to know the rules. Tom tries to explain them to her at one stage, but both Francesca and Trombal stare at him, the latter with hostility.

"Don't even try," Francesca says. "Not interested. Only here because my beloved is leaving tomorrow and this is the best I can get. Baby, this is settling."

She's enjoying herself at Trombal's expense, but it's at Tom that Trombal is directing his hostility.

When she waves at yet another person and jumps out of her seat to say, *"Oh, my God, what are you doing here?"* he feels Trombal's intense stare again.

"What makes you think I haven't tried explaining the rules to her?" Will says.

Trombal has already had a whinge about Leichhardt Oval and what a dump it is and how it doesn't have a screen or even a proper scoreboard. Tom resorts to drinking through the first half, relieved when it's his shout again.

"Do you want a beer?" he asks his father out of instinct, wanting to tear out his tongue the moment he finishes speaking.

"I'd love one, but might just have a Coke instead," his father says, not missing a beat.

And Tom actually thinks his father is having fun at his expense. *Join the Trombal club, Dominic.*

He makes his way to the kiosk bar, where Francesca is finishing up a conversation with a girl in a Tigers jersey.

"I'm making her wedding dress," she says as if Tom is interested.

"Wonderful," he says.

"Thomas, talk to Will," she says. "Just about life and the stuff you won't talk to us about. He is the best listener in the world." When she says the word *best*, she shakes her head and grimaces with emphasis. "You need to get things off your chest and I reckon talking to him would be so helpful."

While she's speaking, he's staring at the line in front of him. He can't believe it. Mohsin the Ignorer is here. Tom waves Francesca away and stands behind him in the line, drilling holes in his head with his eyes and it's as if Mohsin the Ignorer feels the impact because he turns around.

For a moment there is a look of surprise on his face and almost a smile and hello, but Tom's not interested and looks the other way. But after a moment it really begins to get to him and it's the beers he's consumed and having had to sit next to Will Trombal and his father that pushes him over the edge. He leans forward and taps Mohsin on the shoulder.

"You're a rude bastard," he says.

"I'm sorry?"

"Too late to be sorry, *my friend*. But just some advice. Next time someone wants to make your life a little bit easier and befriend you, try actually responding to their hello or to the questions they ask."

The bartender calls out a *"Next"* and Mohsin has no choice but to be served. As he walks away with his drink and hot dog, he looks at Tom as if he's a lunatic.

Back in the stands, Francesca is still speaking to the whole of Leichhardt and Tom is stuck with Trombal and his dad again. Worse still, the Tigers are getting slaughtered.

"You know I'm not interested in her."

It's the type of confession you make at the footy after a plethora of beers and your team is losing. Will Trombal does *not* want to talk to him and gives him a look that says he *especially* doesn't want to talk to him about Francesca.

"I just get the sense that you think I'm going to poach her," Tom continues.

"Like an egg?" Will asks.

"No. Like taking something you want that belongs to someone else."

There is a part of him that's buzzing with excitement because

Trombal has a fist clenched and all this emotion bunched on his face. Best-case scenario, Tom suspects, is a punch-up with this prick.

"But as I said, I don't want to do that."

He's been hanging out with Francesca for too long and her need to explain every statement has caught on.

"It's just that sometimes I want to cuddle up against her and just let her take over, you know. So she can look after everything around me, but when I picture it, I'm never the one doing the holding. It's always her."

This time Trombal does react. *"Fuck. Off,"* he says in a pissed-off, flat tone.

"That didn't come out right. It's the same with Justine. Those chicks are such huggers and every time their arms are out, I'm there."

He leans closer to Trombal because he doesn't want his father or anyone to hear.

"But when I think of Tara, I'm doing the holding. I'm in charge. I'm the he-man. Alpha man. I'm beating my chest. My arms are out and she's there."

Something different registers on Will Trombal's face. Disbelief.

"Tara? *Tara Finke?*" he says. "Dude, you broke her heart."

"Is that what you and Frankie talk about when you're together?" Tom snaps.

Another sound of disbelief. "Frankie and I have better things to do when we're together."

Trombal looks satisfied. Tom doesn't know whether it's because the smart-arse is thinking about what he gets up to with Francesca or because the Dragons have possession of the ball. But then he's looking at Tom again. "Tara told me. When I was in Timor. Her

269

exact words were, 'He broke my heart and I'm not letting him anywhere near it again, Will.' "

Hearing those words, Tom's own heart feels like it's disappeared in a puff of smoke. "Well, that's that, then," he mutters.

Will makes a sound. A hmphing sound. Plus he's shaking his head.

"What?" Tom asks. Behind them, someone's yelling hoarsely and thumping Tom's seat.

"Nothing. It's nothing," Will says, shouting above the noise. "You and I? We're just different."

"How different?" Tom is desperate for anything. Even from Will Trombal. "What would you do?"

Will goes back to the game, but even when the Dragons score, he doesn't react. After a couple of moments, he turns back to Tom.

"If I did something to hurt Frankie and she said that I was never getting near her heart again, I'd spent the rest of my life trying anyway. *That's* the difference between you and me, Tom. I'd go back to the moment it all fell apart and I'd start there."

The one-and-a-half-night stand.

"You know why?" Trombal's on a roll. He's not shutting up. "Because women are elephants and watch the way you say that in front of them because they'll think you're calling them fat and there's no coming back from that moment. But they hoard. They say they don't, but they do. We think that if something's not spoken about again, it goes away. It doesn't. Nothing goes away just like that, Mackee."

Francesca comes back and sits between them, an arm over each shoulder, pushing Tom against his father.

"Missed me?"

Will Trombal doesn't respond. Tom figures he's not into cutesy conversation.

Francesca shivers from the cold and Will takes her hand and tucks it in his jacket pocket and for a moment Tom feels an ache of loneliness for whatever these two have that works for them. He wants to sigh, but he holds back.

Beside him, he hears his father sigh instead.

To: anabelsbrother@hotmail.com
From: taramarie@yahoo.com
Date: 17 September 2007

Dear Tom,
What's with this Mohsin the Ignorer? I think you're getting obsessed. Just go up and ask him what his beef is. Knowing you, you've done something to piss him off and it needs to be resolved rather than crapping on incessantly about how he ignores you or how dare he be a Tigers fan and not respond to you? Who died and made you king of the world? I see it here, you know. If someone doesn't respond to our Aussie mateship, they're the world's worst. How imperialistic is that?

Fix this Tom, and without being a bully either. Ask him to a football match or invite him to the pub. Despite your denial, deep down you'd like to be friends with this guy. So just do it.
Tara

To: taramarie@yahoo.com
From: anabelsbrother@hotmail.com
Date: 17 September 2007

271

Dear Tara,

You're acting as if I have a crush on Mohsin. I'm not going to ask him to a football match!

P.S. Are you going to be a traitor to your country and go for the Brazilians in the World Cup when the time comes?

P.P.S. I don't like the BatangChe font. It makes me feel as if my parents are getting a letter from one of the teachers for not handing in an assessment.

chapter twenty-nine

Georgie and Sam walk home mostly in silence, which is not as common these days, so she knows something's wrong. It's late and they've been out for coffee and *cannoli* in Norton Street and Callum is already asleep in his arms.

"What is it?" she asks.

"What makes you think there's something?"

"Because I know you."

Because she knows him. That belongs to the language of intimacy, not strangers. He looks at her and it's like each time he does it these days, she can't help thinking, *How did I love this man again?*

"Leonie's interested in joint custody," he says, his voice tired. "A week each."

She can't speak for a moment because she doesn't know what it will mean to them.

"How did you answer?"

They stop at the Parramatta Road lights and she thinks of their walk down here earlier, where she imagined the next time they'd be doing this pushing a pram.

"I didn't say anything," he says as they cross. "But if you and I don't have a future together living under the same roof with this baby, I'm going to agree. I can easily arrange to get home by four every afternoon those weeks. Then when the time is right, you and I work out the custody arrangements for our baby. I'll want the same thing. To keep them together on those alternate weeks."

Her stomach churns. "Is that what you want?" she asks.

"No, Georgie," he says. "It's what I'll settle for."

"And if we live under the same roof with this baby?"

And still the bitterness is there on his face. She can see it, or feel it. In this half-lit street close to home. Is it directed at her, or the universe, or himself?

"Then I won't go for joint custody and on the weekends I get Callum, I'll go to my mother's."

Someone beeps the horn and they both wave automatically to God knows who.

"So the ball's in my court?"

"The ball is always going to be in your court, Georgie. Always."

It's like *Sophie's Choice* for him, she thinks. Without Auschwitz and death. But all the same it's about choosing between children or choosing her over Callum, and that makes her feel evil. She's the Nazi.

"Is this because of the boyfriend? Because she wants more time with him?"

"Maybe. Or maybe because I ask for this every year and she's finally giving in."

"Because it suits her," she says sharply.

"Regardless, Georgie, it suits me too. Personally and financially. Look," he sighs, shifting to get comfortable with Callum. "I don't want this to be hard work. Let's talk about it another time."

She thinks of a conversation she had with Tom last night about girls and hard work. They had argued about the terminology.

"Am I hard work?" she asks quietly.

"Yes."

Silence for a moment.

"You could have hesitated in answering that."

"Why? I've never lied to you before," he says. "You do that all the time, you know. You ask me questions when you know the answer will piss you off. Ask me a question where the answer could be yes? Ask me if you're worth the hard work? Ask me if in the last seven years of my life I've woken up in a cold sweat knowing I lost the most important person in my life apart from this kid I'm holding? Ask me if getting you pregnant has felt like the best thing that's happened to me since my son was born?"

She's stunned by the emotion.

"Fuck, Georgie, what do you want me to say? That I regret what happened back then? Look at me," he says, the kid's arms around his neck, his head on his father's shoulder. "I can't do that. That's my punishment. Not being able to give you a complete 'I regret every single thing that happened back then.' This isn't just about you and me." He struggles to grab something out of his back pocket. His wallet. He manages to get it open.

"See this," he says. It's the photo Tom took that time in her backyard when Callum was listening out for the baby against her belly. "It's all there, Georgie. Everything I want in the world is all there."

They're both shaky from the moment and begin walking again.

"Am I worth the hard w—?"

"Yes," he says before she finishes. "*Yes.*"

When they reach her house, she looks up at him. "Why don't you stay the night?"

"With Callum?"

"No, we'll leave him out on the lawn, Sam."

He laughs for a moment. "I can't. Not tonight. If he wakes up in a strange room, he'll panic."

He bends to kiss her, but it's awkward with Callum in his arms.

"But promise you'll ask me again if he's ever awake enough to know where he is."

chapter thirty

Tom's favorite errand for Francesca is driving Will and Luca to the airport, all three squeezed in the front of the Spinelli family ute. Nothing more satisfying than the idea of putting Trombal on a plane that's leaving the country.

Luca Spinelli is pumped and trying to get into his duty-free bag without breaking the seal. Will's subdued.

"Why didn't you just let her come along and get emotional rather than trying to control it?" he asks, because all of a sudden he's the Francesca-and-Will relationship analyst.

No response.

"She could have dropped you both off. What's the worse she can do? Cry hysterically?"

The truck's gears get stuck at the lights, and Will pushes Tom's hand out of the way and shoves it into the correct gear.

"It wasn't her," he mutters after a moment.

"Sorry?" Tom says.

"She didn't cry."

"Then what?"

It's too quiet except for the crap engine sounding like a lawn mower.

"I cried."

Luca bursts out laughing beside Will.

"Yeah, well, I did," Will says. "And it's not the thing you want to do in front of a bunch of engineers. Now my nickname is Will the Crier. We'll be playing footy over there and someone will say, 'Throw it to Will the Crier.' They've actually cut it down to just 'the crier.' Or they used to do this," he says, squeezing two fists over his eyes, "every time they walked past me."

Tom can't help laughing, but only because Will's laughing as well.

"I can't believe you told us that, Will," Luca Spinelli says. "We can blackmail you."

"'Course you can, mate," Will says innocently. "Just like I can tell anyone, maybe even Tom here, the name of the girl you have a crush on."

Luca stops laughing. "I can't believe Frankie told you."

Tom shoves Will back so he can stare across at Luca, but the kid won't meet his eye.

He stops at the drop-off outside the departure area and they get out of the car, dragging out Luca's luggage and complaining about all the stuff his grandmother has packed to send over to relatives.

"Thanks," Will mutters.

"We owe you," Luca Spinelli says, still not looking at him directly.

"No worries. Although Frankie said I might be able to see the *Willy loves Frankie* tattoo if I ask nicely."

"Just say it's on my arse and I tell you to kiss it while you're down there," Will says.

"Show it to him," Luca urges. "It's awesome."

Will hates attention. It's there in his fidgeting face, but he pulls up his sleeve, revealing his arm. The tat is massive and a bit on the spectacular side with not a cliché in sight. Tom refuses to let his respect for it show.

"I don't get it," he says. "I thought it was a Frankie tattoo."

And then he becomes audience to one of those moments when Will Trombal smiles as he looks down at it.

"They mate for life, you know," he says.

"Are you alone?"

He always asks her that. Only once or twice has she told him she "can't talk just now." He never questions whether it's about work or the peacekeeper because he dreads the answer, and today she makes it worse because he can only hear silence on the other side for what seems like forever.

"We're not together anymore," she says. "He reckons my heart wasn't in it."

Tom thinks he hears a choir of *Alleluia* in his head. He wants to skin the guy for even demanding that Tara give her heart to him when it belongs to Tom. He wants to run up and down the stairs to the *Rocky* theme except he's naked and it'll scare Georgie if she comes out of her room. He wants to take a plane to Albury and thank everyone in Nanni Grace's novena club.

But he stays calm. "Hmm. What are you doing?"

"Painting my toenails. You?"

"Clipping mine."

"Listening to?"

" 'Your Ex-Lover Is Dead.' '*When there's nothing left to burn, you have set yourself on fire.*' "

"Very dramatic."

279

"You?"

"Ani DiFranco. '32 Flavors.' "

"Don't know it. Sing."

"No, no, no, no. My voice is shit."

"Nah. Go on."

"Are you sure?"

"Sure, sure."

" '*I'm a poster girl with no poster . . .*' "

"Stop!"

" '*I'm beyond your peripheral vision . . .*' "

"I'm begging you. *Stop* or I'm hanging up, Finke."

"I feel ugly in monsoon season and I need cheering up and you're making me feel like crap," she says, laughing.

"You're just begging me for a compliment."

"And I haven't had a good haircut for a while or my eyebrows waxed, and a facial would be great."

"Send me a photo. Take one with your phone and send it, and I'll tell you the honest truth."

"Okay, but I'll have to hang up so you ring back when you get it."

A minute later the photo comes through and he laughs before ringing.

"I'm calling you Finkenstein, daughter of Frankenstein."

All he hears for a while is laughing.

"Prick."

"I'm just calling it the way it is, baby."

"Send me one of you."

They both hang up and he quickly takes the photo and sends it. She rings back.

"You, on the other hand, take my breath away. I will sleep tonight with it clutched to my breast."

Silence.

"Tom?"

"Sorry. The words *clutching* and *breasts* will render me useless for the next forty-eight hours."

"Then I'm sure you'll be able to find someone's breasts out there to clutch."

"Not interested in anyone else's."

Silence.

"What are you thinking?"

"You don't want to know."

Silence again.

"What are you doing?" she asks.

"You don't want to know."

"Yes, I do."

"Then if you do, I think you already know."

"I've got to go."

"Same."

"Tom?"

He can't breathe.

"Yeah."

"Nothing." She hangs up.

Other times he talks to her for ages, comforted by her *Hmm*s and *Go on*s and by the sound of her breathing.

"This one time," he tells her, "I was thirteen years old and the stand-off at the wharf was happening and I remember my dad came home and told Mum he was going down there because it wasn't just about the wharfies' union anymore. It was about every worker in the country. Anyway, Mum said there was no way she wasn't going if he was and she started ringing around to see if someone would babysit, but every person she spoke to said, 'If Dom's going, we'll go too.' So they took Anabel and me with them. My grandmother Agnes still goes on about how they put our lives at risk. There had been pretty wild scenes down there and some of the workers had been camped on the docks for weeks and weeks. Sometimes their kids were with them.

"So there we were down at the waterfront and it was packed with people that night and honest to God, Tara, some of them were the most feral I'll ever see. Riled up beyond anything. Thousands. There'd been a massive call around to all the unions to come down and support the wharfies, so hundreds of cops were lined up facing this angry mob, and I heard my mum say, 'Shit, those poor bastards,' because some of those cops were so young and they looked scared.

"I was shaking like crazy and I remember my father took my hand and asked me if I was scared. But I lied and told him I wasn't and he just looked at me and said, 'Well, I am, so you're going to have to hold my hand tight.' I looked around and we were all there. Apart from my grandparents, everyone I loved in the world was there. My uncle Joe with his union's banner, because he was the rep at the school he worked at, and Sam and Georgie, and my mum and dad and heaps of their friends. Everyone around us was shouting, 'The workers united will never be defeated!' and I honestly thought they were saying, 'The Mackees united will never be defeated!' I thought the chant was just for us. That nothing could break us. I felt in tune with every person around me for the first time in my life. And the only time I've ever felt that again is when I'm watching a great live band. Or when I started hanging out with you and the girls and Jimmy Hailler."

He can hear that Tara's crying.

"It's not that sad a story, Finke," he says gently.

"I was there," she whispers.

She'd been there. On that waterfront. With parents like hers, how could she not?

Maybe she'd always been there. Maybe strangers enter your heart first and then you spent the rest of your life searching for them.

He doesn't say anything at all after that and nor does she. But they stay on the line.

And there goes another week's wage, but he doesn't care.

chapter thirty-one

When the phone rings, it's five p.m. and Georgie knows. It's about the timing. Grace and Jacinta always ring at night, and Lucia would never ring during family peak-hour. It continues to ring and she eliminates Sam, because they've never indulged in daily phone calls, and the office has no need to contact her now that she's on leave. Plus Tom belongs to a generation that has no idea how to memorize landline numbers. He usually rings her mobile. So she knows. Dominic does too and she lets him answer, because he's been waiting all his life for this one phone call and is better prepared. She thinks of the way they rehearsed this, from the moment they lay in their beds as children. But back then, they truly believed Tom Finch would come home alive. In their shared dream, he'd walk down the corridor of their home in Petersham and he'd catch them both in his arms and tell them that the memory of holding his twins kept him alive. But it was Bill they woke to each morning. Bill, who they'd convinced each other was the reason Tom Finch couldn't return. Bill, whose expression they had interpreted as cold and bitter in those early years. When all that time it was just grief.

• • •

They both stand lost for a while, in the hallway of her house, neither having a single clue what to do. Until Dominic calls Jacinta Louise and she tells them to ring Bill and Grace and Auntie Margie Finch. But then Jacinta changes her mind and says that Bill probably should tell Auntie Margie and that she'll ring the Queensland mob and that perhaps Georgie should tell Tom, while Dom rings someone from Tom Finch's regiment. Georgie likes having that kind of purpose and when she speaks to her nephew, he's calm and quite contained. "Come down to the pub," he tells her. "Bring my father."

It's packed when they get down to the Union later that night. Uni's winding down for the year and the younger crowd is around. She sees Tom over everyone's head and he waves, and then he's there, hugging her.

"Follow," he says to them, and although he doesn't hug his father, she notices that as he leads them someplace, Tom has a hand at the back of Dominic's shoulder and it stays there the whole while. They reach a large table. "You," she hears him say to a group of kids his age sitting there. "She's pregnant and they're old. Get up, you pricks."

Dominic mutters something about *the little shit* and squeezes in next to her, and Sam and then Lucia and Abe and Jonesy arrive, and she bursts into tears the moment she sees them.

"It's fine. She's okay," Lucia says forcefully the moment Sam suggests they go home.

Georgie wonders if one of them should say something. To make a toast to Tom Finch, but she knows that none of their friends would dare because that was always Dominic's thing. For a moment she catches her brother's eyes and it's as if he's reading her mind, but he shakes his head.

"When are your parents coming down again?" Abe asks.

"Next week," she says quietly. "Grace wants to be here in case the baby comes early."

"How are they?"

She shrugs. "They're with friends and Auntie Margie Finch is driving down so they'll be together. She was pretty emotional."

Because Auntie Margie Finch would never forget her little brother, Tom Finch. "Wives can replace their husbands, Georgie," her aunt once told her. "But sisters can't replace their brothers."

"And when does he . . . get returned?" Jonesy asks, on his best behavior without a mobile in his hand.

"They say it could be anywhere between two to four weeks," Dominic says. "There's a lot of ID rigmarole."

Then some of the vets arrive. Word has got round quick and they've come from as far away as the mountains. They had always frightened Georgie as a child, with their wounded eyes and trembling hands. Although they're of the same generation as Bill and Grace, they look as if they've lived one thousand years more. These fragile men, the last to ever see her father, are so emotional as they squeeze in with them. They want to tell their story of the day they had to move on and leave one of their own behind. Then it gets a bit quiet and she looks up to where Tom is standing on the counter.

"I want to make a toast," he says, his voice so strong, so powerful. There's still a bit of noise and next minute Francesca Spinelli is on the counter next to him. *Shut up,* she yells.

Then there's silence. Francesca is watching everyone like a hawk and Tom is looking over everyone's head, at Georgie's table.

"I want to make a toast on behalf of my family," he says. "On behalf of my father, Dominic, and my aunt, Georgie, and my nanni Grace and my pop Bill and my sister, Anabel, and my great-auntie Margie Finch . . . and for the guys in my grandfather's battalion."

The silence accentuates the beauty of him. The beauty of this first boy of theirs.

"A toast to Tom Finch and this is the perfect place to make it. Because he fell in love with Nanni Grace here when he was twenty years old, and the day he went off to Vietnam, he had a drink with his best mate, Bill Mackee, here. He made Bill promise to look after Grace and their twins and Bill's been doing that ever since. So here's to Tom Finch, who's finally coming home to our family."

Georgie can hardly breathe.

When the toast is over, some of the uni kids approach them shyly and ask the vets and Dominic and Georgie if they could buy them a beer and she's anxious the whole time that Dom will want one. Of all times, he'll want one now because he's shaking from emotion. And then Tom's there, squeezing in between her and Dom, shaking the vets' hands and she sees the tears in the old men's eyes, the same tears she sees in Auntie Margie Finch's, because opposite them is the young Tom Finch they remember, sitting alongside the Tom Finch he would have grown up to resemble.

When they get home, she sits with Dominic on his bed in the study. They can't speak about Tom Finch because only Bill and Grace can provide the memories for them, so they speak of the one they haven't been able to get out of their minds since the phone call.

"There are probably a million things I'll never forgive myself for," Dominic says quietly, "and one is leaving you to take care of bringing back Joe. Sam's told me some of it. About the hospitals and the press and the other families. And the survivors. And what they remembered and how the worst thing he's ever had to tell you is that there was no body. He said he'd kill me if I asked you anything more now. But I need to know, Georgie."

"Even if it'll break your heart?"

"I need to know if he had regrets," he says. "We'd seen him upbeat all his life. I need to know if he was having a good life. Was he happy that week? Was he in love with his girl as much as we thought he was?"

She wonders how to tell him the good and the bad, because it's what Joe's last couple of hours were about. Fate too. Bill told her a story about fate once. That he had known Tom Finch from the time they were born. It was how their mothers met. In the hospital. One was born before midnight, the other after. Those hours between them meant nothing at all for most of their young lives. Until the draft.

"The day before . . . he had a fight with the great Ana Vanquez," she begins. "Ana couldn't remember what it was about. I think he had stayed out too long or had been drinking after indoor cricket and she wanted him home and they had a big blue. So he left for work that morning with both of them so angry at each other."

Georgie takes his hand because he's going to need her strength now, more than ever.

"He went back, Dom. He went back to say he was sorry. You know Joe. He hated any kind of conflict. How many times did he say, 'Let it go, guys. Not worth it'?"

Dominic nods and there's a smile there too and it kills her to see it. "And because he went back to make things right, he missed his train, Dom. And he got on the other one."

And she doesn't realize how much she needed to say those words to Dominic. That those words bring her solace. That's what he would have been thinking of, her little brother. That he had made good with his love, the great Ana Vanquez. He would have had a cheeky grin on his face thinking of her, the same grin he would have had as a kid, when they told him he had done good. He would not have known the anger and rage of a young man standing next to him. He would have been oblivious.

"Remember when we were kids at the Easter show," Dominic asks, "and Bill ripped into me for losing Joe? Shit, that was the belting of a lifetime. But do you want to know the truth, Georgie? I didn't lose him." He's shaking his head. "I didn't lose him. Not accidentally, anyway. I let go. On purpose. On *purpose,* Georgie. I let go of Joe's hand on purpose because I was so pissed off at Bill."

And then Dominic's sobbing. "I let go, Georgie. I let go of Joe's hand and he was so small. It shouldn't have been him. It should have been—"

"*Don't.* Don't you dare say it, Dom."

But he just shakes his head and says it anyway and she cries at the sound of those words spoken.

"It should have been none of us," she says fiercely. "None of us. We didn't deserve it. No one does."

"Christ, Georgie, just say I lose Tom," he says, beating a fist against his temple, as if he wants to hammer the thought out of his head. "Just say I lose my boy."

chapter thirty-two

Since his talk with Will, he finds himself itching to e-mail Tara and ask her about that night in her parents' house. He doesn't like this thing called fate getting in the way. Worst-case scenario is that she'll stop speaking to him again. Except the one thing he's come to realize over the last couple of months is that worst-case scenario is the last thing he wants. So he chickens out. He's not sure he can go through any more emotion this week. Last night he had sat on his front porch listening to Georgie and his father talking about Joe. Sometimes the way Georgie cries rips holes into Tom. Hearing what his father said was a thousand times worse.

He goes outside for a smoke and a moment later Mohsin the Ignorer is there.

"Didn't know you were a smoker," Tom says after a while, because they are both just standing there.

Mohsin clears his throat. "I feel we have misunderstood each other—"

"No misunderstanding on my part," Tom says coolly.

Mohsin belongs to the Stani school of intense gazing. Tom hasn't noticed it until now.

"When I was a young boy . . . in my town, there was a very big explosion—"

"Look," Tom says, interrupting him. "Mohsin, I'm not responsible for what happened in your country. It doesn't give you a reason to see us as the enemy."

Mohsin is shaking his head; he's confused. "See who as an enemy? I am speaking of fireworks. The explosion. They were fireworks, Tom. And now for many years, I have not been able to hear from this ear." He points to his right ear. "So I am very sorry for not hearing what you were saying when you sat here," he says, pointing to his right side, "but when you speak, even when you stand here," he says, pointing to his left side, "you sound like this." And Mohsin the Ignorer does an impersonation of him. The same one his father would do when imitating Tom's mumble at the dinner table.

"So all I see is this face," Mohsin says, doing another impersonation of a frown, "and hear this voice," and then he does the muttering. "You need to speak English better, Tom."

Tom could probably count on the hands of every member of his family, and extended family, and the city of Sydney, how many times he's felt like a dick this year.

"You finished?" he asks, trying to clear his voice because he has absolutely nothing to say and he's trying to buy time.

Mohsin shrugs. "No, not really. What happened to us on the weekend, Tom? If they do not get Benji Marshall back from injury, we are finished."

Tom's furious. "Say that again and I don't know what I'll do. *So what?* We lose a few games, big deal. Souths have been losing game after game for years and their fans don't give up on them."

Mohsin is sighing and shaking his head.

"I have supported this team since I came to this country and I will continue to support them, but I am very disappointed and one day I may stop going to the game and only watch it from my TV."

"You going Sunday?" Tom asks.

"Yes. And you?"

"I usually make it a point not to go to Brookvale because Manly are a bunch of . . . well, you know what they're like, but if you're going, I might tag along. My father goes as well."

"As does my uncle."

At work one day, Tom checks his e-mail and sees Siobhan Sullivan's name. He's not sure what to expect. Part of him isn't in the mood for a tongue lashing or whatever it's called when someone lashes you in cyberspace. But he opens it all the same because chances are that Siobhan may shed some light on what Tara's saying about him these days.

To:	anabelsbrother@hotmail.com
From:	siobsullivan@yahoo.com
Date:	20 October 2007

Dear Tom,

Frankie wrote and told me about your grandfather coming home after all this time. My father texted me, too. Isn't that strange? My father and I have a texting relationship and I kind of enjoy it. He even does those smiley faces.

Anyway, it seems strange to give my condolences and even stranger to say congratulations. But tell your family I'm thinking of them. I always do, you know. I didn't want to tell you this because I was angry about how you treated us, but for the last two years I've been to the anniversary service down at Kings Cross Station to put some flowers there for your uncle. I thought perhaps your family would like that. Some of his students turn up, you know? They reckon they'll come for the rest of their lives, for "Sir." That's what they call Joe.

Do you know if anyone's heard from Jimmy? I don't like to ask Frankie because I know she gets upset. She thinks we're never going to see him again, or that he'll end up in Guantánamo, and we'll have to begin a *Free Jimmy Hailler* campaign. Maybe if you try to contact him, Tom. He always seemed to understand why you didn't want to have anything to do with us two years ago. He said we had to learn to stop crying in front of you, but none of us could. We tried. I promise.

Love,

Siobhan

P.S. I don't recall the word *dick* or *head* being in Frankie's text to us that day you turned up at the Union. As you pointed out, I have a brilliant memory, and the exact words were, *I think we're getting our Tom back*.

Later, the computer-illiterate woman who sits opposite him wants to be taught how to save old e-mails into folders and it's while he's showing her on his own computer that he sees Joe's last e-mail. The one his uncle sent that week after his father was in the backyard crafting a table for the whole Mackee family to fit around. When his mum and Anabel still lived in Sydney. After Tom had been with Tara in Georgie's attic and was about to spend the Saturday night alone with her in her parents' house while they were away. That time.

To: tomfmackee@hotmail.com
From: mackee_joe@yahoo.co.uk
Date: 1 July 2005
Subject: Nothing Comes of Nothing Part Two

Damn, Tom. I don't know what kind of advice to give you from here. Make sure you know where it's going because you've become a bit of a tomcat when it comes to the opposite sex, and this girl doesn't seem the type who plays your games.

It's all a bit of a gamble, mate. That's all I can promise you. And we never get to see what that other life would have looked like if we don't take chances. You know what I did on the day before I started at this job? A practice run on the Tube from Convent Garden to Arsenal. I was miserable Joe sitting on the Tube, homesick for you all, honestly thinking of packing my shit up and flying back to Georgie's place and meditating in her attic for the rest of my life. I'd been here for almost six months and nothing had happened. And I was praying, Tom. I was praying for a sign. I was so close to being a no-show the next day. But thank God I went through with it because every day, now, I sit on the Tube and think I almost missed out. Just say I didn't know I was twelve minutes away from the rest of my life. Twelve minutes away from meeting a bunch of the most decent kids I'll ever teach. Twelve minutes away from meeting my girl.

Anyways, enough of this sentimental crap. Just do the right thing. Don't be a little man, Tom Thumb. Give a kiss to Anabel. Why is it that the sanest member of our family is an eleven-year-old? She played me "The Last Post" on the trumpet over the phone the other day and I fucking bawled my eyes out.

See you in twenty-three days for the great Finch and Mackee reunion. Can't wait. And I mean that.

Love,

Joe

Nothing comes of Nothing.
Tom starts writing.

To: jameshailler@gmail.com
From: anabelsbrother@hotmail.com
Date: 20 October 2007

Dear Jim,

I feel like a c-bomb for not being around when your granddad died and I know that Frankie and her mum have dibs on you, but know that when you come back, you'll always be able to crash wherever I'm living. Always. And I don't give a shit if you think I've got sentimental in my old age.

I just wanted you to know that.

Tom

P.S. I'm thinking of going to Walgett in December to help build something long overdue. I heard you could be out west, so if you're not doing much, we could do with the help.

To: taramarie@yahoo.com
From: anabelsbrother@hotmail.com
Date: 20 October 2007

Dear Tara,
Tell me if you remember everything about that night in your parents'
house like I do. I need to know.
Love,
Tom

    His finger has never been so powerful. It presses the send button,
and he knows it's going to be a waiting game now. But the new Tom
is patient. It's what boredom has taught him to be. He'll wait and
if she doesn't respond, he might just have to plan himself a holiday.
Step out of that grid.

chapter thirty-three

The place is full to the brim and he can see Stani behind the bar, where Justine and Francesca are serving with Pitts, the new guy. Georgie and his father and Sam are here and so are Francesca's parents and Luca, back from overseas, and Justine's brothers. And so is every other drop-kick band in town who thinks they're performing tonight. He pushes his way through the crowd and jumps the counter.

"He's here," Justine shouts to him above the noise.

"Who?"

"Ben the Violinist. Near the door, wearing the Ramones T-shirt."

The violin guy is as nondescript as any other guy Justine's been interested in. He stands between two somber-looking guys who share a feral alikeness and some Asian dude. All four are either holding guitars, violins, or a saxophone.

"Don't like him."

"Tom!" She laughs. "You don't even know him."

"Don't like who he hangs out with. Look at them. Pissed-off looks on their faces. He's too short for you, anyway."

"Don't listen to him," Francesca says, squeezing between them to hand back someone's change.

"We're the same height," Justine says, her voice weakening.

"Justine!" Francesca says, irritated. "You are not going to lose interest in him just because Tom doesn't approve. *Stop pushing in!*" she snaps at the guy who's just shoved to the front. She points to one of the regulars over his head and serves him next and when the shoving guy gives her lip, she sends him to the back of the line. Tom doesn't know if the guy's pissed off or turned on.

"I can't believe you convinced Stani to do this," he says to her.

"I kind of lied a tiny bit," she says, grabbing a bottle of wine out of the fridge and pouring it. "I told him it would just be our band. Five covers. Five originals. Do you think he's okay about it?"

He looks over at Stani, who's staring at all the musical equipment being dragged in. The moment Stani sees an amplifier, he sends a scathing look toward Francesca.

"I probably would keep away from him for the rest of the . . . year," Tom says.

Later, the three of them join Ned in the kitchen while there's a quiet moment.

"He hasn't come near me," Justine says. "He's only here to play. He's not interested. I think you're right, Tom. I think he's gay." She heads straight to the toilet.

Francesca punches him hard in the shoulder. And it hurts.

"It's exactly what you told me about Will when we were at school."

"No, I didn't. It was Siobhan telling you he was going to join the priesthood."

They watch most of the action from the doorway and when the first band goes up, there's silence, which is a pity because they're crap and he'd like noise to drown them out.

"I reckon Ned should go out there and accidentally hand the T-bone to the violinist, and if he has a vibe, then we'll know Justine's guy is gay," Tom says.

Ned utters a sound of disbelief. "There's no such thing as gaydar, dickhead."

Francesca is looking at Tom and nodding for a change. "Go on, Ned. Even if there's not gaydar, there's this . . . I don't know . . . thing."

Ned is still looking horrified. "What am I to you people?"

"For Justine," Francesca pleads. "She's in the toilet, Ned. Let's lay this violinist thing to rest tonight."

Tom massages Ned's shoulders and then chops at them like he's about to meet an opponent in a boxing ring. Ned shrugs him off aggressively, grabbing the two plates of T-bones and walking out into the crowd while Stani's barking out Francesca's name to get back to the front and serve.

Minutes later Ned comes back all red-faced and a sinking feeling comes over Tom.

"You had a moment with him, didn't you?" he asks flatly.

Ned is focused on the order as if it's the most perfect piece of writing he's ever seen.

"No," he mumbles.

Ned begins chopping up the vegetables.

Tom's confused. "No moment with the violinist?"

"No."

"Yessss," he says, punching Ned's arm. "Then what's wrong?"

Ned is agitated and he walks to the doorway and peers out. "There was a bit of a . . . moment . . . with one of the retard lookalikes."

"Which one?" Tom asks, looking over Ned's shoulder.

"God, I don't know. The one who looks like the other one. Is he looking this way?"

Francesca races in with plates and plonks them in Tom's hands.

"The violinist is all clear," Tom explains to her, "but Ned had a moment with one of the guitarists."

"Ned, don't make this all about you," she says before walking out again.

When half the bands have played, Justine introduces them to the violinist.

"Tom and Frankie," she says politely, her face reddening instantly.

The violinist has a cocksure way about him and introduces his band.

"And who are you?" Tom asks.

He receives an evil unseen pinch from Francesca.

"Ben."

"Are we on next?" one of the brothers asks rudely. Tom can't tell the difference between him and the other brother. They have the same sour look on their faces. "We have a seven-hour drive in front of us and we have to get the car back first thing in the morning."

"Why? Is it stolen?" Tom asks.

The brothers stare at him.

"Who told you that?"

Justine looks at Ben, slightly alarmed.

"It belongs to a friend," he explains.

They're called Deluge and their original piece is pretty impressive. Violin, sax, acoustic guitar, and bass guitar. It's a bit of a wild number, mostly a show-off instrumental piece, but the crowd loves it and Justine's violinist is one of the many musicians in Tom's life who make him feel inadequate in the talent department.

But then it's time for the cover and things go downhill.

Francesca and Justine gasp. Actually, Tom does as well, but he hopes his gasp gets lost with the girls'. Ned's there too. "What?" Ned asks.

"Car thieves and song thieves. They stole our cover."

But it sounds near perfect with just one vocal, two guitars, and the violin, and he hears Francesca and Justine sigh. Actually Tom does as well, but hopes that his gets lost just as much.

"It's our song. Will's and mine," Francesca says.

"Yeah and everyone else's in this room," Tom says. "The violin player just looked at you, Justine, during the line about not being able to take his eyes off you."

"And the guitarist looked at Ned."

"He's the one with the bass guitar. Remember that, Ned. The one you had a moment with is holding a bass guitar," Tom says as if he's speaking to a moron.

Ned mutters something and walks away.

"We need a cover," Justine says. "You guys choose."

"Tom?" Francesca says.

He chooses Paul Kelly's "How to Make Gravy" and looks out to where his family is sitting, knowing the choice won't be lost on them. The harmonica in his hand quavers from everything he's putting into it, and Tom plays it for Joe. For introducing him to his first note, his first strum, his first understanding of the solace a song or instrument can bring. For placing a pick in his hand, because he

301

knows he would never have met these two alongside him if it wasn't for music. When they finish, it's Stani who calls *encore*, and who are they not to take advantage of another five minutes onstage when the boss orders it? Francesca beckons her brother up to play drums and then she belts out "Union City Blues" as if her life depends on it. The crowd goes wild, her voice is so perfect in its ability to hold a note forever, making it hers and mixing it with every one of their emotions. He catches Justine's eyes and she's shaking her head in awe. Tom realizes that the universe must have changed in some way because he's not just wishing Tara was there but that Will was too.

Later, he shares cigarette time against the front wall of the pub with the saxophonist and two guitar players from Deluge.

"Impressive," the saxophonist says.

"Same."

"You cheat when you go for Paul Kelly, though." This from one of the guitarists. They're not holding their instruments, so he can't tell who's who again. "Specially in front of a bunch of old-timers."

"Had no choice. You stole our cover," he explains.

The three of them lean forward from the wall and look at him.

" 'The Blower's Daughter'? With an accordion? Don't think so," one of the lookalikes says.

"We're pretty experimental. Our accordion player's gifted."

The others lean back again and mutter something about "the accordion player." Tom doesn't like their tone.

"Problem?" he snaps.

One of the guitarists peers into the window and shakes his head. "We have to sit in a car for the next seven hours with Mr. I'm-in-love-with-the-accordion-player."

"And in one year he has made no progress from 'She could like me' to 'I think she likes me,' " the saxophonist complains.

"We're over it!" This from the second lookalike. "Back home, the girls are going to be like, *Did you ask her out, Ben? Did you? Did you?* And we're going to spend the whole time in therapy with him."

There's a banging sound on the window and it's Stani.

"Got to go. Back to kitchen duty."

Then Tom pauses. "With my friend, Ned," he says for emphasis. He nods, looking at the guitarist. Actually both of the guitarists, because he doesn't know which one had the moment with Ned. "Ned the Cook. Tall guy. Hair over his face. Kind of a bit shy? *Ned.* Hands out T-bones."

They don't say anything. Look at him suspiciously, actually. Until one of the guitarist grins, wolfishly.

"Tell Ned, Alex said hi," he says.

"You?" Tom asks.

The guitarist points to his brother. "Him."

Him's a bit embarrassed. Him's doing a Ned and looking everywhere but at them.

Inside, Justine and Ben the Violinist are awkwardly playing that game of her-fiddling-with-her-hair and him-talking-a-mile-a-minute-with-a-lot-of-hand-gestures.

Tom puts an arm around both of them. "He wants to sleep with you. She wants to sleep with you. Just do it."

Justine stares at Tom in horror and he recognizes the look that says she's about to cry and then she walks away leaving him with an incredibly hostile violin player.

303

"They made me do it," he says, pointing to his friends.

Tom follows her into the toilet where Francesca's standing by, a filthy look on her face.

"Oh you are so dead, Tom."

The Deluge wins the beer and drive away in the stolen car. It takes them forty-five minutes to get everyone out of the pub. Justine begins cleaning, while Francesca goes into damage control.

"He didn't mean it, Justine. Tara's always said that Tom's the last bastion of arrested development."

"I thought you'd like that he was into you," Tom says, confused, as he mops the floor. He wished, with all his might, that there was a guidebook to life out there that he could follow.

Justine stops cleaning and looks at him. "I like him, Tom. A lot. I knew he probably liked me too. But that's not the way it's done."

"Let me make it better."

"*No,*" they all say at once, even Stani. "Bloody bastard," he had muttered when he saw his niece in tears. Tom believes it was most probably directed to him and not the violin player.

"How long's he gone for?"

"Until uni begins again. *In March!*"

"I reckon—"

"No more suggestions, Tom," Francesca orders.

"I just want to—"

"*No more,*" she says, holding up a finger. "Or I'm telling Tara and Siobhan."

"You're going to tell them anyway," he argues.

"Yes, but I was going to give you enough time to go to a place where they can't track you down."

"Stop!" Justine says.

"I didn't say anything," he argues. "Geez! Can everyone stop telling me to *stop*?"

"*Stop,*" Francesca says, holding up a hand to listen. "*Shhh.*"

Strands of music come from outside the door and they all rush to the window to peer out, even Stani tries to push them out of the way.

And while the violinist is playing his tune, the car thieves sit on the hood waiting.

"What is it?" Tom asks her.

" 'Calliope House,' " Justine answers.

"Are you going to go out there?" Ned asks. "He's good."

Justine shakes her head. "I'm so embarrassed. Everyone's watching. I have to do this in my own time."

"Justine, it's been a year," Francesca argues.

"I know," she says honestly. "But not like this. Everyone's watching and I just want to talk to him, alone. Or on the phone. Not with an audience."

"Do you have his mobile number?" Tom asked. "I'll go out and . . ."

"*No!*"

Justine backs away from the window.

"Great. Now the cops are here, and Stani, you're going to get a fine for noise pollution."

"Bloody bastards."

When the violinist finishes, he walks to the window and slams his hand against it.

"He's Post-it-noted the window," Tom says, peering to see what it reads. "It says 'Call me' and his mobile number. I might just do that," he muses. "He's kind of cute."

Justine and Francesca laugh. Ned does too. And there it is. The knowledge that it makes him happy to hear it. So simple. They laugh and it makes Tom happy.

He closes up and Stani hands him his pay. He started getting it a month ago. He can feel it's too much and when he looks inside the envelope, he stares back at his boss.

"Back pay," Stani explains.

"You don't owe me back pay."

"I do. What your friends did? Not your debt to pay."

"Yeah, it was."

"No."

Tom flicks through the money.

"You earned it with the floorboards, anyway," Stani says. "Don't try to give it back or leave it behind, because you won't have a job here if you do."

Tom shakes his head but puts the envelope in his pocket.

He holds out a hand to Stani and they shake, then he turns and walks away.

"It's been good to see your father again," Stani says just as Tom reaches the door.

"He was a good in-between man, Dominic Mackee. A good union man. Kept the peace. Kept the dialogue going."

He walks into the house later, into the kitchen, where his father's sitting. Tom mutters a greeting and stands at the fridge door, staring at Georgie's shit organic stuff as if it's the most interesting thing in the world.

"I liked your choices tonight," his father says.

Tom shrugs. "We didn't know what else to play."

But he's lying and there is a part of him that hopes his father knows that too. The part that doesn't have to explain away sentimentality. That doesn't have to tell him the way he feels. He hopes, somehow, that ten minutes on a stage does that because he doesn't think he'll ever be able to say it with the proper words. They'd all sound contrived and forced.

He feels the wad of money in his pocket. "Do you want me to come along?"

"Where?" his father asks.

He shrugs, facing him. "With you and Bill. To bring Tom Finch home."

His father stares at him. "To Hanoi?"

Tom nods. An in-between man. Keeping the peace and dialogue going. That would be a good profession to go into. Union reps to keep families united. Maybe that was his calling.

"I don't have the money for both of us, Tom."

"Got my own. And Bill reckons the government will pay anyway."

His father doesn't speak. Just nods and then says, "I think Nanni Grace would love that."

Tom goes to walk out again, but something stops him.

"Would you, though?" he asks his father.

"Would I what?"

"Love it? Not just Nanni Grace. Would you love it?"

His father seems confused by the question, but then Tom realizes it's not confusion he reads on his face; it's disbelief.

"How could you ask me that, Tom? I'd give anything for you to want to come along with my father and me."

Tom doesn't ask which father Dominic's talking about. It can't be that confusing loving more than one.

At work the next day, Mohsin shows him the course he's applied for at Sydney University.

"Hmm," Tom says. "Molecular science. Sure you don't want to aim higher?"

He goes online and finds himself looking at the deferment rules for the course he dropped out of two years ago. And then he sees the number 1 next to his in-box. Anabel's at school camp, so it can't be from her. He knows exactly who it's from.

To: anabelsbrother@hotmail.com
From: taramarie@yahoo.com
Date: 8 November 2007

Dear Tom,

I'll tell you what I remember, seeing as you asked. That after we made love that night in my parents' house, you asked me to get out of bed, naked. Remember how I felt? I mean we had just had sex, so that's as intimate as I thought it got, but it's funny that I don't remember that part as much as you making me stand in front of you with nothing on and we were freezing cold and I felt so exposed, like I felt you could see inside the guts of me. And remember, I cried? And you were like, *Shh, shh, don't. You're beautiful*, and I can't believe I'm writing this now, but I don't think I'll ever forget your voice when you said that. I think I loved you at that moment.

But then Joe happened, and you didn't ring or anything. You didn't let me see you exposed from all your pain. You hid and you left me there, starkers, and for so long, *for so, so long,* I felt raw. Don't ever ask anyone to do that again, Tom. Don't ever ask them to bare their soul and then leave it. It's fucking cruel and no matter how much pain you were in, you had no right. Because sometimes it makes me want to shudder, because sometimes I still think I'm there in my bedroom standing naked, except it's like the whole world can see me, and they're laughing like sometimes I remember people laughing at me behind my back in high school. And it makes me just want to cry with shame.

She doesn't sign it off and he doesn't even give himself a moment to think.

To: taramarie@yahoo.com
From: anabelsbrother@hotmail.com
Date: 8 November 2007

Dear Tara,
If you think I've forgotten anything about that night, you, most gorgeous girl, are laboring under a great misapprehension. I remember everything. I remember your petticoat . . . slip . . . whatever the hell it's called, and how you let me take it off. You made me close my eyes and that was even more of a turn-on.

You've always seen through me and that's freaked me out. You saw the stuff I didn't show other people. The part of me that sometimes can be a bully, because I come from a family of it. Learned behavior because I think my dad was taught by Bill and Bill was taught by his father and sometimes I feel it inside me as well, except we're not actually comfortable with it, but it's there and it frightens all of us. And that night you saw the fear. You made it go away for just one minute and then Joe happened and I couldn't speak anymore and the numbness—please, God don't ever let me feel that numbness again. I think I was scared that you wouldn't be able to make the numbness go away and if my mum and dad and Anabel couldn't, and then you couldn't, I didn't know whether I could handle that.

I know I stuffed up and I know your peacekeeper probably treated you like gold and I've treated you like crap, but I want you to know that I remember the conversations we had in Year Twelve, when you told me you wanted to do a cultural studies degree because you believed in trade, not aid, and you believed that the only way was to ask the questions and listen to the needs of the people and I remember thinking that exact moment, I want to change the world with her. And I remember feeling that again in Georgie's attic. That's a pretty powerful gift you have there, Ms. Finke. To make the laziest guy around want to change the world with you. So next time you remember standing in your bedroom naked, know that it is the most amazing view from any angle, especially the one where we get to see inside.

Love always,

Always,

Tom

chapter thirty-four

Georgie's water breaks during breakfast one morning. It's all pretty calm. She just says, "This is it, kids," and then she picks up her phone and texts Sam.

"You can't send him a text telling him his baby is about to be born," Tom argues, looking around for Nanni Grace's support. Nanni Grace has already gone up the stairs to collect the bag Georgie's had packed ever since she read one of the books that told her to always be prepared.

"I don't want to get into a phone conversation with him," Georgie says. "He'll ask really stupid questions and then we'll get into an argument and I don't want to be stressed."

The phone beeps back.

"See," she says, showing Tom the message. "Stupid question."

It is a pretty stupid question, but Tom doesn't give her the satisfaction of agreeing.

"I'm starting up the car," Bill says, standing up.

"See?" she says again. "Starting up the car. Are we living in the mountains where it snows, Bill? Does the car need warming up? Or are we robbing a bank?"

Nanni Grace is pretty calm when she returns. "I think we should walk anyway. It's only fifteen minutes and she's been a bit of a blob these last couple of days."

Deep down, Tom is really stressed. The women are not acting the way he thinks they should be acting.

"Bill, go outside and wait for Sam and warn him that Georgie doesn't want to be stressed."

"Why does everyone think that all of a sudden Sam's going to act like he's crazy?" Tom asks.

Outside, someone has their hand on the horn and doesn't let up.

"Bill, go outside and tell Sam to get his hand off the horn," Georgie says.

Tom thinks it's a ridiculous idea that they walk. Apart from the fact that he will never get over the humiliation if she gives birth on Carillon Avenue in front of his ex-flatmates, and knowing Georgie, she'll do that to spite him, he's scared something's going to go wrong and he just wants her in hospital as quick as possible.

It ends up a bit of a procession, like something out of those foreign movies where they have weddings or funerals tunneling through the town. Georgie leads the way with Nanni Grace and Tom and his father, and Sam and his kid and Bill follow.

"Baby's coming," he explains to Sam's kid, in case no one's told him.

"How?"

"Sam?" Tom asks. Because he knows that Sam will be pragmatic and sensible without using the word *vagina*.

"I told you already, Callum," Sam mumbles. There's a very stressed look on his face, too. The whole walking thing isn't working for him either.

Tom looks down at the kid. "What did he tell you?"

"A gift from God."

Tom can't believe that Sam would use such terminology. He actually thought Sam was an atheist. Sam gives Tom one of those threatening looks that promises a universe of pain if he says anything other than that.

"How old are you?" Tom asks the kid.

"Six."

Tom nods. "A gift from God delivered by the angels."

Georgie gives orders over her shoulder. "Tom, call your mother and Anabel and tell them what's happened. They'll want to be kept updated. Sam, you call Lucia and Abe." They cross at the lights at Missenden Road.

"What about Auntie Margie Finch?" Grace asks.

"Maybe when it's born. You cover the family, Mum. Sam, have you called your mother? She'll be hurt if Grace is there and she isn't."

She waves to one of her neighbors, who's walking home.

"Having the baby," she calls out to her.

It's long. Longer than he imagines, and it makes him think the worst. It makes everyone think the worst—he can see it on their faces, especially Nanni Grace. They have to get used to not thinking the worst. It's so long that there are discussions about who comes and goes and if someone should take Sam's kid home to his own mother, but then everyone decides to stay except for Lucia, who has to get home to her kids. She nudges Tom and points discreetly to Nanni Grace and Tom goes and sits with her, because he can see her hands are trembling and she won't let Bill hold them. He knows she won't slap Tom's, so he takes hers in his. But then Sam's there, hours later, with a bundle of blue hospital blanket in his hands and everyone's crowded around him and he looks a bit shell-shocked, but he bobs down in front of his kid and shows him the baby. The kid looks at it and begins crying, because of all the attention. And then Nanni Grace is crying and it doesn't look like happy crying either. She buckles and Tom's dad catches her and they sit his nan down. Bill goes and gets a glass of water and Tom's there in the midst of it all, clutching Nanni Grace's hand because he wants to make it better. He wants to make his whole family better, but he knows he can't.

"I want to be with my Georgie," Nanni Grace is crying. She hasn't even looked at the baby yet. Sam helps her up.

"And Georgie wants to be with you, Grace," he says gently. "Can you take Callum's hand?"

"I want to hold your hand," the kid says, and Sam takes his son's hand.

And it's like no one knows how to celebrate just yet.

"What's his name?" Dominic asks.

Sam looks down at the baby for a moment.

"Bill," he says huskily, looking up at them all. "Bill Finch Thompson."

When she wakes up, the first thing she sees is the humidicrib. Then she sees Sam sleeping in the armchair, holding Callum. They had both decided that his son shouldn't miss out on any of the excitement. And for the life of her, Georgie can't imagine wanting to wake up to more than this. Granted, she'll want more than this during her day, but this is what she wants to wake up to.

As if he senses her, Sam opens his eyes, a half smile on his face and then a bit of pain as he tries to stretch without waking up Callum.

"Ask her for joint custody," Georgie says, and it takes a moment of misreading his expression for her to understand that he's actually misreading her. "I want you to move back in. We need to bring up these boys together. I need happiness. I deserve it. No more than anyone else, but I'm no good for this baby if I'm all self-sacrifice and restraint, and nor are you."

She stops speaking, knowing the power she possesses in this moment. Wasn't that what it was all about? Who grabs the power and holds on to it and uses it for the rest of their life? But Georgie has never seen power on someone's face look beautiful. She's seen it look smug and twisted, with a squint of the eyes, a haughtiness and arrogance, but never beautiful. This kid deserves beauty. Both these boys do.

"I actually wouldn't mind getting married," she says. "What are your thoughts?"

He doesn't speak and when she looks up at him again, she can see Sam's crying.

chapter thirty-five

Francesca drops Tom off on Devonshire Street at Central Station and he grabs the pack from the boot.

"You'll get a fine," he tells her. She has a total disregard for all street signs that begin with *No*.

"Try to enjoy yourself, no matter how sad it is." She kisses his cheek, unemotional and practical. She even pats him on the back and gives him the thumbs-up.

"Cheers," he says, and walks away, amazed at how effortless it all is.

At the bottom of the stairs, he turns to look up. She's still there and he can't help walking back up to her, because he thinks he'll never be able to help himself when it comes to the girls. He holds her against him and they stay like that for a long while.

"No listening to the news every hour," he says. She nods, and he feels her tears trapped against his neck. "And tell Justine that if she doesn't ring the violinist, I will."

He kisses her and wants to beg her and the others to never give up on him. *Ever*. But he gets a feeling that he would be preaching to the converted.

•   •   •

He's lying on the couch at his grandma Agnes's flat when his phone rings. He wonders when he will ever stop feeling excited at the word *Finke* appearing on his screen, or *taramarie* in his mailbox.

"Hey," he says and he's grinning. Like an idiot, he's grinning.

They haven't spoken since the e-mail exchange about the one-and-a-half-night stand and the mayhem in-between of baby Bill.

"Hey to you, too," she says, and he can hear laughter in her voice. "Guess what? My dad is flying me to Sydney for a couple of days for the election. I'll be in tomorrow, until Monday."

The euphoria sails out of him and frustration sets in. More than frustration. Anger at the universe.

"I'm flying out to Hanoi tomorrow with my father and my grandfather," he says flatly.

"What time?" she asks, the laughter beginning to leave her voice. "I'm not coming in until late in the afternoon. We might be able to see each other at the airport," she adds.

"I'm in Brisbane, Tara. I'm with my mother and Anabel. My flight tomorrow connects with my father's and Bill's."

"Okay," she says quietly and now there's nothing in her voice.

"Shit . . ."

"It's okay," she says. "It's fine. I'll be back in six weeks . . . after Christmas . . . and we'll have a drink. . . . It'll be cool. . . . I've got to go. . . . I've got to go, okay."

And she hangs up on him. Just like that. Just when he wants to say a thousand other things, but she hasn't let him. Tom's had enough and he lies back, refusing to allow himself to dwell on whatever he's done wrong in Tara Finke's eyes. Again. He vows not to give it another moment's thought. Not. One. Single. Moment's. Thought.

•   •   •

"And I promise this is the last time I'm going to bring up this situation," he says to his mother with frustration the next day. They're at the indoor sport center in New Farm, where Anabel is filming a mini documentary about blood sport and focusing on an indoor netball team for over-thirty-fives.

"It's not as if I chose to go overseas at this point. How did I become the bad guy here? I think I made her cry and I don't know what I did."

His mother is staring at him. There have been moments when her eyes have glazed over, but he just puts that down to her being tired and not the fact that he's gone on about this Tara thing since he woke up this morning.

"You're a bit clueless, aren't you?" she says. "Which is strange, because Dominic was never clueless about women. He really knows how to read people."

"Oh, yeah, he's fantastic with people," Tom says. "That's why he's living with his *sister* and his *parents* at the moment, at the age of almost forty-three. While his *wife* is in Brisbane and his daughter is covering a blood feud between the goal shooter and goalkeeper of this ridiculous sport."

People are staring and he realizes that you don't criticize netball in a room full of women wearing pleated sports skirts with whistles around their necks.

"Tom, think about it," his mum says patiently. "She finds out she's coming home for a couple of days and apart from seeing her parents, she knows she's going to see you. She can't think of anything she wants more, and then what happens? You're not going to be there. She cried because she's built up this moment and it's gone. I'd be shattered. I used to hang out at Manning because I knew where

318

Dom and his first-year law mates went when we were at Sydney Uni. I didn't even care if I got nowhere close to him, as long as I saw him. If he wasn't there, I'd go back to my room at the college, *crying*. Because I missed out on seeing him for one night! Could you imagine if I was overseas and my one window of opportunity to see him slipped through my fingers for the next few months because of circumstances beyond my control?"

"You think she was upset because she really, *really* wanted to see me?"

"Oh, Tom," she sighs. "Am I going to be playing lawn bowls with your father and still be giving you advice about this girl?"

He doesn't know what makes him happier. The idea of him knowing Tara forever or his parents playing lawn bowls together when they're old.

Anabel approaches with a satisfied look on her face.

"The *center* just called the *wing attack* a . . . very rude word. Perfect television."

She senses the tension.

"Is everything okay?"

"Yeah, fine."

Anabel looks at him closely.

"Is this about a girl?"

"*No,*" he lies. "Yes."

"Is it the psycho Tara Finke?"

"That's a very rude thing to call her," Tom reprimands. "Did you hear what she called Tara?" he asks his mother, outraged.

"It's what you used to call her," Anabel argues. "I used to think psycho was some Japanese name, like Seiko-Tara."

His mother is laughing. "Look at that deadpan expression."

319

"I like her," Anabel says, making herself comfortable next to Tom. "Always have."

"Who?" he asks, surprised. "The psycho Tara Finke?"

"See?" she says, pointing with exasperation. "He called her that!"

"Last night," their mother explains to Anabel patiently, "Tom received a call from Tara saying she was flying into Sydney an hour before he's flying out to Hanoi. So they are going to miss seeing each other because Tara will be gone by the time Tom returns. And they really want to see each other."

He was very impressed by his mother's ability to articulate it. In his head it had been a mess of *What? Why? What did I do? Shit. Fuck. What the hell?*

Anabel shrugs. "Then take an earlier flight today so you get to see her at the airport, stupid."

He shakes his head. "How bloody disrespectful is generation zed?"

It's not as if he hadn't thought of taking an earlier flight. But he wants to be with his mother and Anabel too. He shakes his head. "I came to see both of you. To spend time with my womenfolk because I miss you like hell."

They're both smiling and he knows he has said and done the right thing and that's enough for him. Anabel reaches over and hugs him. "You're the best brother in the world, Tom."

He's amazed at how sentimental she's become. As much as she loves him, she would never have said anything that cheesy in the old days. When she pulls away from the hug, she slaps him on the cheek.

"Are you over it now?" she snaps. "Let's go!" she says, grabbing their mother's keys out of her hands. "I'm sick and tired of you people living interstate and overseas from people you want to be with. You're ruining my life! All of you!"

They drive back home to grab his backpack and as he bends and kisses his grandma Agnes, she scrunches a one-hundred-dollar bill in his hand. "Buy yourself some chocolates, Tom."

It's what she'd say to him as a kid with a twenty-cent coin.

"I'd prefer you spend it on getting your hair set, Nan," he says. "You look like a babe when you get it done."

"Don't you worry, Tom. I've always got money put away to get my hair set."

At the airport, the three of them hold on to each other the whole time it takes for everyone to board the plane.

"Have I ever begged you for anything?" he asks his mum quietly.

She won't look at him.

"I'm begging you," he says. "Please don't let Dad and me get off that plane in Sydney with you not there."

Anabel walks him all the way up to where he's the last to board.

"I'm counting on you, 99. If she tries to send you down to Sydney alone, chuck a tanty."

"Agnes of God says tantrums are my forte," she says proudly before throwing herself at him for a hug. Then she's crying and he can't handle this much crying and he's forced to do what he vowed he never would.

"Luca Spinelli said to say hi."

She recovers in an instant, fixing her hair as if Luca Spinelli has materialized miraculously.

"What were his exact words?"

321

"Say hi to your sister. . . . No, no, no . . . say hi to Anabel."

And the memory of the expression on her face has him grinning all the way back to Sydney.

His plan was never to run through the airport like one of those scenes in the movies. Too much anticipation, leaving things open for too much disappointment. He could already imagine what would happen. Tara would look at him and say, "Oh, hi, Tom," as if they just met up in the school corridor at lunchtime. But she's at one terminal and he's at another and then he has to get to the International one, so he starts running like a stress head, almost knocking people out of the way. He figures she's coming from Darwin and finds the right gate lounge, then looks around to see where Justine and Francesca and Tara's parents are. But they're nowhere to be seen and when he turns around, Tara's standing there in front of him, with a backpack on.

"Oh, hi, Tara," he said nice and matter-of-fact, like they had just bumped into each other at Coles in Norton Plaza.

She stares at him with her airplane hair that looks slightly greasy and her eyes bloodshot from the cabin pressure. She's darker and he wants to say, "Nice tan," but remembers that she hasn't been on holidays. He gives her a quick hug, patting her on the back, and for the whole time she looks at him, her face is on the brink of . . . something he can't put a finger on. *Say something. One of us, say something.* Just because you can talk to a girl all night about everything doesn't mean she's going to feel the same. It's like she's lost her voice.

"Want me to stick around *here* while the others turn up?" He points to the ground when he says *here*. He does a whole lot of pointing and can't understand why. He keeps his face neutral and she's just staring at him with that look of . . . is it disappointment?

He's miserable. There's no coming back from this moment and they're just staring at each other, not starry-eyed or with tears welling up in their eyes. She has that "What is your problem?" look of hurt on her face. He hasn't a clue how to fix this. How many great love stories in history go down the gurgler because the right thing wasn't said at the right time?

He stops pointing and holds up his hand as a good-bye. See you later. Have a good life. Not that they'll never see each other again, because they will. Always. But she'll belong to someone else and so will he, and the girl he'll end up with won't like his friends, for some reason. And one day he'll think that balancing them both is too much work and they'll all start seeing each other every couple of weeks, instead of every day, and it makes him feel like shit to think that. Like his insides are in revolt. Tara looks like she's about to cry, shaking her head as if to say, "Thomas, what am I going to do with you?" But that's all he needs. The hope that she wants *him* to do something. So he talks.

"This is the deal, Finke," he says firmly. "I'm getting on a plane with my pop Bill and my father and I can tell you this, *Apocalypse Now* has nothing on what will take place in Vietnam in the next couple of days, so you look after yourself and have fun with the girls, but don't let anyone introduce you to engineers or peacekeepers, and whatever you do, don't hang out with Ned on your own. Don't let anyone take care of you. Can you maybe leave that for me to do? I mean, take care of you? Feel free to take care of me in return . . . because I think I'll need you to do that."

Why can't he just kiss her and stop this talking crap?

323

"I've been an inexplicable fool," he jokes. And then from behind him, he hears screams and Francesca and Justine are all over her.

"Oh, my God, look at you," Francesca says.

Tara looks at the girls.

"My hair's shit," she says, and then burst into tears.

Tom can't believe it. He's just spilled his guts all over the floor in front of them and she's crying about her hair.

Justine and Francesca are looking at him furiously.

"Did you make her cry, Thomas?" Justine asks.

"What did you say to her?" Francesca demands.

But they don't wait for his answer and then her mum and dad turn up, wearing Kevin 07 T-shirts, and there's no getting close to her, so he walks away.

Georgie rings him while he's on the line going through immigration.

"I'm breast-feeding," she explains, because he really needed to know that. "We've checked them in so they should be somewhere in immigration now. We're already in the car."

He looks around and he sees Bill and his dad a couple of people behind him and he waves.

"Did you get in your postal vote?" she asks.

"Uh-huh," he says.

"It's a pity I didn't get to see you today," she says.

"You saw me yesterday, Georgie."

"I know, but I wanted to see you today."

"Why?"

"Because seeing you makes me happy. I was telling that to Billy when I couldn't get him to sleep this morning."

"Maybe he couldn't get to sleep because you were talking to him."

324

"That's what Nanni Grace says. She wants to kidnap him because she reckons I kidnapped you when you were born."

He hears something said and he figures it's Nanni Grace in the car with them.

"Hold on, I just have to swap breasts." When Georgie explains why, he just blocks it all out. He's seen Georgie's breasts more times in the last week than he'll ever care to see in his lifetime. And she talks on and on, but it brings him comfort and somehow he figures that when she gets off the phone, he'll try to ring Tara and make things right. There's something about Georgie's voice that makes him want everything to be right in the world.

"Auntie Georgie?" he says just as he gets to the top of the line in immigration.

"Yeah?"

"Sometimes . . . sometimes I thought I'd . . . deck myself in the last couple of months . . . and if it wasn't for you . . . if it wasn't for seeing you every day . . ."

He doesn't know where that comes from, but he knows he has to say it, even if it's going to make her cry. But she doesn't cry. She's silent for a moment.

"You don't have to move out, you know."

"Yeah, I do."

"The Europeans have been living together in multigenerational households for years. And the Chinese and the Vietnamese. Everyone does it except for us and do they look any more miserable?"

Tom swears he hears something mumbled by Sam beside her.

"I love you, Tom."

"Same." And he hangs up before it gets too messy.

• • •

325

His phone rings again. Comes up anonymous.

"Hello?"

"When I got off the plane, I was so churned up because there was this really small part inside of me that hoped you'd somehow be there, even though I knew you were in Brisbane, and when I came out, you were there but you had your back to me and then you were pointing . . . what was with the pointing, Tom? And you were shrugging and matter-of-fact, and I thought it was just like the one-and-a-half-night stand and I just wanted to slap you, Tom, because I can't believe I have to wait another six weeks to see you and I'm kind of sick of this bad timing, so when I get back, *no excuses,* do you hear me? I'm going to be following you like a bad smell."

"Who is this?"

And then he can hear her laughing. "Why can't you make this romantic?"

His father and Bill pass him toward security.

"I spilt my guts out all over the arrival lounge at Sydney's domestic airport, Tara. It's as bloody romantic as you'll ever get from me. Where are you?"

"At a public phone in arrivals. I've run out of credit. I used my reprimanding voice and told my parents and Frankie and Justine that they couldn't come near me for the next five minutes. I can see the four of them from here. They're talking about me. They have a look of fear on their face. Even my parents, who created me, are afraid. I see that look on a lot of people's faces when they see me, Tom. Never yours."

"I keep it hidden, but it's there. Believe me, you frighten me to death, but for different reasons."

There's silence for a moment.

"Can you promise me something?" he asks.

"I'll promise you anything."

The air kind of whooshes out of his lungs.

"Okay, when I get back, I need to go to Walgett with my father. Something he promised my auntie Margie Finch a couple of years ago. I'm probably going to move in with Mohsin, who's enrolled to do molecular science, as one does when they've worked as a data-entry zombie for a year. He's sharing a house in Summer Hill with a bunch of international students and I'm thinking of picking up a few construction subjects and taking Frankie's dad up on his offer, but before I do all the moving bit, et cetera et cetera, I thought I'd come and, you know, kind of check out what you do over there in Same. Wouldn't mind hanging out in Dili for a couple of days and watch you get chucked out of salsa classes. And then we can fly home together."

Silence.

"Are you still there?" he asks.

"A thousand times yes," she says quietly. "To everything you said."

Maybe it's because he hasn't had a cigarette for a week. Maybe it's because he's seen Anabel and his mum and spoken to Georgie. Maybe it's because Tara Finke is his girl, but all of a sudden, Tom feels as if he can breathe properly for the first time in a long time.

"I've got to go. They're making my pop take off his shoes in case he's got traces of explosives and my father's just about to chuck a mental."

He sits between Dominic and Bill for the sake of sanity, bladders, and maybe because he just wants to. His dad looks shell-shocked. Tom doesn't know what to say to a guy who's about to bury a father he has never known, but Dominic's gripping onto the two scapulars Georgie's given him as if his life depends on it. Georgie says they should be buried with Tom Finch.

The hosties do their thing and Bill wants them to listen to the security instructions despite the fact that Tom's listened to them twice in the last twenty-four hours.

"How were your mother and Anabel? How did they look?" his dad asks.

"Beautiful," Tom says.

"Do you think they'll be there when we come back?"

"Dunno. I think so."

"I do too."

His father still hasn't budged, so Tom reaches over and grabs Dominic's seat belt and secures it tightly. For a moment their hands touch. When he was a kid, it always turned into "This Little Piggy." But this time they don't need words.

And he knows that everything's going to be fine.

Because he and his family are on their way.

Acknowledgments

Thank you to those who answered my questions about politics, passion, and work: Julia Clements, Jill Finnane, Phil Glendenning, Mark Halsted, Patrick Devery, Jan Murphy, Robert Thorne, and those who work at the Edmund Rice Centre for Social Justice. Your generosity gave substance to many characters in this novel.

Many thanks to Amy Thomas, Clair Honeywill, Anyez Lindop, Kristin Gill, Marina Messiha, Gabrielle Coyne, and everyone at Penguin for your support. Especially to Laura Harris for your friendship and ability to pick the best part of my brain.

Thank you to those who read the manuscript and provided feedback: my mum, Nikki Anderson, Marisa Brattoni, Anthony Cantazariti, Adolfo Cruzado, Patrick Devery, Jessica Flood, Jill Grinberg, Sophie Hamley, Tegan Morrison, Raffaela Pandolfini, Brenda Souter, Maxim Younger, Deborah Wayshak, and Kate Woods.

A special thanks to Jim Bourke, who answered my very naive questions about the work involved in returning to their families the six Australian servicemen left behind during the Vietnam War.

All of the characters appearing in this novel are fictional creations. Any resemblance to real people, living or dead, is entirely coincidental. Some aspects of the rugby league matches referred to in this story have been fictionalized for the purposes of my narrative.